A. G. von Suttner, H. M. Jewett

Djambek the Georgian

A Tale of modern Turkey

A. G. von Suttner, H. M. Jewett

Djambek the Georgian
A Tale of modern Turkey

ISBN/EAN: 9783743335561

Manufactured in Europe, USA, Canada, Australia, Japa

Cover: Foto ©Andreas Hilbeck / pixelio.de

Manufactured and distributed by brebook publishing software
(www.brebook.com)

A. G. von Suttner, H. M. Jewett

Djambek the Georgian

DJAMBEK
THE GEORGIAN

A TALE OF MODERN TURKEY

FROM THE GERMAN OF
A. G. VON SUTTNER

By H. M. JEWETT

WITH AN INTRODUCTION BY
MANGASAR M. MANGASARIAN

NEW YORK
D. APPLETON AND COMPANY
1890

INTRODUCTION.

THE story of "Djambek, the Georgian," as related in the following pages, furnishes the American and European reader with a glimpse of the social and civil institutions of the Orient. The author proves himself minutely and accurately informed of the peoples and places he describes. To a native of the Orient the picture drawn by Von Suttner appears in every detail exact and trustworthy. Our thanks are due to him for presenting phases of Eastern life little known in the West.

It will in no way detract from the merit of the work, however, to add that the author has not succeeded in concealing his nationality. He is a European, and sees only as a European. His book, therefore, is bound to be appreciated by the Western people more than if it had been written by a native of the East.

Georgia is one of a group of countries which form the isthmus that divides the Sea of Azov and the Euxine—its shores studded with Greek colonies—from the Caspian. It is also one of the border lands of Asia and Europe. This part of the globe has always been prolific of traditions, fables, and myths. The mountains, "tinged with the rosy hues of morning," which skirt its northern horizon, have been supposed to have cradled the human race at its birth. The first emigrants spread their tents in its rich and picturesque plains. Here was the nursery of civilization. The story of Noah and

his ark and of Prometheus chained to the rock have been
handed down to us by the inhabitants of these regions. At
the foot of Mount Ararat is the lake where Nimrod is supposed to have met with his death at the hands of the Circas-
sian dalesman.

The geographical position of these countries has been the
cause of all their misery and misfortune. Being the tramp-
ing-ground of marching hosts and invaders, they have never
enjoyed security or the opportunities of peace. Odin and
his Asæ marched through these lands when in search of the
shores of the Elbe and the Baltic. Emerging from these
valleys, the barbarian Scythians poured themselves upon
western Asia. Cyrus the Great and Alexander have left their
footprints upon the soil. Timurlane and Genghis Khan en-
acted their inhuman *rôles* in these parts of the world. Here
blazed the star of Mithridates, and here it went out in darkness. The Ossmanlee and Muscovite met on these plains to
express their unsurpassable and eternal hatred of one another.
Such are some of the truths and traditions which the reading
of "Djambek" * calls to mind.

The physical and natural aspects of Georgia, "the terres-
trial paradise," are described by a masterly hand. The picture of the Pasha of Batoum with his gorgeous train, sailing
up the river to Djambek's home through a country of incom-
parable beauty, is exquisite. Indeed, Georgia is one of the
most lovely spots in the world. It is the land of the olive,
the ilex, the pine, and the cedar ; the land of rich farms
nestled in the bosom of luxuriant plains ; of vineyards and
antique castles ; of cool springs and charming hills ; and of
gardens laden with flower and fruit. Georgian dress and
manners are described in language at once felicitous and
faithful. Truly there is a charm about the Oriental costume.
It is calculated to enhance graceful movements and to add to

---

* Pronounced 'Jambek, with *D* silent and accent on second
syllable.

the beauty and expression of the features. The Eastern people seem to understand the rhythm of dress. Let us hope that the day will never come when these people will substitude the Occidental for the picturesque costumes of the East.

The characters of the principal Georgians in the book lead us to question Gibbon's estimate of this ancient race. "A handsome but worthless people" is the judgment with which the illustrious historian dismisses them from his pages. "Handsome" they are, especially their women—erect, symmetrical in form and figure, with delicately cut features and sparkling black eyes, and a complexion like silk and satin. The harems of Constantinople have from of old received their Guzel Kizlar—beautiful maidens—from Georgia and Circassia. Even to-day the most handsome houris in the imperial palace on the Bosporus have been brought from these "gardens of God."

As to the moral worth of this people, opinions have differed since the days of Gibbon. The Armenians have forced both Georgians and Circassians out of all mercantile pursuits, being themselves almost the only shopkeepers and traders of the land. The Georgian cultivates the soil or lives on the large estate which he has inherited. In the absence of these he takes to begging, as the streets of Tiflis, the Georgian capital, will show ; but another occupation within his reach is that of highway robbery in Turkey. The Oriental caravans dread more than all to fall into the hands of Georgian robbers. Unlike other brigands, so numerous in the lands of the sultan, the Georgian fires on his victims from behind the tree or stone without any warning or notice. He must kill before he robs. "The fierce, fighting Kurd" among the mountain passes in Armenia is more merciful than these mean and cowardly assassins.

Notwithstanding, there are thousands of Georgians who are industrious and honest. Their immigration into Ottoman lands has perceptibly added to the wealth and civilization of the people. Better roads have been built, and the means of transportation are to-day far superior to those of former times. Surely the impetus given by these Georgians is one of the causes of the improvements in the interior of the Turk-ish Empire.

And now one word about the Osmanlee Government. The prevailing opinion in Europe and this country has been that Turkish rule is synonymous with everything that is monstrous and wicked. Turkey is looked upon as the land of oppression, intolerance, and despotism. The Sultan is represented as an Oriental tyrant, under whose iron heels the people, especially the Christian races, groan and perish. I do not propose to enter into this discussion here. But there is another side to this picture, and some day I have no doubt the whole truth will be known. As our author has very clearly shown, the cardinal vice of the Turkish Government is venality. This has completely corrupted the officers, judges, and rulers. The ends of justice are thwarted, favoritism is shown, robbers are allowed to plunder and to escape —all through bribery. Who can contradict this immoral and degrading condition of affairs in Turkey? But the subjugated Christian races, so loud in their complaints, must acknowledge their share of the responsibility. Instead of encouraging the virtues of the Turks, the conquered people, thinking Islam incapable of any goodness, have appealed only to their passions, and not unfrequently cultivated and supported bad customs for their own gain. The reformation will come when the Christians begin to set a good example to the Turks.

Mohammedanism, however, has produced some excellent results, and is not in itself the enemy of civilization. The power of the religion for good is seen in the life of every *honest* Mussulman. In the Islam quarters of any city or village in Turkey there is less drunkenness, gambling, or direct violation of law than in those inhabited by Greeks, Armenians, and Franks.

The charming impartiality of the author is seen in his description of the character of the muezzin Ahmed. He too is a Mohammedan, but how unlike the Pasha of Batoum, the caimacam, or Murza-Khan ! We can not condemn a religion which, when sincerely followed, will make men honorable, honest, and peaceable. The words which the author puts in the mouth of Ahmed, the conscientious believer in Allah and the Prophet, do not at all surprise us. It sounds very much like a good Moslem. The muezzin says : "I do not think it is so hard for one to do his duty. There are many temptations to every man to do some wrong ; but if he only thinks, 'Shall I break the commands of Allah to enjoy a brief pleasure and forget that he will severely punish all unfaithfulness ?' then it is not hard to withstand."

The curse of the Orient is not Mohammedanism. The salvation of the people will not come from the Russians. Rebellion will not help the conquered countries. The great source of all the wrongs and crimes and sufferings is the want of *moral education,* which, unfortunately, neither the mosque nor the church as they exist to-day can give.

We hope that the reading of "Djambek" will make new friends for a country whose needs are many.

MANGASAR M. MANGASARIAN.

NEW YORK CITY, *March, 1890.*

CONTENTS.

DJAMBEK, THE GEORGIAN.

CHAPTER I.

THE PASHA OF BATOUM.

THE chain of the lesser Caucasus Mountains forms a natural line of demarkation between the province of Batoum and the Turkish provinces of Asia Minor, as well as of Armenia and Georgia. The original inhabitants of this section, stretching from the mountains to the Black Sea, were originally, as far as historical evidence goes, of the pure Georgian race, and, though Islam has for five centuries sought with every means in its power to crush out the national feeling, there still remains on every foot of the land the evidences of the old Georgian nationality. Long before the Christian era the valleys of the chief river, the Tchoroch, its tributaries, and all the country around, received the names which they bear to-day, and which are almost all of Georgian origin. Throughout this region one finds at every step ruins of churches and fortresses bearing inscriptions which, though now unfortunately hardly decipherable, are unquestionably in the old Georgian or Cartalinean language; and the name of the mighty queen, Thamar, is as well known here as it is beyond the mountains, where this Semiramis of Caucasus once held her royal court.

At length, at the beginning of the seventeenth century, the followers of Islam became complete victors, after having instituted a most cruel persecution against everything called Christian, and after leveling to the dust every monument which recalled the once flourishing period of the land's history. For the most part the people resigned themselves to their fate. With unwonted energy the Mohammedan rulers had organized a government which held as in iron bands the whole country of Klarjetia and Adjaria. Batoum became the residence of the pasha, under whose rule were eleven *kazas* or districts, presided over by *caimacams* and *mudirs*. The *Medjilis*, or State-council had its seat in Batoum as well as the tribunals and the customs-officers. A battalion of troops was also stationed there.

After the districts along the coast of the Black Sea had accommodated themselves to their new position, and even in large part had accepted Islamism as their religion, the Klarjetians and the people living along the river Tchoroch followed their example. Even some of the Adjarians submitted to the new rule, in so far at least as outwardly recognizing the Turkish sovereignty. But in their own hearts, the Adjarians for the most part clung to the old faith, and remained true to the old race to which their ancestors had proudly belonged.

Still there were oft-recurring signs of unrest in some of the provinces. Many of those who had been called to office found it advantageous to look less to the interests of the state than to their personal profit. Each *caimacam* felt himself to be a little king within his own district, responsible only to his immediate superior, the Pasha of Batoum. Many of them found it more comfortable to let matters in their districts go as they would rather than take the trouble to see that they went right, while many, too, after a few months of attempts at good government, decided it more to their advantage to make common cause with the corrupt minor officials under them and divide with them the spoils wrung from the people in the way of bribes and unjust taxes. As to making complaints, where could the good people present their complaints? The pasha was absolute master, for Stamboul was so far distant that any cry of injustice would die away before it reached there.

Toward the end of the sixth decade of the present century, as a result of the ever increasing corruption and misgovernment, an insurrection arose among the Adjarians, but it was speedily crushed out. Soon after that, the ruler in Batoum died suddenly, and hope arose that with his successor there might come a change for the better in the government of the unhappy country. And, indeed, as far as promises went, Cherif-Pasha left nothing to be desired, though he always gave these promises with a mental reservation that he would carry them out only so far as doing so did not interfere with his personal comfort and ease. "By Allah!" he used to say to himself, "a man who for forty years has had but few hours of ease, who has been constantly on the journey on government business, to-day in Roumelia, to-morrow in Egypt, next year in Asia Minor, has won the right at last to rest"; and it was for this reason as much as for any that he gladly accepted the post in Batoum.

He took but a small following with him, for the

fewer there were the less was his domestic quiet liable
to be disturbed. Thamar, his grand-niece, who had
been educated at first in Stamboul, and later in a
French institution in Trebizond; Daria, her friend
and companion, and finally Russudan, a distant relative
of uncertain age, formed the female portion of his
household, while his male attendants consisted of
Osman, an old servant, and his assistant Panyoti, a
Greek. The numerous hangers-on which are necessary to the oriental ideas of greatness could be got
later in Batoum.

Cherif-Pasha was a man of some sixty years of age,
of middle stature, and of so heavy build that he had
some difficulty in moving about. A short, gray, full
beard covered the greater part of his face, to which the
heavy, sleepy eyelids gave an expression of extreme
apathy. But even this quiet, stolid mien found favor
with the people, and the amiable expression with which
he listened to their complaints, nodding his head now
and then as if in sympathy, gave them the assurance
that this new governor was a man who would let people talk to him, and under whose rule affairs might
perhaps improve.

When Cherif-Pasha arrived in Batoum, his first
care was that his house might be arranged with all
possible comfort. He found to his agreeable surprise
that the most difficult work had already been done
without any care on his part, and done so well that
the artist who had so cleverly brought it about was at
once taken into his good graces.

Totia Nitscheladze, as the man was called who had
undertaken on his own responsibility to so comfortably
arrange these matters for the pasha, was a Mingrelian,

who had played a very inferior role in the household of the former governor, and after the latter's death had remained in the house, ostensibly to look after it, but really because of want of money necessary to procure other means of living. As soon as he heard of Cherif Pasha's appointment, like the clever fellow that he was, he made a tour among the shops of the city and boldly gave orders in the name and on behalf of the pasha, for all the necessary preparations in making ready the house for his arrival. He selected carpets, rugs, draperies, furniture, utensils, in short all that was necessary for newly furnishing the residence, and gave his orders with so confident an air that no one ventured to decline furnishing whatever he called for. He procured laborers too who carried out all his directions, so that Cherif-Pasha entered a house fully prepared for him.

A satisfied nod and repeated expressions of "Good!" "Excellent!" showed Totia that his speculation had been a successful one, and his satisfaction was increased when the pasha speedily called for the list of expenditures in order that he might make a draft on the Treasury in payment.

The merchants and laborers were paid without any questioning, and Totia had suddenly become a distinguished character. With this fortunate stroke he was able to silence all the disagreeable talk that had been floating about concerning him. For, indeed, it had been whispered that while in the Russian service he had allowed his accounts to become so confused that the only choice left him was to either turn his back upon his home or spend some years in the seclusion of a prison. But now all were ready to believe what he himself said, namely, that while a Russian officer he

had struck one of his superiors who had ill-used him,
and in order to escape the sentence of the court-mar-
tial had been obliged to flee.

Toward the pasha, Totia showed himself as one
whose only object in life was to make his chief's existence as agreeable and comfortable as possible; and
this suited the other so well that the Mingrelian in a
short time had become indispensable and the factotum
of the house. While the pasha reclined in comfort on
his cushions, with the amber mouthpiece of his *nargile*
always at his lips, the ladies of the household busied
themselves with arranging their new home. Thamar,
a girl of twenty, with black eyes and tall, slender
figure, had European blood in her veins. Her mother
was French. The girl inherited from her the light,
delicate complexion, the small hands and feet, and a
talent for dressing herself becomingly with limited ma-
terials, and for arranging the rooms of the house in a
way that was at once elegant and home-like. The inter-
course between her and Daria was that of two sisters,
while toward Russudan she showed more of a formal
etiquette. The elderly lady belonged to the fanatical
party. She looked with hatred and contempt upon
anything new or foreign to Turkish customs, and
reckoned it impious for a woman to be seen with her
face uncovered. Many were the lectures the young
girls were obliged to listen to from her when they returned from the French school dressed in European
fashion. Had it been in Stamboul, Cherif-Pasha must
have admitted that she was in the right; but here, in
this out-of-the-world place, he paid little attention to
her complaints and implied that it was as well to keep
one eye shut in regard to such matters. When she

threatened him with the anger of the prophet, he would raise his heavy eyelids and pointing in the direction where Constantinople lay in the far distance would say :

"My good Russudan, the prophet has so much to look after over there that he will have but little time to turn his attention to us poor worms. Let us rather let the matter rest and not disturb the quiet peace of our household."

The citadel where the pasha lived was upon a height which formed a part of a promontory extending into the sea. Here the air was fresh and mild, and the view over the city and surrounding plain and the sea beyond was a beautiful one. The vegetation was almost tropical in its luxuriance. The groves were filled with plants which in Europe are cultivated with care in greenhouses but here grow like weeds. Rhododendrons of most gorgeous coloring, soft green mixed with flame - like blossoms, olive trees and fig trees, all shades of green and all colors of flowers, thick grape-vines and climbing roses, all blended in one of Nature's fairest pictures.

The two friends spent hours together in the gardens that surrounded the buildings. They usually brought their books with them — those wicked and dangerous types of the unbelieving West, as Russudan called them; but their reading did not usually continue long, for the beauty of the scene around them was apt to draw their attention away.

Though Cherif - Pasha sought to avoid being troubled with affairs of business, still he was not one who loved retirement and solitude. On the contrary, he liked to have people about him and to join in con-

2

versation, so long as it was not of a character to tax the
brain too much. His house was always open to those
who might like to come to drink a cup of coffee, smoke
a cigarette or *chibouk*, and talk over the latest events
in the city. There were even regular evenings when
his acquaintances assembled there in large numbers
to spend an hour or two in social conversation, quite
in European fashion. Those who wished could even
play cards, and the evening always closed with a sup-
per, in which the food and drinks were not always
regulated according to the command of the prophet.

The liberal minded governor, indeed, looked on
Batoum as being not a part of his own country so much
as an advanced post which lay in neutral ground. In
fact, commerce with other nations began to assume
considerable proportions, so that several of the great
powers found it advisable to send their consuls to
Batoum, and these officials, with their families, gladly
took advantage of the opportunity to make the mo-
notony of life there a little less irksome by the social
evenings at the pasha's. Both the Russian and English consuls had wife and daughters; and in their
honor the pasha could not do less than have his niece
and her friend take part in these official gatherings,
though Russudan used every means in her power to
prevent so gross a breach of Moslem customs. The
other officials of the city were for the most part men
grown old in the service, who had little taste for Western novelties, and therefore seldom took advantage of
their chief's hospitality; while, on the other hand, the
younger generation found these evenings very pleasant, and contributed all they could toward banishing
all remembrance of old Turkish fanaticism.

The soul of the whole was, next to Totia, the chief of the battalion, Hassan Bey, a man in the prime of life, who was for a long time attached to the embassy in Italy, and had there tasted too often of the forbidden fruit to willingly withdraw again into the narrow ways of his fellow-believers. So that, altogether, the evenings passed right merrily, and Russudan had reason enough to shake her head gloomily and prophesy the swift vengeance of heaven.

Little by little the circle increased, and several of the more prominent natives of the city were drawn into it. Among these was a young man, whose uncle, Artschil Tagniridza, was a member of the tribunal and a man of considerable prominence.

Djambek Tagniridza, the nephew, had lost both parents in his early youth. He busied himself with the management of the extensive estates which he owned in the elevated plain of Adjaria. He was body and soul an Adjarian, and so, in a wider sense, a Georgian, and at first held aloof from the pasha's coterie, whom he regarded as the instruments of unjust oppression, and toward whom he nursed a silent hatred. But as the impression gradually extended that Cherif-Pasha was a man who loved justice and his fellow men, he allowed himself to be persuaded one evening to visit the citadel in company with his uncle. To his pleasant surprise he found little trace there of the strict Turkish element which elsewhere made itself so sternly felt, and he enjoyed himself so much in this mixed company of foreigners and liberal - minded Turks, that henceforth he became a regular visitor. Having received a good education, partly in Tifles and partly in Odessa, he could speak Russian and even in case of necessity take part in a French conversation, when Thamar introduced it, with the wives and daughters of the European guests.

Djambek gave no more of his attentions to the pasha's niece than to the other young ladies, he even held somewhat aloof from her when he saw that Hassan Bey was anxious to gain her good favor, and was encouraged in doing so by Cherif-Pasha.

Totia—who since he had become the pasha's factotum considered that he must make himself as prominent as possible—paid most devoted attentions to Thamar's friend. He received, however, no encouragement. On the contrary, she gave him every opportunity of seeing that his society was distasteful to her. But this only made him the more assiduous and the more importunate in his attempts to gain her favor.

Cherif-Pasha showed himself on many occasions well disposed toward Djambek. This encouraged the young man to refer now and then to the many cases of misgovernment and abuse of power which were taking place in the province. Especially was it the caimacam of Adjaria, whose conduct of affairs left much to be desired, and whom Djambek often complained of to the pasha. But this sort of conversation was not at all to the pasha's liking. He would indeed shake his head and admit that things were not all as they should be, but he would soon manage to change the subject after assuring his caller that these matters should be looked into.

CHAPTER II.

Two years had passed since the arrival of Cherif-Pasha in Batoum. The people had come to understand their governor, and saw that as little was being done for the good of the country and the interests of the people as in former times. No one was sanguine enough now to hope for any improvement. In many places complaints became loud.

Among the most dissatisfied was Djambek, who had learned very quickly that the pasha promised readily but never carried out his promises. The only result of his intervention had been to make the caimacam of Adjaria his bitter enemy. The pasha had treated this official in a friendly way, and had advised him to be on good terms with the young man, as he had made complaints against him. This confidential information had aroused the anger of Ali Bey and he sought revenge by spreading suspicions that Djambek was a political agitator and a friend of Russia. Some small occurrences happened in the province just at the time, which enabled Ali Bey to make charges against his enemy though Djambek had in reality had nothing whatever to do with the matters in question. The result was that the pasha began to show himself less

friendly toward him, and as he hated telling people
directly what he meant, he intimated to the young
man's uncle that it would be well for him to talk to
his nephew and bring him to his senses. Artschil
hastened to carry out his superior's instructions, and
warned the young man from mixing in political matters.

"Ali Bey has never injured you personally, and
why should you risk your head for other people," said
he. "It is a thankless business which can only harm
you, while others will use it for their own advantage."

Djambek was greatly astonished at the lengthy lecture his uncle favored him with on this subject. He
admitted that he had often made complaints against
the caimacam, but denied being the leader of the dis-
contented faction.

"In that they have simply lied to you," he said
quietly. "It was I that sought to keep the people
quiet, and advised them not to incur the disastrous results of a forcible opposition. Furthermore, I shall
speak to Cherif-Pasha myself, for if it ever comes so
far that I am obliged to disturb the peace of the land,
as I hope will never be necessary, I shall not do it
behind his back while showing a false friendship to
his face."

He carried out this intention at once. He went to
the pasha and gave him a clear account of the matters
in question. At the same time he did not hesitate to
repeat his charges concerning the misgovernment and
official oppression practiced by Ali Bey in the district
under his charge, and as Cherif-Pasha, who was in exceptional good humor that day, voluntarily proposed
visiting the district to see for himself how matters

stood, Djambek took advantage of the opportunity to get him to fix a day for the visit, in order, as he said, that he might arrange the necessary preparations that the Pasha might make the journey as comfortably as possible. The next week having been fixed on, Djambek betook himself home in order to make his arrangements at once. The pasha, on his part, hastened to let the caimacam know of the projected visit, in order that he too might be prepared, and not leave a place exposed which might bring his superior into the disagreeable position of being obliged to give a reprimand. So the whole matter resolved itself rather into a pleasure excursion which the Pasha sought to make more agreeable by inviting some of his Batoum friends to accompany him.

In the meantime great preparations went on in the *kaza* for the distinguished visit. The caimacam used his utmost efforts to arrange matters in a favorable light, and as he possessed a considerable following among those of the population who had lost their remembrance of the ancient regime, he felt confident that he would be well prepared for any investigation that the easy going pasha might make. Djambek, on his part, made extensive preparations to receive the governor in a worthy fashion, and to repay the many hospitalities he had received at his house by making the visit as brilliant a one as possible.

The situation of the young man's house was in a beautiful valley, which enjoyed a wide reputation for its excellent fruit. The family mansion was upon a gentle rise of ground above the village of Scalta. The pasha would make his headquarters here with his fol-lowing, and proceeded the next day on the official inspection through the *kaza*, while the master of the house would entertain the other guests who remained behind. A large part of the trip through the *kaza* would have to be up the river in boats and would require at least two days. While Djambek busied himself with seeing that his house was fitly prepared for the distinguished guests, his friends and neighbors attended to the preparations for the river excursion. They found that three boats or *caiques* would be necessary. The newest and largest were chosen and fitted up as comfortable as was possible. One was intended for the pasha and his friends during the day, the second for the ladies of the party at night, and the third for the attendants without whom an eastern dignitary can not travel. All the cushions and carpets that could be spared from the different houses were brought together. A gayly colored awning protected against the rays of the sun, while on the night boat for the ladies, a regular house was built, and under Djambek's personal supervision was fitted up with all the comforts and conveniences which this out of the way place could afford.

Djambek's house, a two-story building, stood upon a hill commanding the river. As he belonged to one of the most distinguished families of the land, his house was superior to the others of the village in size and in the care which had been bestowed on both its interior and exterior ornamentation. Finely carved work on the gables, pillars and verandas gave it an appearance of lightness and elegance, and the walls and ceilings within were finished with no little taste. In the reception room stood an immense stove of marble, whose fine carving gave evidence of the skill and artistic taste of the native stove-workers. Around the four sides of the room ran a shelving of fragrant cedar wood which was a masterpiece of filagree work, and on it sparkled the valuable silver plates, cups, bowls, and spoons which dated from the time when the owner's family openly reckoned itself as belonging to the Georgian people and stood in close connection with the Caucasian capital. Divans of various shapes, covered with fine rugs of Teker and Daghistan and soft cushions which seemed to invite to repose, were placed along the walls, while the six covered *tabourets* of inlaid mother-of-pearl stood near so that one half-reclining could comfortably reach coffee cup or cigarette.

Djambek had arranged with a few friends to meet the guests at the mouth of the Adjaria in gayly decorated boats. Early on the appointed day they started on their way, having some five hours of distance down stream.

The caimacam, with a numerous following, was at the rendezvous before Djambek and his friends arrived there. The two parties, however, after formal greetings, held themselves aloof from each other, as neither of the opponents felt like taking the first step toward the other.

A boat with two of the villagers was sent farther down the stream with directions to fire guns when they saw the pasha's party approaching. Before long the shots were heard and the little boat came back rowed at full speed. The boats intended for the reception of the guests were quickly manned, while Djambek's *caique* flew swiftly through the water and shot ahead of the caimacam's.

Cherif-Pasha came with his friends on a cutter belonging to the customs office, and he was not displeased to hear from Djambek that the party was to change boats here and make the rest of the journey in more comfort.

The finely decorated *caique* waiting by the shore called out expressions of general admiration, and when at length all were comfortably seated on the soft cushions under the awning, and coffee was handed around, Cherif-Pasha declared that everything was beautifully arranged, and that his young friend, Djambek, was a most excellent host. Thamar, too, spoke a few friendly words in praise of the arrangements, and the daughters of the European guests were enthusiastic in their admiration of everything.

Djambek, who, after seeing his guests started would have withdrawn to his own boat, was compelled by the governor, to remain with him. The pasha also invited the caimacam to stay near him.

The course up the river was slow, but no one was in a special hurry, for the whole company was in such good spirits, that all declared the voyage might last a week without any one having need to wish it at an end. As the boats approached the first village a *caique* put out carrying the elders accompanied by their attendants, while the other inhabitants, in holiday dress, lined the shore and filled the air with shouts of welcome and salvos from their guns. This was repeated at each village they passed. As noon approached, a landing was made at a village for lunch.

The governor conversed in a jovial way with the representatives of the people, listened to all their complaints, and unhesitatingly promised to right all that was wrong, agreeing to everything in the friendliest way possible.

After an excellent meal, the party proceeded on their way, and, as each village contributed one boat or more to the escort, the train toward evening became an imposing one. With the approach of darkness torches were lighted, while bonfires along the shore reflected in the stream, and, lighting up the groves and villages along the banks, made the scene a brilliant one.

On board the governor's boat the best of spirits prevailed, and no one thought of retiring. Refreshments of various kinds were placed on a table for whomsoever wished to help himself, while a company of musicians discoursed the plaintive minor music peculiar to the East.

Thamar sat at one side, away from the others, and dreamily watched the changing scenes along the banks lit up with a fantastic light by the torches and bonfires. Djambek reclined at her side, telling her of the peculiar customs of the people, customs handed down from remotest time.

" I did not think when we landed in Batoum that we were to find here a real fairy-land," said the young girl.

Djambek smiled. " It appears to you so now, under the influence of this excursion, which has something romantic in it," he said, " but I can assure you that, as a rule, life here is prosaic enough. The struggle for personal interests requires so much of one's energy, that there is little time left to indulge in romantic ideas. In former times it was different."

Thamar glanced up with some surprise. " You speak as if you were a relative of Russudan, who is always bewailing the loss of the good old times when strict rules prevailed and every infraction of ruling

customs was looked upon as a high crime. I must
admit I do not mourn for the loss of these so-called
good old times, for then, instead of enjoying this
pleasant trip, I should have the doubtful pleasure of
sitting behind lock and key, nibbling *helva* or count-
ing my string of amber beads. No, I was not created
for that sort of life. The blood of my mother would
revolt against it."

"You misunderstand me," said Djambek; "I too
have tasted enough of Western customs to have no desire for the revival of our old, strict ideas of life. I
only regret the existing conditions which force us to
be incessantly on our guard if we would not be crushed
in the battle for existence. It is just that that robs
life of its pleasures, and forbids us from taking time
for thinking of anything else but the merely material.
In former times one would go cheerfully about his
day's work, and, when that was ended, meet with his
fellows for an evening of quiet pleasure with dancing
and singing, and so dream away a few hours free from
the strain of life's cares and labors. But, now, each
goes gloomily to his hut, to count on his fingers how
much remains to be done, and how hard he must labor
in the sweat of his brow to satisfy the demands constantly made upon him by those above him, and to
put off the evil hour when he will be driven from
house and field, because his earnings are not enough
to meet the obligations imposed on him by the state.
Formerly, each enjoyed for himself the fruits of his
labor; now, they fall into the laps of those who have
done little or nothing to deserve them. But I am
wrong to spoil the pleasure of the day by such unpleasant talk. Forgive me."

" You do me wrong if you think I care to talk only about light and trivial matters; I can also sympathize with others' hardships, if I could only do something to help them. From all you say, I judge you blame the existing government. Is my uncle—"

" Your uncle is a good man," interrupted Djambek, fearing he had introduced a subject that was painful to his companion—" perhaps, indeed, he is too good. He wishes to make things pleasant for everybody, and that is a difficult task.—See there," he cried, " they are burning Bengal-lights. The light reaches to the distant mountains. You can even see the snow-covered summits, if you look close."

Thamar looked in the direction he indicated. " Yes, indeed, I can see the glimmer of the snow."

" There is an old tradition connected with that mountain," continued Djambek. " It happened, as in all fairy tales, ages and ages ago. A prince of the land, at the bidding of his mother, went to the mountains to seek a bride. He soon returned, bringing a young girl with him. Accompanying her was a most beautiful woman. 'Who is this woman?' demanded his mother, looking with jealous eyes upon the stranger. ' The friend and protector of my bride,' replied the son. ' Then,' cried the mother, in anger, ' she is a creature that will bring woe to thee and thine! No! I will not endure her!' and she uttered a furious curse which changed the bride and her companion into stone where they stood. The following morning the husband of the beautiful woman came, and when he learned what had happened he broke forth in dreadful cries, so that the whole valley was filled with the noise, and the hills echoed back his lamentations unceasingly. The inhabitants of the place were terror-stricken at the frightful clamor, and called to their assistance a giant, who chained the husband to the rocks. But when the unhappy man swore by all his gods that he would cease his cries, the giant released him from his chains. As soon as he was free, he sprang at one leap over the mountains to that snow-clad pinnacle yonder, and there disappeared. But on the rock to which he had been chained one may see to-day the impression that his foot left as he made that mighty leap. A primitive tale, is it not?"

"But perhaps with some meaning for those who can read it aright," said Thamar, musingly.

"Yes, you are right. I have often thought over it, wondering if there were not some historical event for its basis, or whether, perhaps, it had some allegorical meaning taken from the long-vanished past."

"And have you come to any conclusion?"

"Not with certainty; for there are so many meanings that might be attributed to it that it is difficult to say which is the right one. It seems most probable that it is the form of the Promethean myth that obtained in this land. The rock to which, according to the myth, the unhappy hero was bound, lies not far distant from here. It is a mountain in Imerethia, now called the Chwamli; that is to say, Smoke, probably because its top is often covered with clouds. But it is also possible that, in the first instance, the legend was intended to teach that one must be constantly on his guard against the encroachment of foreign elements, and, to avoid unhappy results, one must see that he be not carried away with the witchery of beauty and splendor."

"I suppose by 'foreign elements' we are meant," said Thamar, smiling.

"You? Your name clearly marks you as belonging to us. Thamar was the greatest queen that ever lived, and under her rule naught but good came to the land."

"That is very flattering of you. Very well, will you choose me as your queen? I certainly would accept the throne," she replied, laughingly.

"As my queen? Instantly! With all my heart."

The words escaped his lips without his will, and he drew back half frightened at his boldness. The girl, too, startled at the meaning given by her harmless jest, let her eyes seek the ground, forgetful that the darkness hid the blushes that colored her cheeks and brow. Both were silent with embarrassment; and neither knew how to begin the conversation again.

Daria solved the difficulty by approaching her friend and telling her that the ladies were about to withdraw to the other boat where their sleeping quarters had been arranged. The company dispersed, and soon nothing disturbed the stillness of the night but the regular dip of the oar and the ripple of the water.

CHAPTER III.

AN EXCURSION AND INVESTIGATION.

THE sun was high when the party reassembled the next morning on board the governor's boat.

The day was beautiful. A cool breeze from the west tempered the heat of the sun and made it practicable to use the sail and so increase the speed of the boats. The pasha saw to his satisfaction that the boats accompanying him had much increased in number overnight so that his was at the head of quite a numerous fleet of larger and smaller boats and *caiques*. On all sides were songs and music and cheers of welcome from the people along the shores; so that he felt himself quite like a king making a progress through his land and receiving the plaudits of his people. As they were now in the region celebrated for its fruit, at many of the villages the tributes of respect brought by the chiefs took that form.

At length they reached the end of their journey, and, as they approached Scalta, they could see a great crowd of people assembled on the bank in holiday attire. As the boats neared the landing-place, loud cries went up from the people, mingled with the reports of fire-arms, which echoed and re-echoed among the hills.

Landing at the impromptu stage laid with carpets, the pasha and his friends mounted the horses which stood ready. Djambek assisted Thamar to mount, and in doing so held her pretty foot perhaps an instant longer than was strictly necessary for the purpose, and all proceeded in gay procession to the house.

The more distant villages not less interested in the event than the Adjarian highland had sent most of their men to join in the honors paid the distinguished guest, so that there was such a multitude in the little village as certainly had never been seen there before. Cherif-Pasha observed this with no little self-satisfaction as he looked down from the carved balcony on the crowd below.

" I thank you heartily, my dear young friend," he said, pressing Djambek's hand. " You have given me a reception, and through me our august sovereign, the padishah, which speaks eloquently for the excellent feeling of the people."

Then turning to the caimacam, he added :

" Let the people be told that the rest of the day is to be devoted to pleasure, but that to-morrow I shall be pleased to listen to any petitions or representations they may have to make, and for that purpose it will be more convenient for all if they choose representatives to speak in their name."

The banquet-table was spread under the giant lindens with places for fifty, as, besides the pasha's party, the leading men of the vicinity had been invited. Parallel with this table was another for the village elders and the lesser officials. As for the others, they sat about in groups on the grass around the fires where the food was being prepared.

3

While the guests were still at table, and coffee and
cigarettes were being handed around, the villagers
commenced their national songs and dances. All were
in holiday dress, and each had taken pains to deck
himself out with the best his wardrobe afforded.

The Adjarian costume, together with that of the
Guriens, is the most attractive of the Caucasus. A
jacket reaching only to the waist, open at the breast to
show the bright-colored *caftan*—a garment between a
vest and shirt—covers the upper part of the body.
The trousers are wide at the waist and narrow at the
ankles; a wide girdle of bright-colored silk is bound
many times around the waist. The feet are covered
with shoes of soft leather, pointed and embroidered.
Like all Caucasians, the Adjarian prides himself in
his weapons: a dagger and pistol, often two pistols,
richly inlaid with silver, are thrust into the girdle, the
latter generally behind the hips. Two rows of metal
cartridges, fastened in a band of filigree-work, sparkle
across the breast. A small pouch of leather embroidered in gold thread and attached to a gold cord which
passes around the neck, carries flint and tinder and a
small box of grease for use in loading the cartridges,
while at the girdle hangs a flat drinking-cup of metal
or leather. The every-day dress is usually of gray or
light brown, but on festivals occasions brighter colors
are brought into use, particularly blue, of which one
may see every shade in the different costumes. The
head-covering, a sort of turban, is of some bright
color—red, blue, or yellow.

The women and young girls wore veils over their
heads, with the ends drawn over the face; but here and
there, in the excitement of the dance, the jealous cov-

ering would fall down, revealing glowing cheeks, sparkling black eyes, and rich red lips. Nor indeed were the young women very particular about hiding the charms of their faces, especially as the ladies with Cherif-Pasha gave the example of fullest freedom in this respect.

The couples turned in graceful movements to the more melancholy than joyous strains of the native stringed instruments. There were war and weapon dances too, which gave opportunity for much address and skill, as the dancers held their sharp daggers to breast and throat, when a misstep or mistaken movement might give a serious wound. After the dancing came wrestling-matches and foot-races. When these were over, darkness was approaching, and the servants dispersed to prepare the lanterns of colored paper to hang about the verandas and grounds, and to prepare the fire-rafts which were to be floated down the river.

While these preparations were going on, Djambek found opportunity to exchange a few words with Thamar. When she complimented him on the success of the *fête* he had arranged, he replied, with Oriental extravagance, that the honors they had tried to show her were, to his regret, far below what was due her rank and beauty, but that they came from devoted hearts, and that this day, which had brought the queen of the fairies to her home, would be remembered forever in all Adjaria.

Thamar smiled at the extravagant words. " Do you forget that we were not brought up in this country? " she said, with a slight reproof in her tone.

" I do not forget it, but the customs of the country will have it so. And in any case, my thoughts remain the same, though they are clothed in our Eastern garb. I feel myself really indebted to you for coming and the every-day phrase—'I have been much pleased'—gives too little expression to my thought."

" Especially as these customary expressions of pleasure often mean the very opposite."

" Very true ! So we will keep to our Oriental forms—"

" Which also do not always come from the heart," she said, smilingly, " but are better in keeping with the place."

" Shall I take a solemn òath that to-day they are the expressions of the fullest truth ? "

" I will believe you," she replied, with a laugh. " As far as concerns myself, I came with the most friendly feeling, so there is no reason why you should wish my visit had not taken place; and, as for my uncle, I can assure you that he is friendly to you, and undertook this trip with the best intentions."

" May his visit bear the hoped-for fruit!" he replied.

The other young people now came up to them; and as Hassan Bey, the commander of the garrison, seemed to have something particular he wished to say to Thamar, Djambek yielded his place to him and fell into conversation with Daria and the European ladies. All agreed in saying that the whole excursion had been like a visit to fairy-land ; and, if Djambek had been open to conceit, he might well have drawn conclusions very favorable to himself from the flattering words and bright glances that fell about him.

Totia, the pasha's factotum, sought from a feeling of jealousy to weaken the effect of the day's festivities by a glowing description of how magnificent had been the reception given the Russian Czar on his visit to the Caucasus. But his descriptions found little favor with the company, who all declared that it was doubtless very well in its way, but could not have equaled what they had enjoyed to-day.

A shot now rang through the air. A few seconds later sparks glittered all along the shore, and then a shower of fire fell upon the water, and the river was covered with thousands of dancing lights. A second, a third report followed, until the whole river as far as the eye could reach glowed and glistened with shimmering points. The concentrated light threw a crimson glow upon both shores, so that the giant trees whose branches overhung the water stood out in strange colors, and suddenly seemed to be on fire to their very tops. Then the dark form of a boat glided out on the glowing surface of the river, to suddenly become wrapped in colored fire and then spring into the air with a loud report.

This was the signal for the music and dancing to commence again. By the mild light of the colored lamps, the couples glided about in graceful circles, at first with measured movements, but then, quickly becoming excited, they flew faster and faster, until the whole company was in a confusion of leaping, whirling, singing, shouting dancers whose movements the eye could not follow. Suddenly, a figure, which in the half-light looked gigantic, leaped over the heads of those in the outer circle, seized one of the girls in his arms and with powerful blows made a way through the crowd to disappear with his burden, like a flash, in the darkness. The mysterious personage had pushed

his way close by where Thamar was standing with her
friends, and now as a crowd of men with drawn daggers and wild cries rushed by her, she grasped Djambek's arm in terror.

" A bold fellow," he said, quietly. " This is in
earnest. It was not a part of the programme."

" What is it ? " she asked, in agitation.

" A peasant has carried off his sweetheart, so that
he may marry her in spite of her relatives. It behooves
him to be quick and clever now, unless he wants to
pay for his boldness with his life."

" You think that "—loud and angry cries were
heard from the river-bank—" Listen ! Ought not some
one go to his help? "

He grasped her hands tightly, that she might not
be carried away by the crowd which rushed by them.

" Oh, I know the man. He is one of the strongest
and cleverest young peasants in the highlands. Any-
way, he is certainly not alone. His friends will know
how to turn the pursuers off from his track. It is their
affair, and it would go hard with any third party who
tried to interfere. He would draw down on him the
vengeance of the whole crowd. If I thought he was
in real peril, I would go to his help—to assist true love
in distress, for I do not believe that any one has the
right to interfere in another's love-affairs. It is quiet
now—a sign that they have found no trace of them
yet."

The whole company had by this time thronged to
the banks of the river, as it was thought the fugitive
had taken to a boat. Even Cherif-Pasha and his company had been drawn there by curiosity with the
others. Djambek and Thamar stood alone under the

lindens. The murmur of many voices came to them from below, with now and then a loud shout from one of the pursuers, giving directions to those in the other boats.

Suddenly, from one of the hills on the other side of the river there rang out a shot and a loud shout.

Thamar anxiously pressed Djambek's hand, and her voice trembled as she whispered :

" They have killed him ! "

" No ; on the contrary," cried Djambek, joyfully, returning the pressure of her hand, " he is out of danger and is in safety now. He was clever enough to choose the difficult and dangerous way over the mountain instead of trying to escape down the river. He is a long way ahead now, and knows every path, and it will be impossible for them to overtake him." And, as if to vex the others, he drew his pistol and fired it, at the same time giving a prodigious shout of exultation.

Thamar now noticed for the first time that he was still holding her hand. She drew it away, blushing, and turned into the path which led to where the others were.

" These are fine goings on," said Cherif-Pasha, shaking his finger at Djambek as he approached. "Kidnapping !—elopement ! " and he broke into a hearty laugh. " Well, I must close one eye, and believe that our host has arranged this little piece of acting for our amusement. But, if they had caught the rascal, by Allah, I would have given him a good lecture and locked him up for a month."

" You would hardly be so severe as that," said Djambek, smiling.

" Indeed I would. I should certainly have made an example of him."

"That is, supposing they had brought him back alive!" added Djambek.

"It would be a fine state of affairs if they killed him for such a piece of foolishness."

"So, if any one dared, for example—your niece—"

"That, my friend, is something different," interrupted the pasha in evident displeasure. "I represent here our august lord the padishah, and any one that would commit such a crime against him is certainly ripe for the gallows. But it is getting late and I must be up early to-morrow, to listen to what the good people have to say and to carry out their wishes. So, thanks, friend Djambek, for a delightful day, and—good-night!"

It had been arranged that the pasha and suite with the caimacam should go to the government-house of the district, distant some hours' journey, where the representatives of the different communities were to meet them. The other guests in the mean time were to visit a friend of Djambek's to attend the celebration of a wedding.

The programme was carried out the next day, the pasha with his suite, Ali Bey, Hassan Bey, and Totia going to hold the inspection, while Djambek and his other guests betook themselves to the scene of the wedding.

The host and his guests passed a pleasant day at the wedding festivities, and toward evening were escorted home by the bridegroom and his friends. The pasha arrived about the same time. He was in excellent spirits, and assured Djambek that everything had gone off finely. "The people are all satisfied," he said, loud enough to be overheard by Ali Bey, who compla-

cently stroked his beard and regarded Djambek with
an ill-concealed look of triumph. He had every reason
to be satisfied at his victory, though it had been easily
won, as he had himself chosen the representatives who
were to speak in behalf of the others. These naturally
had no complaints to make, and vied with each other
in praise of the caimacam who, according to their version, was a most upright man, always ready to assist
the well-disposed and peaceable.

Djambek contented himself with a shrug of the
shoulders. It was evident that a trick had been played
him; but to-day he was unable to guess how Ali Bey
had been able to make the dissatisfied and wronged
members of the community keep silent. What could
he then say to the pasha? But it was bitter for him
to think that he had incurred all this trouble and expense, only to bring about the triumph of his enemy.

He retired with the feeling of a man who has
staked all his fortune on a card, and sees his opponent
drawing it in with a grin of triumph. From what he
knew of the pasha, he knew that he would now be satisfied, and assured for all time of the satisfactory state
of affairs. There was no longer any hope of convincing him that his subordinate had misused his office to
amass wealth. If justice was to be obtained now, it
must be sought farther off than Batoum—and, even
there, there was but little hope—for who in Stamboul
would trouble himself about an insignificant province
in the Caucasus, of which even the name was hardly
known? And even if he were listened to, the first step
would be to ask for a report from Cherif-Pasha, and
one could harbor no illusion as to what the character
of the report would be.

Djambek arose early the next morning, hoping that he might have an opportunity for a talk with Cherif-Pasha; but, in answer to his inquiries, he was told that his guest was still peacefully slumbering. So he occupied the time walking up and down before the house, and, while doing so, he saw his relative Artschil at one of the open windows. He beckoned to him to come out, and poured forth his grievances to him.

Artschil listened quietly, and, when the other was silent, said:

"What will you have, then? Ali Bey is a sly fox, who knows how to turn things to his own advantage. There is nothing you can do now. It is hopeless to try and win the pasha to your side, since he has, as he thinks, investigated matters for himself. You would only make him regard you as a slanderer and busy-body whom it would be well to keep at a distance. If you follow my advice, you will act in a friendly way toward Ali Bey, and, for the present, let matters rest where they are."

"Never!" cried Djambek, excitedly; "I will never so demean myself as to make common cause with a man whom I look upon as a thief and an oppressor of the people, and whom I despise from the bottom of my heart."

Artschil waved his hand back and forth in a gesture peculiar to the native Georgians.

"What will you do? You can't change nature and make trees grow downward. Cherif-Pasha has heard only good reports concerning the caimacam. You see, therefore, that your own associates have left you in the lurch. Believe me, it never pays to sacrifice yourself in the interests of others."

The other shook his head.

"It would be cowardly to allow one's self to be frightened from his purpose because momentarily his opponent has the advantage over him. Let Ali Bey beware! If I can not obtain justice from those who are appointed to do justice, I and my countrymen know how to obtain it for ourselves."

"You are too hot-headed, Djambek," retorted Artschil. "Beware of trying to meet force with force. They are too strong for you." He paused, and, shading his eyes with his hand, looked in the direction from which a band of horsemen was seen approaching. "What people are those?" he asked.

Djambek strained his eyes to see, for the men were still at some distance.

"It is Murza-Khan. Probably he is coming from the mountains, where he sent his cattle a few days ago."

Murza-Khan was a prominent character in the land, and one that was feared. His ancestors had been freebooters in further Asia, who in times of war took every opportunity to plunder, irrespective of which side they robbed. In this way they had in the course of time amassed great riches, a large part of which was in landed estates which they had forcibly taken possession of. Murza's father, however, sold the larger part of these when the Russians began to get possession of the country, and with the proceeds removed to Turkish territory, where he acquired extensive estates, which brought him in large profits in silk, oil, and wax.

After his father's death, Murza-Khan came into the possession of the estates, which constantly increased in value, so that at length he came to be a personage looked upon by his neighbors as a little king. He owned pasture-lands in the Adjarian highlands, and thither he sent every spring his extensive flocks and herds, to remain there until winter. His estates proper were situated north of Batoum. There he had his own residence in a castle called Kardjeti-Tziche, situated on a rocky eminence overlooking the sea.

Murza-Khan had no need of robbing others to add to his riches; but it was whispered that by means of his boats, of which he owned a perfect fleet, he occasionally imported goods upon which the government collected no duty. The authorities winked at this; for the northern district to a man swore by the name of Murza-Khan, and it was as well to keep so powerful a man for a friend.

Djambek went forward to meet the stranger, whom he had often visited with his father when a boy. "I sent you word that Cherif-Pasha was coming here on a visit," he said, after the usual salutations; "but perhaps my messenger did not find you at home."

"Yes, I know it," replied Murza-Khan, indifferently. "I knew of the visit, but it was of more importance to me to look after the welfare of my herds than of Cherif-Pasha. I can assure myself as to his health any day if I want to."

"But you will rest here, will you not?" said Djambek, with a hospitable wave of the hand; and, as the governor is returning home soon, it will be pleasanter for you to go the shorter way by boat with him. We can arrange a boat for the horses."

"That will suit me, though you know I have no special love for high society." He dismounted, and again saluted Djambek and Artschil. "If you can give me some breakfast, Heaven will reward you, for I have eaten nothing for six hours."

Djambek at once gave the necessary orders, and Murza-Khan soon sat down to a bountiful breakfast. "That was good," he said, after satisfying his hunger. "I feel more good-natured now, too," and his bearded face was drawn into a friendly grimace, showing two rows of powerful white teeth. "Now I will make his High Mightiness one of my most respectful salaams."

At this moment Cherif - Pasha came out of the house, and, as soon as he recognized Murza-Khan, he hastened toward him.

"What! is it you?" he exclaimed. "It is well that you let yourself be seen. You have been a rare guest of late."

"Unfortunately," he replied, affecting a tone of deep regret. "Business gives me no rest; it is always driving me."

"A happy lot, when it drives into riches," said the pasha.

"Riches! He only is rich who carries his wealth with him. I envy these strolling singers, who have no cares, are welcome everywhere, and get food and lodging at the only cost of letting their songs be heard."

"Perhaps you are right, Murza-Khan. We who are called rich have more cares than pleasures."

One by one the others of the party came from the house, and preparations began for the return journey. Murza-Khan, who was accustomed to be waited on, left to Djambek the responsibility of arranging for the transport of his attendants, and chatted with Thamar, whom he had met once or twice at her uncle's house.

He also tried to converse with the other young ladies, but with indifferent success, as he could only speak Turkish. But they took pains to try and understand him, and to make themselves understood, for he was an interesting man, whose reputation as a nabob and powerful lord had come to the cars of even the European residents of Batoum. The daughter of the Russian consul, particularly, took pains to make known her interest in him, and, when she could not find the right word, Daria would good-naturedly act as interpreter, and had to repeat several times that Murza-Khan was exactly like the portrait of her ideal hero, Abdulla-Kader. At this he would show his white teeth, stroke his black beard complacently, while his flashing eyes, wandering from one to the other, seemed to say: " You may all fall in love with me in turn. I am very willing to share my heart among you."

At length the signal was given to embark, and the company entered the boats. As the course was now down-stream, the boats went rapidly. Batoum might be reached by evening. Some stops were again made at different villages, to allow the elders to pay their respects, and at length the point was reached where the pasha's party was to take the cutter. Here Djambek took leave of his guests, after promising the pasha to attend a festival which he intended giving in return for the civilities he had received. The young man waved his white turban in a parting salute as long as the cutter was in sight, and then turned the bow of his boat toward home.

Murza-Khan and Hassan Bey vied with each other in polite attentions and gallant speeches to Thamar, but the young girl's glance rested dreamily on the distant mountains, and her ears heard only detached phrases of what they said to her. It seemed to her as if she had been torn away from a sunny land of romance and brought back against her will to the dull routine of every-day life.

CHAPTER IV.

MURZA-KHAN AND THAMAR.

Now that the pasha had found everything in good order, the caimacam naturally became still bolder and lost no opportunity of doing what he could to spite Djambek.

Not far from the young man's house there was a small dwelling which a former female servant of Djambek's father had received from him as a gift. She lived there with her husband, and got along very well until one day her ill fate would have it that her husband fell seriously ill and afterward became a cripple. He was now unable to earn means of subsistence, and the poor woman found it impossible to provide for both. Djambek, indeed, was generous with his help, and also the woman's brother, although himself but a poor devil earning the meagerest of living as muezzin * at a mosque in Batoum, did what he could for them. In spite of these helps there were times when the couple lacked the necessities of life, for the sick man needed various medicines, and they were dear.

The poor woman was too modest to call on Djam-

---

* The caller to prayer.

bek for help, and managed to exist for a while on the price she got for her little crop, sold in advance at half its worth. This was soon gone, and again they were in abject want, and that too just at the time the government taxes fell due. The tax collector notified Ali Bey of their default, and he, knowing that the two people were *protégés* of Djambek's, gave order that they should be turned out of their house.

The poor woman was obliged now to go for help to the son of her old master, but, as it happened, he was at the time on a visit to a friend in the mountains. No mercy or pity was to be had. The caimacam's order was peremptory, and the unhappy couple saw themselves thrust into the street, while an individual of bad repute, a tool of Ali Bey's, took possession of their house, ostensibly as keeper for the government.

Ahmed, the muezzin, on receiving the news of what had happened came and offered to pay a part, all he could, of what was due for taxes. But Ali Bey refused. The government was not a trader to accept payment in little sums; either all must be paid or the house would be seized in default. And so it was.

Fortunately Djambek came back the next day and brought succor. A tenement of his happened to be vacant, and was at once placed at the disposal of the poor couple, rent free. Ahmed could therefore go home in peace, knowing that his sister was provided for, and, as he thanked Djambek, with tears in his eyes, he swore never to forget his kindness.

Ali Bey was not entirely pleased with the outcome of this affair. He had hoped to seriously vex and harass his opponent, but saw that his blow had fallen on the empty air. But he would not so lightly leave the

4

victory with his enemy. So a few days later the old woman received a summons to attend and answer on a charge of unlawfully carrying away certain articles from the house. The process did not last long. It was shown her that she had grossly injured the state, and the end was a sentence to prison.

Djambek, when he heard what had happened, was so carried away with angry indignation that at first he thought of storming the prison and rescuing the poor woman by force; but then he reflected that such a course could only help his *protégée* for the moment, and he decided to go direct to the pasha with his complaint. He took an early start the next morning, for he had other business in Batoum, and intended too to make a call on Murza-Khan. The supercilious way in which the latter had spoken of the pasha had struck Djambek, and he had come to the thought that much might be done if this influential man could be won to his side.

His business in the city was soon disposed of. He also visited the muezzin to tell him of the injustice done his sister, and that he was about to lay the matter before the governor. Then he swung himself into his saddle and turned his face toward the north.

After a two hours' rapid ride he arrived at the castle. Murza-Khan received him warmly, and as Djambek had not been there for a long time, there were many new things to see and talk over. At last the wished-for moment came when both sat at their coffee and smoked. Murza-Khan, who had been talking a long time on business matters, became silent, and gazed thoughtfully out upon the sea. Djambek used the opportunity to speak of the unhappy state of affairs in the country, constantly becoming worse, and likely to end in the ruin of the land. He intimated that it was the duty of the children of the soil to attempt a reformation while yet there was time, and that this could only be done by a bold union of all their forces.

Murza-Khan shook his head. " You are young," he said, " and, like all at your age, think you can take the world by storm. I am a man of experience, my good Djambek, and tell you that that is not the right way."

" But we can try, and much depends on who is at the head of the movement. A man like you, for example."

" No, no ! " cried Murza-Kkan, with a gesture of refusal. " I feel no inclination to attempt bringing about a new order of things with weapons in my hands."

" Who speaks of weapons ? I believe your personal influence is enough to compel the attention of the officials."

" There you are in error. Do you know what is the best means of making these good people like clay in your hand ? Money. Throw a handful into their laps and they are your most devoted servants, but come to them with soft words and they will laugh in your face. I can do here as I please, because at the proper times I convince the caimacam and his band with clinking arguments. It is, as a matter of fact, a tax like any other, and I find it is one that it is profitable to pay. Why should I then stir up strife when I have nothing to complain of ? Follow my example, my friend. Ali Bey is doubtless as approachable as the honest and honorable Osman here. You will soon see

that everything goes as you wish. It is just as it is in
Nature. Go up the Adjaria and it will cost you much
time and exertion to reach your goal; perhaps even
your strength will give out; but let yourself be carried
down stream, and you can let your hands lie in your
lap and enjoy the beauty of the scenery."

"I thought from your manner recently that you
were dissatisfied with Cherif-Pasha and his troop."

"Dissatisfied? I despise the whole lot, that is all.
Cherif-Pasha is a lazy bear, who looks on his present
position as a post where he can comfortably rest. He
wishes to be friends with everybody and at the same
time get his profit. As to the thieves below him, I have
told you what is the best way of getting along with
them. It is the only way to live in peace and quietness."

"I am sorry you have such views. In your position
it would be easy to do the land a great service. A
word from you, and your adherents in this district
would flock to you to lend their weight to your demands, while at the same time I would engage myself
to bring my lands-people to your side."

"As I have told you there is no reason for doing
so. Why should I disturb myself for other people,
and that, too, in a hazardous matter. As long as no
one injures me I have no need to injure others."

Djambek saw that it was useless to seek for an
ally here, so he let the subject drop, and soon after
took his leave.

Much depressed at his ill success, he rode back to
the city, pondering on what Murza-Khan had said.
Perhaps he is right, he thought. It is always a
hazardous business to oppose those in power. Indeed

MURZA-KHAN AND THAMAR. 47

he had not thought of any resort to force. He had only intended the use of moral influences on those in authority, not to resort to weapons. He felt no personal enmity toward Cherif-Pasha; on the contrary, since this visit he felt drawn toward the man, although he had so slyly avoided his responsibilities instead of going to the root of the matter and redressing the evils as he had promised to do. Yes, if Cherif-Pasha had no relative, or if his relative were not so charming and lovable, then, perhaps—he interrupted his reverie for a moment. Had then Thamar made so deep an impression on him? He hardly knew; he only knew that he often thought with a strange pleasure in his heart of the day he had passed in her society, and that he was very far from wishing any evil to the old man who had been so friendly to him then. In how far the young lady was responsible for his friendly feeling toward her uncle, he could not clearly determine.

He soon reached the city, and first going to Artschil's house he got him to accompany him to the pasha's.

Guests had already arrived in considerable numbers, and he had to content himself with saying to Thamar only a few words of formal greeting as she stood the center of a little circle. It appeared to him as if there were a shadow of trouble on her beautiful face, which vanished as he approached, and then quickly came back again.

Cherif-Pasha at once discovered him among the other guests and called him to him. This seemed to him a good opportunity for bringing forward his complaints, and after the first words of greeting, he plunged at once into the matter.

The governor at first could only answer with a
"hm-hm." Finally he said, "My dear friend, the
law prescribes what an official has to do. I will not
deny that it depends much on the good or evil will of
the official as to whether he will carry out the law in
its fullest severity. But that is his own prerogative,
and I have no influence in the matter. I am sure if
you had gone to Ali Bey and spoken a few friendly
words to him he would have tempered justice with
mercy. And, any way, I advise you again to be on a
more friendly footing with him. It is very unpleasant
when you live in the same district to have such
strained relations with each other. Disputes and
troubles are sure to follow in which I can not interfere. Only think, what would be the result if I should
always be mixing in the caimacam's business and
championing the cause of every private individual."

"I thought you might make an exception in this
case. The poor people stand very near to me, and—"

"Well, well," interrupted the pasha, "we will see
what can be done, only let us not spoil the pleasure
of this pleasant evening. Rest easy; I will let Ali
Bey know what my wishes are. You find me to-
night in good humor—your petition shall find favor."
And he hurried away to greet a new comer.

Djambek was satisfied with the governor's promise.
He again approached the place where Thamar stood,
but contented himself with watching her, as she was
still surrounded by a group of admirers. The milk-
white robe she wore to-night made her slender figure
look almost tall. Her bearing and movements were
those of a queen giving audience to her subjects, but
with it all there was something so kindly and winning

in her ways as to draw all hearts to her. But for the second time Djambek noticed that it seemed to require an effort for her to smile, and an expression of anxiety fell upon the corners of her pretty mouth when she thought herself unobserved. What was it that troubled her? he asked himself. It could hardly be a family disagreement, for Cherif-Pasha had just expressed himself as being in excellent spirits; it was doubtless some trouble from outside and one which she had confided to none of her intimates.

" Why so preoccupied?" said a voice near him. It was Daria who had approached him and was following the direction of his eyes.

" I was thinking that—that—there are a good many guests here to-night."

" Really! Were you not just for a moment thinking of something else, too?"

" I do not know."

" For example—that Thamar is, if possible, more beautiful than ever?" she continued with a smile.

A flush passed over his cheeks.

" You know that in our country such thoughts are not allowed—to be spoken."

" But to have them is allowed, as may be judged from your answer. I did not know that you are so conscientious an Oriental. On the contrary it has appeared to me as if you have more taste for the Occidental idea which sees nothing wrong in one's owning to his admiration of beauty."

" True! if you will promise to take my freedom in good part, I will permit myself to reproduce an Oriental picture in the Occidental manner." He made a gesture toward Thamar. " There, a white lily—here, a pomegranate flower ; happy the hands that may pluck them ! "

" At least that is more prettily said than Russudan's comparison. She thinks Thamar very much like a ghost and me like a boiled crab."

" *I* tell you you are both most charming."

" Thank you. You would make your mark in a French *salon.* But now go and say a few friendly words to Thamar. I believe you have not even said good evening to her."

" Do you think that she has any desire that I should ? " said Djambek, casting a glance where Hassan Bey was engaged in a lively conversation with the young girl.

Daria shot a glance at him from beneath her eyelids. " Ungrateful man ! " she exclaimed, and turned hastily away.

This expression started a new train of thought in Djambek's mind. What hidden meaning was there in the words ? As Thamar's intimate friend she must have some reason for accusing him of ingratitude. " Ungrateful ! " He could think of but one meaning, and that made his heart beat like a trip-hammer. He could not remain in these crowded rooms. He needed the fresh, cool air which came from the sea. He looked again toward where Thamar had been standing, but could not see her. Probably she had gone with some of the guests into the refreshment room.

A pale moonlight hung over the landscape. Grass-plot and grove shimmered in a gray-green light. In the distance the forest-clad hills were covered with a light mist that rolled up from the low-lands, or seemed to shrink back into the blackness beyond. A delicate perfume filled the air, renewed by every breeze that softly swept over the blooming arbors. No other sound was heard but the regular beat of the waves on the beach below.

Djambek took a path which led to a point where the view was finest. Here there was an open grass-plot around a group of magnolia trees. As he came out of the shadow of the trees he saw a white figure sitting on a bank beneath the fragrant trees. His first impulse was to turn back, but something seemed to draw him on and he could not resist. Daria's exclamation was in his mind. Perhaps now chance had given him the opportunity to learn its meaning.

Was she asleep? Her head rested on her hand and her eyes were closed. A twig broke beneath his feet and the sound aroused her. She started up in agitation, then sank back again as she recognized who it was.

"Forgive me for disturbing you," he said softly. "You were so surrounded with your guests that I waited in vain for an opportunity of speaking to you."

"Yes, it has been a tiresome evening," she said, "and especially so as I did not feel in the humor for lively talking."

"Then I was right in thinking that something is troubling you."

"You noticed it? And I thought I was a good actress! Then you probably know the reason, as I saw you speaking to my uncle."

"No, he said nothing about it. I remember he spoke of being in particular good spirits, but that—"

"Then I will be myself the herald of the joyful news—I am engaged to be married."

" You—engaged to be married ! "

She nodded, and her voice trembled with excitement.

" Yes, my uncle has arranged the matter—just as if it concerned the selling of a good horse."

" And who is the person with whom they have— been bargaining about you ? "

" Hassan Bey."

" I thought so," cried Djambek bitterly. " It was not without reason that a voice within me whispered, ' In this man you will one day find your worst enemy.' "

A glad smile which she could not conceal passed over her face at these words, and the glance she flashed at Djambek revealed to him clearly the meaning of Daria's exclamation. " Thamar ! " came trembling from his lips, but it was all he could say. He sank at her feet and grasped her hands whose answering pressure told him more than any words could have done.

For a long time neither spoke, while a dark figure that stood in the shadow gazed at them curiously and then noiselessly vanished among the trees.

" I must go now," she said suddenly ; " if we were seen here it would bring heavy misfortune on us both. Let me go, dearest. To you, you alone, shall my heart belong." She sprang hastily up and gently disengaged her hand. " Farewell, dear."

As if lost in a dream, Djambek gazed after the bright figure which glided over the turf and in the moonlight seemed like a being from the fairy world. He wished to cry after her to return, not to leave him yet ; he wished to tell her how happy, how blessed this moment had made him, to talk with her of what they should do now—how they should demean themselves before others to ward off the threatening evil and counteract her uncle's plans—these and many other thoughts filled his brain, but his tongue cleaved to his mouth, and when at length he uttered her name she was gone.

CHAPTER V.

ELISBA AND ALI BEY.

A FEW days later Djambek again went to Batoum. He had returned home after the festival to collect himself and quietly think how he could bring it about that Cherif-Pasha might relinquish his plans regarding Thamar. But these quiet thoughts would not come. There was ever one picture before his eyes. He ever seemed to hear but the low words, " To you, you alone, shall my heart belong," and so the happy present would always prevent any planning for the future. He had but one wish, one thought—to see her again, to hear again the tones of her sweet voice; and as impatience consumed him, he hurriedly decided to go back to the city.

To his unpleasant surprise, he was told that the pasha was not at home. So he went into the city and strolled about the harbor, as he knew Artschil was still at his bureau. He met several friends and chatted with them a while, and then tried his fortune again at the governor's, but unsuccessfully. He concluded then to go to Artschil's house and wait for him to come home.

At length Artschil came, and Djambek, who felt the necessity of talking about the beloved one, sought to bring the conversation round to her, but his uncle had not seen her since that evening, and could tell him nothing about her. He related, on the other hand, how he had met Cherif-Pasha the day before, and how the governor was in a most disagreeable temper, and without any apparent reason had launched into a fierce diatribe against women, declaring they were only created to bring dissension and trouble into households.

This bit of information made Djambek's heart beat quicker. He concluded from it that Thamar had had a talk with her uncle, and declared her determination never to marry Hassan Bey. That was surely a long step. It might be hoped that in time Cherif-Pasha would abandon his idea, and then, perhaps, some day Djambek might try his fortune. What was there, indeed, to be said against him? Hassan Bey occupied a high position, and had the prospect of a brilliant career before him; still, Djambek was in nowise behind his rival. Was not his family one of the oldest and best in the land? Did he not own wide domains which offered every possibility for the playing of a prominent *rôle?* Why, then, should not Cherif-Pasha bid him welcome? There was to his mind but one answer to these questions, but he might have put them even to himself with less confidence had he suspected the powerful reasons which bound the pasha to the cause of his rival. It would be no joking matter if the story of certain embezzlements came to the ears of those in authority at Stamboul—and as Hassan Bey was the only person who in some inexplicable way had obtained knowledge of these shady matters, the simplest way to preserve the secret was to make him a member of the family, and then—carry on the affairs in partnership.

As this was the evening for the pasha's weekly reception, Djambek determined to attend; perhaps he might find an opportunity for a word with her of whom he dreamed day and night.

His reception by the governor was a chilling one—a bare nod of the head was the only greeting he received—no jokes, no amiable grimaces, as was usually the case. Djambek felt at once that matters stood differently from what he had supposed. Thamar was nowhere to be seen. Daria seemed anxious to avoid him whenever he approached near her. He was just thinking of leaving so inhospitable a house when he heard his name called in a low tone. He looked in the direction whence the voice came, and quietly approached the side of the veranda, which was thickly screened with orange and lemon trees. There he heard Daria's voice.

"Stay where you are—you must under no conditions be seen with me," she whispered from behind the thick branches.

"Is Thamar ill?" he asked in a low tone.

"No; but she dare not leave her room. Some one has been listening to you two, and that is the reason for to-day's icy coldness. If you want to know who has been playing the spy, you can see him in the house; he is playing chess with Hassan Bey. Enough for to-night; we might be overheard."

"One thing more," pleaded Djambek. "How can I obtain news in future? According to what you say, the house will be closed to me hereafter."

"I know of no one whom we can take into confidence. So you can only be patient."

"But just a word now and then—only the simple word 'She is well'?"

"There is no way. All I can promise is to let you know if any danger threatens. But how and through whom?"

"Perhaps through my relative Artschil. No, he is too timid." He stopped a moment to think over his acquaintances. "Murza-Khan?" He, too, would not do. After what he had said there was no assistance in this matter to be looked for from him.

"Well?" asked Daria impatiently. "Quick, I hear voices."

An idea came to him.

"In the mosque by the harbor, the muezzin Ahmed; he is devoted to me."

"Very well. Go now."

He returned into the house and looked for the man whom Daria had told him was the traitor. Not far from where he stood he heard the rattle of dice, and with a quick glance he recognized the man who was playing with Hassan Bey. "Totia! the miserable wretch!" he muttered, clenching his fists. Then he turned and left the house without taking leave of any one.

He went directly to Ahmed. Next to the slender minaret stood the humble dwelling where the prayer-singer lived.

"What, is it you?" cried Ahmed, in surprise, as Djambek entered; "you bring me good news, do you not?"

"From your sister? No, neither concerning her nor myself. I too have fallen under the pasha's displeasure. He promised me, it is true, to give orders for your sister's release, but as yet he has done nothing, and now I am afraid my interference in any one's behalf will work more harm than good. But she will, at the worst, be free in a week, and in the mean time her husband is well taken care of. And she shall be, also."

"I thank you. You have already done more than a merciful man is bound to do; we are deep in your debt."

"It is not worth talking about; but if you really feel under obligation to me, you can perhaps do me a service in return. Such debts rest heavily on good men's hearts, so possibly you will be happy to remove them."

"I could have no greater pleasure."

"Listen, then. Word will be sent you verbally, or by letter, concerning one who is dearer to me than all the world besides. This word I beg you will send to me at once by a swift messenger."

"Is that all?"

"All! do not think it is a small matter. There may be danger connected with it. So you must be cautious. And do not forget that upon the immediate forwarding of this news may depend my life's happiness. So be careful; high personages are concerned in it."

"Have no fear. Lazar, who comes every week from Skalta with fruit, is a trustworthy fellow, and, if the matter presses, I know some one here whom it will be safe to trust."

"I thank you, Ahmed. Be assured I will repay your services."

"To make me again your debtor?"

Djambek pressed the muezzin's hand and left the house. He determined to pass the night at Artschil's, and return home early the next morning.

A whole week passed without any news, and his impatience and anxiety kept him in a fever of excitement. Elisba, his friend and neighbor, whose wedding he had attended with his guests, said to him one day as he met him : " Is there anything I can do for you in the city? I am going there to-day, and will return to-morrow."

Djambek would gladly have given him a commission which lay very near his heart, but how should he put it so as not to excite suspicion, and without exposing the person from whom he so longed to hear.

" If you find time," he said at length, hesitatingly, " to call at the harbor mosque and inquire after Ahmed? It is only to see whether he has any news for me."

" It is well. I will not forget it. Have you heard the latest? "

Djambek shook his head.

" I learned yesterday that the caimacam had declared that the finest part of my estate belonged to the government. That is why I am going to Batoum, though he has never ventured to say any such thing in my presence."

" Nonsense ! " said Djambek, " he might as well claim that my house belonged to him."

" Well, I always find that caution never harms. I will get an official declaration of my title to the land. It is just that part that my father purchased from the government, but I can find no papers referring to it, and I think it best to at once have the matter put in

5

order, while there are witnesses of the transaction still
living."

"You are right, perhaps, to be on the safe side, but
it is hardly credible that the caimacam would attempt
a thing so sure to fail."

"He has already done incredible things. We shall
see. I will not forget your commission."

The next afternoon Elisba returned.

"It is tiresome business having anything to do with
the authorities," he grumbled ; "I thought it would be
sufficient if I represented the facts to the pasha. But far
from it. He told me that the right and legal way was
first to institute an inquiry with the authorities of this
district; and when I gave him to understand that I
had reasons why I wished to have nothing to do with
Ali Bey, he could only advise me to get a lawyer and
have him take the necessary steps with the caimacam.
I had half a mind to tell the good man that there must
be something wanting with his good sense if he failed
to see that it was impossible for me to get my rights
from the very man who was disputing them. But what
good would that do ? Perhaps there was more ill-will
than stupidity in what he said. So I left him and
went to Artschil. He went with me at once to see if
there were any papers referring to the case among the
official documents. But, think of it ! Three rooms
full of official papers from top to bottom ! It was too
much to think of looking through them all, one by
one, and so I found myself obliged to employ a man to
find the document, if indeed it exists. I can only
reckon on its taking several weeks, and then, possibly,
I shall learn that there is nothing there referring to
my matters."

"That is very annoying certainly," said Djambek.
"but that is the way things are with us. Instead of
the officials feeling that they are appointed to assist
and aid those at whose cost they live, the case is re-
versed, and they imagine we are here for the purpose
of being humiliated and worked by them. 'A world
upside down,' my dear Elisba."

"I saw Ahmed as you wished me to, but he had no
news for you. He received me very coolly and in
answer to my question said he did not know what
there was to tell you of."

"So?" said Djambek, unpleasantly impressed.

Had Ahmed perhaps thought it over and concluded
it would be better for him not to mix in an affair which
was attended with danger? But no, Djambek could
not but believe that it was more probably caution on
the muezzin's part; he could not know whether Elisba
was really acting in Djambek's service or in that of his
enemy.

"And you heard nothing new of interest?" Djambek asked, after a long pause.

"Nothing of special interest. For want of anything better the people in the city are gossiping about
Cherif-Pasha suddenly becoming less hospitable than
he used to be. Formerly his house was open to everybody, but now he receives only a few particularly intimate friends. They assign all manner of reasons, but
it is generally supposed that he has received a hint
from Constantinople that it would be better for him
to more closely observe the Mohammedan law."

Djambek knew that the reasons were far different,
but he refrained from contradicting the general opinion.
His friend took his departure and left him to his own

thoughts, which were not of the most agreeable nature.
At a late hour that evening Lazar was announced—
the man whom Ahmed had indicated as being a trustworthy messenger.

In deep agitation Djambek hurried down to see
him.

" I have brought something for you, sir."

Djambek eagerly took the packet and handed the
messenger a piece of money.

" When do you return to the city," he asked.

" The first of next week."

" Are you prepared to go earlier in case I wish to
send a message ? "

" Certainly."

" It is well.   In case I do not send you word, you
can go at your usual time.   But do not fail to inquire
regularly at Ahmed's."

Djambek returned to the house to open the packet.
In an unsigned letter was a note which he looked at
first.   It contained but a few words.

" Although shut out from the outside world, it is
well with me.   I think of thee.   T."

A sigh of endless relief and delight came from his
breast, and it was some time before he could lay aside
the note to look at the other paper.   This too was very
brief :

" Inclosed is the expected news.   This morning one
of thy neighbors came to me, but I thought it best to
answer him evasively as I could not be sure in what
character he came.   Know that for the future I shall
only give answer to him who brings me a proof that
he comes from thee.   Sendest thou therefore another
messenger, let him bring from thee, as a sign, one of

the silver cartridges—those that thy father used to carry."

The word he had received from Thamar quieted him for a few days. He gave Lazar a letter for her together with a few lines to Ahmed, and to his great joy the messenger brought back another note from her. From this time the exchange of letters became regular, and little by little Djambek learned the particulars of Totia's treachery, the pasha's anger, his stormy interview with her, and her firm reply that she would never give her hand to Hassan Bey in marriage, which led to her imprisonment in her room. Russudan was specially charged with the duty of watching and of seeing that no one approached her. At first Thamar had laughed over the whole "real Turkish affair," as she called it, and found that this little adventure was not without its charm. But now that she had been shut up for several weeks and allowed to see no one but Daria, the matter was becoming too serious for a joke. The spirit she had inherited from her mother was aroused, and one day she declared to her guardian that she was too little a Turk to endure this treatment any longer. Unless it was changed something unpleasant would happen. She wrote in similar terms to Djambek, and her complaints started an idea which became more and more formulated until one day he wrote to her:

"If they push matters too far, I shall carry you away by force. Then all our troubles will be at an end."

Her threats to Russudan seemed to have an influence, as she next wrote to Djambek that she was allowed to receive visits from some of her girl friends in the city. This concession meant something certainly, and it was to be hoped that Cherif-Pasha would soon come to a sensible view of matters.

Ahmed's sister returned after her term of imprisonment was ended to find her husband in sorrowful circumstances. In spite of the good nursing for which Djambek had provided, his illness had taken a turn for the worse, and it was easy to see that he could not live through the summer. The end, however, came sooner than was expected.

Djambek offered the widow her option of staying where she was or living at his house. She chose the latter, and undertook the domestic management of the household. The cottage which she had lived in rent free was rented to another couple, and Djambek insisted on her keeping the rent for her own.

The days passed in comparative quiet now, and Djambek began to be more hopeful that his heart's wishes would be fulfilled. Thamar wrote that she now enjoyed full freedom, but that her uncle received but few visitors. The disputed question between them was never alluded to by him. He spoke to her again in friendly terms. Her chief grievance was that Hassan Bey spent nearly the whole day at the house, and constantly followed her about. Once she told him plainly it would be better if he would give up his idle hopes, but he only smiled and bowed low without making any reply.

Between Djambek and the caimacam there was a cessation of hostilities; not that the latter had satisfied his vengeance, but he could find no way in which he could materially injure him.

But this state of quiet was not to last long. One

morning Elisba came to his friend in a state of great excitement.

"Just think of it! the rascal! the wretch!" he exclaimed as soon as he came in.

"What has happened! Whom are you speaking of?"

"Who else could it be but Ali Bey? He now formally declares that a part of my estate belongs to the government and that I must either give it up or pay rent for it. He does not dare to say it himself to my face, but his mudir brings me a notice just as I am making arrangements with my tenant for reuting it another year."

"Do you know what I believe? The shameless rascal only wants to force you to stop his mouth with a purse."

"That I would never do for the very reason that it would be tacitly admitting that he was in the right."

"You are right. The whole matter is an absurdity —a piece of blind malice on the part of Ali Bey."

"But I must beg you to write to Artschil to press the search for the missing papers, for you know our position and that wolves eat each other only when they have no other prey. So long as Ali Bey here and Cherif-Pasha in Batoum can make enough money the latter will leave the former alone and give him a free hand to plunder as he will."

"He dare not!" said Djambek firmly. "If he so far forgets his duty he must be formally accused before the Stamboul authorities. But I will gladly do as you wish, and will at once send word to Artschil."

"Do so and if anything new occurs I will inform you." The something new was not long to wait for.

The very next morning one of Elisba's people came to Djambek breathless with running.

"Quick, sir, a misfortune has happened." The man was so excited he could say nothing more intelligibly, and so Djambek hurried to see for himself what had occurred. As he came to the gate of his neighbor's place, he came upon a crowd of tenants and peasants who were talking and gesticulating wildly, while nearer the house the caimacam's guard were seen standing before the door with weapons in their hands. Without regarding the shouts of the people, he rode up to the guard.

"What is it?" he asked.

"What is it?" one of the men replied. "Nothiug, except that a murder has been committed here."

"Who has been murdered?"

"Ali Bey."

"Impossible." Djambek was about to rush into the house, but the guards barred the way. "Let me in," he cried; "by what right do you prevent me entering the house of my friend?"

A crowd of the peasants too now came nearer, their numbers constantly increasing.

"They wish to take Elisba prisoner," cried some of them to Djambek.

"Have you any order to do so?" he said, turning to the guard. "If not, then go your way and wait until you get one. Now let me pass or you will regret it."

"That is right," shouted the people, who had come very close to the guard and placed their hands threateningly on their daggers, while the caimacam's guard made ready their guns more for defense than attack.

"If you dare bring on a conflict, it will go hard with you," said Djambek threateningly.

"Yes, do it if you dare," seconded the others. "We are tired of being treated like dogs. The caimacam has got what he long deserved."

"And now let somebody explain to me all the circumstances—some one of you," said Djambek, turning to the peasants.

A number stepped forward, and one spoke. "As you know, sir, I am the man who for many years has rented land belonging to Elisba. Before me my father, and before him my grandfather were settled here. The old man is living yet, and can prove that the land belongs of right to Elisba. He and some other people were present when the purchase money was paid. He has often told how the caimacam who was here said to Elisba's grandfather, 'I give thee here, before witnesses, the possession which thou hast acquired as the law provides. Thy ownership extends to here,' and at the same time the charcoal baskets * were buried in the presence of witnesses. Now yesterday we were going to renew the rental for another ten years, when the mudir came and in the name of the caimacam forbade the business, saying the land belonged to the state. We did not stop for such nonsense, but did as we had the right to do. To-day Ali Bey came and commanded me to leave the premises, saying, if I did not go he would have me removed by force and put in prison. I ran to Elisba to tell him what was going on. He came back at once with me. The caimacam would not

---

* Instead of boundary stones, baskets filled with charcoal were buried in the earth.

let him speak, but abused him with shameless words,
and as Elisha too at length lost his patience, they got
into a furious quarrel until Ali Bey lifted his whip to
strike him, when Elisba drew his dagger and Ali Bey
fell."

" All this happened on your premises? "

The man nodded.

" And what are these men doing here at Elisba's
house ? "

" He has fled, and they think he has hidden here."

" I will tell you something," said Djambek, turning to the guard; " it is your duty to give notice of
what has occurred, that Elisba may be brought to
answer. No one has authorized you to besiege his
house, and I demand, therefore, that you leave the
passage free. We are not in the mood to endure illegal
action, and know how to protect ourselves against it."

" Are you prepared to give surety for the murderer?" said the leader of the armed band. " Will
you be responsible with your person that Elisba shall
not escape from the house if we withdraw ? "

" No. I certainly will not. If he intends to flee
I shall be the last person to hinder him. Who tells
you, indeed, that he is here ? You are standing here,
and he is perhaps already in safety."

" We saw him running through the copse-wood in
this direction."

" Very well, then. Let me go in the house, and
see if he is there. There will be no danger in that
for you. If I find him and he has anything to say
I will let you know what it is."

The soldiers consulted together a moment, and
then the leader said :

"It is true. Your going in will not help him to escape."

They made way sufficiently for Djambek to enter. The door opened on a slight pressure, to close again immediately and be fastened with bolt and chain.

It was evident that some one had been listening, and had opened the door as soon as Djambek had approached it. Elisba's old servant Bessarion received him. Djambek entered the well-known room. Elisba was standing by the fire-place, while his young wife had fallen at his feet, and was sobbing bitterly. All the blood had left Elisba's face, and his hands played nervously with the gun, which, cocked and primed, lay upon the mantel. The appearance of a friend seemed to calm them; at least the woman ceased her sobbing, and her husband went a few paces toward Djambek.

"This is a bad affair," said Djambek mournfully; " I will not reproach you, Elisba, for, before God, I would have done the same had I been in your place."

· "And now that the unhappy deed is done, I feel the keenest remorse. You can witness, Djambek, that I never sought a quarrel. Is he dead ? "

"I do not know. But now is not the time to talk of it. Whether he be living or dead, the thing has happened, and we must determine what is to be done. What do you think ? "

"My first thought was to give myself up to the authorities, but Eka begged me not to do so. She was sure that it would be signing my death-warrant."

"Hardly that, perhaps, but a heavy sentence would doubtless be the result."

"He must fly," interjected Eka. "His only hope is in flight."

"But the house is closely guarded, and the guards can not be induced to withdraw. It is true we are the stronger party, but it would only make matters worse if—"

"No; no more lives must be hazarded on my account. I would rather give myself up on the spot," said Elisba.

Djambek was silent. He was considering how a plan for escape might be put in action. At length he seemed to have decided on a way. He drew the couple close to him and told them his plan in whispers.

"It will be for you to arrange matters here inside the house," he then said in a somewhat louder tone. "I and my friends will wait with the horses by the large linden tree in Deer Forest. You understand?"

Both nodded, and Djambek, pressing their hands, departed.

"Elisba is in the house," he said, as he came out. "He agrees with me, however, and says he will only give himself up to those who have an order of arrest for him. You see, therefore, that it will be simpler if you give the formal notice, and get full powers from your superiors."

"The mudir will not return from Batoum until to-morrow," said the leader of the guard. "Before that the murderer might be the other side of the mountain."

Djambek shrugged his shoulders.

"I can give you no better advice," he said.

"We will arrange it so," said the police officer. "One of my men shall go to obtain the order, and in the mean time the rest of us will guard the house."

"It might be well for you, first of all, to look after your caimacam."

"It has been done."

"Is he alive?"

"He lives, but is wholly unconscious."

The leader spoke to his men, and one of them volunteered to go to Batoum. The other seven took up their positions so that each side of the building could be watched.

Murmurs again began to be heard among the peasants. "They act just as if they were on a bear hunt," cried the tenant. "Come on, men, let us show them that Elisba shall not be caught in a trap so long as we have arms to help him out."

Djambek now stepped forward and addressed his fellow lands-men.

"Elisba prays you not to bring on a conflict on his account. You will make his situation worse if you do so, and bring down the vengeance of the mighty on yourselves." Then he added in a low voice to the tenant. "I shall want you with me in an hour. Your help is needed elsewhere.—So," he continued again in a loud tone, "let us go now. The messenger can not return before morning, and we will then be here to see what can be done."

"And suppose while we are away they break into the house?" said one of the peasants.

"They won't be so reckless as to do that. Elisba and his servants are on their guard and will repulse any such attempt."

Djambek mounted his horse, and at a sign from the tenant, the peasants slowly left the premises.

CHAPTER VI.

A LESSON IN TURKISH JURISPRUDENCE.

TOWARD midnight Djambek left the house in company with the tenant Yordane and a number of his people. The party took horses, and going a round-about way, so as to not alarm the villagers, proceeded to the rendezvous. On the way Djambek said to the tenant:

" I fear that this affair will have serious results for Elisba. In case the caimacam dies, the sentence is sure to be a severe one, and if Elisba succeeds in escaping, they will seek satisfaction from those connected with him. You must make it your business to-morrow to see that his wife is taken to some place where she will be safe."

" I see other things coming," said Yordane, the tenant. " They may let Elisba go free and seize his goods, and I shall lose my farm."

" It is very possible ; I had not thought of that."

" Well, we shall see," said Yordane with a sigh.

An hour's ride brought them to the large linden tree. Djambek himself picked out the strongest horse, saw that his saddle was firmly fastened, and tied him loosely to a tree.

The night was not particularly clear, but the guard

around Elisba's house could plainly see all sides of it. On each of the three sides two men were stationed, while on the fourth there was but one. This latter, to pass the time, was smoking one pipe after another and humming a song which he had gone through at least a hundred times. At length drowsiness almost overcame him, and he had to make strong efforts in order to keep his eyelids open.

He had just fallen into one of these spells of sleepiness, which, in spite of himself, would at times overcome him, when a slight noise aroused him, and his first glance fell on the house, whence a grating sound proceeded. He saw at once that one of the windows in the upper story had been opened, and could see a figure standing there. He cocked his gun and made ready to fire.

For a moment the figure quietly stood at the window, as if considering what was best to be done, while the guard kept his eyes fixed upon it, waiting for a decisive step. It came. The figure crawled out of the window, hung for a moment on the ledge, and then slowly came down by a rope fastened to the window-sash. A shot rang out in the night air, and the figure fell heavily into the bushes that surrounded the house. The guard called to his companions, who ran up at the sound of the shot, that Elisba was lying in the bushes wounded. At the same time, a door on the other side of the house opened softly and a figure sprang out and swiftly disappeared in the darkness; in the mean while the guard dragged the supposed corpse out of the bushes, to find too late that they had been deceived by a figure made of straw, dressed in Elisba's clothes.

The captain of the guard broke out in loud curses. He saw at once that the fugitive had used this stratagem to call off their attention from the other side of the house, and that he had now doubtless escaped. His men hastily ran in different directions, to see if there were any traces of the fugitive, but they were too late, and could only return to the station and report that Elisba had, through flight, escaped the hands of justice.

Before daylight Yordane knocked at Elisba's door, after making sure that the guard had evacuated the premises.

Bessarion asked who was there.

"I, Yordane," was the answer. "Quick! tell your mistress to make ready at once for a journey. Tell her to take everything she will need for her person. The carts will be here soon to carry away the rest of the stuff. The hangman's helpers shall find nothing but empty walls when they come."

In a little while all the jewelry, plate, and valuable articles were put into a cart, and Eka, mounted on a horse, rode off under the escort of Yordane and several of the neighbors. Three hours later carts carried away the rest of the furniture, and all was still about the house.

As soon as he had seen his friend in safety, Djambek went home, snatched a brief sleep, and at an early hour was in his boat, bound for Batoum. On arriving there, he went at once to Artschil.

His uncle shook his head doubtfully after Djambek · had related to him all that had occurred.

"Elisba has tied a fine weight about his neck! Go at once to Serop-Effendi and get him to undertake the case. He is a clever Armenian who has carried through some doubtful cases. Perhaps he can get Elisba out of the net. But do not forget that Serop is a very soul-seller for money. If you want his services you must put a roll of money in his hand before you say anything."

Djambek first went to the man who acted as his banker, and then hurried to the lawyer's residence. Remembering his uncle's caution, he placed a roll of gold on a side-table as he entered, and the result was immediate. Serop-Effendi, who had regarded him rather mistrustfully on his entrance, at once sprang up and greeted him as if he had been his warmest friend.

"Why, how glad I am to see you!" he cried. "You were only a boy when I saw you with your father—you are the son of—hm, hm—"

"Yes, the son of Dimitri Tagniridza," said Djambek, to help him out; for he knew the lawyer had never seen him or his father.

"Yes, yes, a fine man, Tagniridza; he is still living?"

"No, he has been dead a long time."

"Is it possible? Such a fine man! You see, my dear Demetr—"

"Djambek," corrected the other.

"I meant to say Djambek. You see, my dear Djambek, I see so many people that I can't always tell at once who is who. It is very good of you to come to see me. Perhaps you want my services. Command me, I pray you." Djambek related the particulars of Elisba's case, and the lawyer listened attentively. Then, Serop-Effendi took a sheet of paper on which he wrote several names, and opposite each name some figures.

6

" So ! " he said, after a little calculation, " the affair
will cost your friend, outside of my fees, about twenty
thousand piasters."

" What ? " exclaimed Djambek, in astonishment.
" I hardly understand."

The other playfully shook his finger at him. " You
understand very well. You know well enough that
everything here costs money. Your friend has killed
or half killed the caimacam. That is a serious crime,
and involves a heavy punishment, unless there are
mitigating circumstances. Now, you know, that by
nature men are not inclined to be merciful. One
must assist them artificially to be kind, and the surest
method is to use money. We have six judges, includ-
ing the president of the tribunal. Reckoning each at
two thousand piasters, a low figure, makes twelve thousand. Then there are two secretaries at five hundred
each, makes thirteen thousand. In addition, there is
Cherif-Pasha, that he may say a good word, and several
subordinates—"

" Enough—" interrupted Djambek, " I will have
nothing to do with bribery. Simply say what your
services will cost."

" I can not tell that with certainty now. Perhaps,
however, I might give you an estimate." He made a
few figures, and then continued : " Something like fifteen thousand piasters, with the understanding, however, that at those figures I can not guarantee success."

Djambek shrugged his shoulders—

" Then we had better let the matter be," he said.

" As you please," replied the other indifferently.
" If your friend estimates his neck as not worth fifteen
thousand piasters, I can have nothing to say."

Djambek, leaving the money on the table, took his leave. "That is the way justice is dispensed," he muttered bitterly. "Such people dare to sit over us in judgment, and decide matters of life and death; and to such miserable wretches we must bow in deference. Shame on such a government! shame on such a society!"

He was still in a rage as he entered Artschil's house again.

"I will have nothing to do with this Serop, nor with these courts! Where one has to pay men for doing right there can be no hope of justice," he said.

"I understand," said Artschil "what you refer to. But Serop-Effendi carries it too far. I, too, have in my official capacity, to decide what is right, and no one can say I was ever induced by a bribe to act contrary to my convictions."

"With you it is different. You do not belong to this brood; in your veins flows Georgian blood."

"And there are others here like me, who know how to distinguish between right and wrong; not many, it is true," he added sorrowfully, "but enough to give us hope that Elisba will not be betrayed and sold."

"Then that lawyer deceived me shamefully!"

"In part, perhaps. How much did he ask?"

"Fifteen thousand piasters."

"Then he intended to take the lion's share for himself. We must take some other course. After you left, I thought of a young man who has recently come from Trebizonde. We will try him."

They accordingly visited the young lawyer together, and after a short discussion, he agreed to undertake the case, and Djambek returned home feeling more satisfied.

Ali Bey lived, and it was hoped that his wounds would be healed. This made the case less serious, but there was always the doubt how the judges would consider it; whether they would take the view that the caimacam had gone to the other in his private or in official capacity, and whether the deed was one of self-defense or of attempted assassination.

By order of the mudir a detachment of soldiers had gone to Elisba's house to take possession of it in satisfaction of the crime, the criminal having fled. A few days later Djambek heard that the government had offered a reward for the capture of the fugitive. This increased the gravity of the situation, and Djambek went to Batoum to consult with Artschil. Both agreed that Elisba had done wrong in fleeing.

"There is no justice for one that is absent, is a true proverb," said Artschil. The lawyer also told Djambek that Elisba's absence worked much to his prejudice, as his enemies could give what version they pleased of the affair, and there was no one to contradict them. For example, the caimacam, who was improving, stated that the assault on him was entirely unprovoked, and had followed from his merely saying that he could not allow the state's interest to be injured. The guards, too, had declared that they had been threatened, and they pointed out Yordane, the tenant, as the leader of a mob. It was therefore resolved to imprison him. Further, Djambek heard that Elisba's property was to be confiscated. In fine, matters could not be worse.

But his duty to his friend led Djambek to make

one more attempt in his favor, though he hoped for little good from it. He went to see Cherif-Pasha. As he had always been accustomed to go and come as he pleased in the hospitable house he intimated to the servant that it was not necessary to announce him, fearing that the pasha might refuse to see him. The servant replied that his orders were to first inform his master who it was that desired to speak to him. Djambek could therefore but wait. The answer was as he had feared—the pasha was too busy to receive visitors.

Djambek drew a gold piece from his pocket.

"Could one meet your master when he takes his customary evening walk?" he asked.

"If you come to the eastern gate after sunset, you will find it open," replied the servant as he pocketed the money.

The sun was just setting as Djambek returned. He found the garden gate open. He entered, and walked up one of the deeply shaded paths. As he turned a corner, he uttered an exclamation of surprise, which was immediately echoed. He stood opposite Thamar.

"You!" came from the lips of both.

"Quick, this way," she said, and hastened up a by-path. Djambek followed her, scarcely able to restrain his joy. A few steps brought them to a grotto shaded with vines, and there Thamar fell upon his breast.

"Oh, dearest, how blessed I am to see you again!" He covered her face with kisses and clasped her close in his arms.

"If only this moment were longer," she sighed.

"I can stay but a few minutes—the danger is too great."

"For you?"

"For us both."

"Then I must not stay. Were only my own safety concerned I would gladly pay for each moment with a drop of my heart's blood."

"Speak not so. We must hope that fate will give us many hours, days, years of happiness."

"Tell me, Thamar, how do they treat you now? Conceal nothing, dearest, and remember that I am ready at any moment to free you from the hands of your jailors. What an opportunity for that this would be!"

"No. All I have to complain of is that I can not see you," she replied, and then she asked him regarding the Elisba affair, in which she felt a warm interest, as it was his marriage she had attended with Djambek and the other friends at the time of the pasha's visit. He told her all that had happened, the unfortunate position of the poor wife, and how he had come there that day to see Cherif-Pasha in his friend's behalf. Then they talked of themselves, their love, their hopes, as only lovers can, until Djambek suddenly bethought him that if he would do his friend the service he intended, he must go, hard as it was for him to leave her whom he could see so seldom and loved so dearly. With a passionate embrace and lingering kisses, he bade her good-by and hurried away. He bent his steps toward the magnolia trees, where Thamar had told him he would find Cherif-Pasha.

Cherif-Pasha sat alone under the trees. His chin was resting on his hand and he seemed absorbed in thought.

It was only when Djambek stood before him that he looked up. As the pasha recognized him he started as if in fright and looked toward the house as if for help.

"What do you want here?" he said in an unsteady voice.

"In former times I was received differently," rejoined the young man. "Then it was not, 'What do you want here?' but 'Welcome, friend.'"

"The times change," answered the pasha in tones which betrayed his uneasiness. "It is not my fault if feelings of friendship have given place to others."

"I am unconscious of having injured or offended you. But it is another matter that brings me here to-day. I come to ask justice at your hands."

"Speak—I am ready to hear you." The pasha arose and moved toward the house, Djambek walking at his side.

"It would be a waste of time if I told you how Ali Bey managed that time to mislead you and turn your visit to his own advantage. But this I must say to you—he is a hard, unjust, corrupt man; one who oppresses the land and drives the people desperate, as in this last case in which my friend Elisba Alichwari unfortunately played a *rôle* which has led you to take legal steps against him."

Cherif-Pasha seemed to listen attentively, but at the same time walked rapidly. The house was now in sight, and this gave him more courage, for at first he had feared an attempt upon his life.

"I could not, if I wished, interfere in the case," he said. "The matter devolves solely upon the court, which must decide the man's guilt or innocence."

" But I know that you have the deciding voice in
the matter. Permit me, therefore, to briefly state the
true facts in the case."

" You are misinformed. The laws prescribe what
is to be done in each case, and my voice can have no
influence for or against the accused."

" You do not understand me. It is true the law
provides what shall be the punishment in each case.
But in a case of murder, for instance, it depends on
the judges whether they will take into consideration
any mitigating circumstances under which one man
has killed another. As in war—is not this murder
by wholesale? and yet the law does not so regard it."

" We will not go into the discussion of such subjects," returned the pasha wearily. In front of the
house Totia could be seen in company with Hassan Bey,
and the pasha's confidence increased.

" Then you do not wish that I should give you the
opportunity of doing justice? "

The pasha shrugged his shoulders; " I have told
you," he said, " that this is a matter beyond my jurisdiction and that I have no right to interfere in any
matters pertaining to the courts."

" Have no right! " repeated Djambek irritably; " as
if one did not know that the Vali Pasha can exert his
influence in any and every thing if he chooses! I demand nothing from you but justice. I ask but one
favor—if it can be called a favor—a thorough investigation of the case. Thus far you have heard but one
side, and that the side whose interests it is to injure
Elisba as much as possible. The case has been entirely
misstated to you. My friend, who is the most peaceable of men, must appear to you as a savage bloodhound

to whom a man's life is as nothing. But that is not so. It was not against your representative, the caimacam, but against the private individual Ali Bey, who would rob him, that he was striving to protect his rights. And you know what it means when one raises his hand to strike a free man. Have I not a right in such a case to prevent the blow with any means at my command? Would you do otherwise if I now said to you, ' The half of your land is mine; you must give it up'? And if when you indignantly repudiated such a claim I should threaten you with bodily harm, what would you do? "

" You forget that I do not stand on the same level as your friend. In a certain degree, I am placed above the law, while you must defer to it. It was Elisba's right to justify his case before the court, but not to make it more doubtful by an attempt at murder. Furthermore, he has sought to escape his responsibility through flight, and the law takes cognizance of that. You people may always demand your rights, but no more. I find that you are altogether too fond of imagining that you can play the master in everything. But I must leave you, for I have business to attend to."

" Then nothing will induce you to provide against a miscarriage of justice? "

The pasha shook his head. "You have said enough," he said sharply.

Djambek raised his hand warningly. " Mark this well, Cherif-Pasha. If one day my oppressed, mistreated people rise against their oppressors, against your brood of blood-sucking officials, the responsibility will be upon your head ! "

"We shall know how to protect ourselves," returned the other in mocking tones. "My good Djambek, you were always a dreamer. You have that to thank that I do not take your boyish threats in earnest. My forbearance is great, and I consider it the duty of hospitality to let you leave my grounds in peace, though I did not invite you to come and shall not hereafter. But I tell you now in all earnestness—go! In a few minutes I might repent leaving your threatening words unpunished."

Totia and Hassan Bey were now near by and exchanged mocking glances as Djambek hurried by them to leave the premises of the pasha—an enemy.

CHAPTER VII.

A TURKISH TRIAL.

" You took hold of the matter from the wrong end," said Artschil, when Djambek had told him of his unsuccessful call. " Do you know who is now really the pasha, the one who has the charge of all matters in and outside the house, and whose influence it is all important to have? "

" Hassan Bey? "

" Not at all. It is a much more humble individual —Totia Nitscheladze."

"Are you sure of that? I can not believe that the fellow who a short time ago was only an inferior scribe should suddenly have acquired such influence."

" Nevertheless, it is so. I know it for a certainty. Cherif-Pasha becomes lazier every day—his physician assured me recently it was a disease with him—he finds it much more comfortable to have another do his thinking and acting for him. Hassan Bey, too, likes to be spared work, and so it has been easy for Totia to creep in, and, beginning with small things, get to greater. Who wishes anything from the pasha must first knock at Totia's door. Of course it costs money, but at least one can now accomplish something, where before it depended entirely on the pasha's promise."

Djambek shook his head.

" I will not buy the services of that fellow. I have reasons why I should keep away from him."

" If you do not wish to treat with him personally Elisba's lawyer can try it."

" If he pleases. Only I must not in any way be mixed up in the matter. I would be glad if you would speak to the lawyer about it."

" I would gladly do so if it were in keeping with my official position. I gave you the hint as a relative. As an official it would be wrong for me to do so; and as such I could not speak to the lawyer about it. But he knows all about it—unfortunately, it is no longer a secret. It will be enough, therefore, if you simply remark to him that there is such and such a sum at Totia's disposal."

" Very well. I will do that. Elisba shall see that all was done on my part that could be done."

The lawyer at once understood the hint. He remarked that Totia would be satisfied with a comparatively small sum, and promised to attend to the matter and inform Djambek immediately of the result.

A few days later Djambek received the following note:

" The person referred to declares himself ready to act in the interests of our client, and good news may be expected in a few days."

The caimacam had so far recovered from his wound as to be able to go to Batoum to push the process against Elisba, and thus still his cravings for revenge. He, too, knew that in such affairs the favor of the pasha's favorite was an important factor, and his first visit was to Totia.

Totia quietly allowed Ali Bey to state his case without showing any embarrassment. Then, when he was through, he said in a sympathizing tone:

"I fear the case will not come out as you wish. Cherif-Pasha has been informed of a good many circumstances which make the matter appear in another light. Besides that, I must tell you confidentially that there have been a good many complaints made against you which are likely to injure you very much."

The reply threw the caimacam into great excitement.

"You really think that Cherif-Pasha is hostile to me?" he asked anxiously.

"It can hardly be otherwise when you have no one here to take your part. I, indeed, have tried to smooth over some matters—but you understand how—"

Ali Bey had already placed a purse filled with gold pieces on the table, and now, without any ceremony, he put it into Totia's hand.

"One service for another," he said hastily; "it is possible for you to do an honorable man a service, and as I know your love of justice, you will take my case into your hands. I will call again in a week, and you may be sure of my gratitude if you have good news to give me."

Totia did not hesitate a moment. Ali Bey's present was twice the amount which Elisba's lawyer had left on his table, and besides there was a good prospect of its being repeated—so his resolution was quickly made.

"What depends on me shall be done," he said. "Have no fear. I will make your matter my own."

The caimacam had hardly gone when Totia, taking
out his ink-horn and wooden pen, wrote as follows to
the lawyer:

" After you left me I found a roll of money which
you doubtless left here in absent-mindedness. Here is
your property, which I return."

He folded the note around the money-roll, and
gave it to a servant to be delivered at once. The next
news which Djambek received was not favorable.

" It appears that our opponent has succeeded in
playing us a trick. The amount which I had depos-
ited for the carrying out of our matter has been suddenly returned to me under a meaningless pretense.
Shall I make another attempt and bid higher? The
trial commences next week."

Djambek answered at once:

" I have had enough of this way of seeking justice.
The process may take its course. The witnesses here
have promised to tell the full truth and will appear in
large numbers. Your skill will perhaps enable you to
make it impossible for the judges to give an unjust
decision."

The day for the trial came and Djambek, accompanied by a large number of witnesses in Elisba's behalf,
went to the city.

As he entered the court-room, he saw a number of
his acquaintances, and among them Murza-Khan, who
had taken a seat on one of the rugs in front.

" You are astonished to see me here," he whispered
to Djambek with a grin. " Usually I can find a better
way of spending my time, but this is an exception. I
am curious to see whether one of our people can
hold his own against the little king of the district.

Or has Elisba perhaps allowed himself to be put to some expense? In that case I would rather not wait."

"You can stay. Our side has not spent a piaster, though we came near doing what the others have done."

The judges now appeared and the accusation was read.

The caimacam who was represented by Serop-Effendi answered the question put to him in a weak, low voice, as if he was still suffering from the assault. This little piece of acting had been recommended to him by his astute legal counsel, who smiled in satisfaction as he saw how well his client played the *rôle* of a sufferer. He himself asked a few questions, and in doing so took pains to have it appear as if he strongly insisted on the naked truth, and would allow . no deviation from it.

After Ali Bey had given his testimony and sunk back as if exhausted into his seat, Elisba's witnesses were called. But just then Serop-Effendi sprang up and vigorously objected.

"That witness is dependent on the defendant," he exclaimed, "and so is this one, and that one there, too." And he pointed out in turn several of the men. "And, furthermore, these fellows have dared to take up a hostile position toward the authorities."

At this cue the leader of the caimacam's guard stepped forward with several of his men.

"Speak, what have you to say," said the lawyer to him.

"It is quite true that not only these witnesses, but a whole multitude of other peasants attacked us, and threatened to use their weapons against us if we insisted on doing our duty."

"And did they not go peacefully on their way without disturbing you further?" cried Djambek, springing up from his seat in strong excitement.

All looked where the young man stood regarding the prosecutor with blazing eyes.

"Who dares interrupt the proceedings of the court?" demanded the president of the tribunal. "Who are you, that you presume to interfere?"

"I am Djambek Tagniridza, Elisba's. friend and neighbor, and I deem it my duty to look after the interests of my absent friend."

Artschil, who sat near the president, whispered something to him, whereupon the latter asked in a more quiet tone:

"Were you present at the time of the assault?"

"Not at the moment when the deed was done, but I got there in time to quiet the people, and induced them to go home, as Elisba implored me not to allow the people to oppose the authorities."

A murmur of approval passed through the crowd, and many made gestures of encouragement to Djambek.

"Why did you not announce yourself as a witness?"

"Because there were so many I thought it was needless. But now that their right to speak is disputed I will gladly give my testimony."

"He too threatened us at first," said the leader of the guard.

"He too threatened you, did he," said Serop-Effendi quickly, "then that makes him ineligible as a witness."

"I threatened you in so far as you opposed my going into the house," rejoined Djambek. "When you finally let me in, and I told the people what Elisba requested of them, none were so glad as you that the trouble ended peacefully."

As the man had nothing to say to this, the president called on Djambek to relate all that had taken place. Djambek hastened to tell all he knew regarding the circumstances leading up to the assault. He emphasized, too, the fact of the tenants not being dependent on Elisba, except in so far as the latter had the right after expiration of the term to rent the land to some one else, while during the term of the lease the tenant was as little dependent on the landlord as the landlord on him. As therefore the lease had been renewed before the assault took place, he urged that Serop-Effendi's objections to the witness were not well founded.

"I must earnestly protest," cried Serop, rising, "against one not called in the case taking part in it. The defendant's attorney is here. And furthermore I beg to again call the attention of the court to the circumstances which would seem to make this witness ineligible. He seeks to give the impression that what he did and said was with the simple purpose of preserving peace between the authorities and the people; but I charge that it was primarily with another intention, namely, to enable the accused to escape, and also his wife, who furthermore emptied the house from floor to roof. It is certain that others assisted in this."

"My client's wife, when she left the house, was full mistress of her person and her property," rejoined Elisba's attorney, "and as regards the defendant's es-

7

cape, there was at that time no order of arrest against
him."

"That is a very clever idea," replied Serop-Effendi,
with an evil smile, "but it strikes me that an innocent
man has no occasion to place his person beyond the
reach of the officers of justice. He has in this admitted his guilt. But we will not go into fine distinc-
tions. That he made an attempt on the life of the representative of the ruler of the province and, therefore,
the representative of our august sovereign, the padishah,
is patent and needs no further proof. Now the testimony of the defendant's witnesses is in my view worthless, because a tenant is just as little free from bias as
a servant; and as to the evidence of Djambek Tagniridza, he should rather be held for trial himself, for it
is a hundred to one that he assisted in the defendant's
escape."

Djambek could no longer control his indignation.
What! this man, this purchasable rascal, who had
declared himself ready for a high reward to undertake
the cause of the accused now earnestly defending the
opponent, who had doubtless acceded to his mercenary
demands!

"And now *I* ask," he cried, "whether a man should
be allowed to act as attorney who offered to defend the
very case which he now attacks, and who assured me
of his ability to obtain an acquittal of the accused
through bribery of the judges?"

This outbreak did not fail of effect upon the
judges. Artschil sprung up and spoke with the
president with excited gestures, while the other members of the court whispered among themselves. Serop-
Effendi was the only one who remained calm. He

shrugged his shoulders and smiled scornfully, but as
he saw the uneasiness which prevailed among those
who had the decision of his case, he turned boldly to
Djambek and said in a loud voice:

"Such accusations are easily made, but they must
be proved."

"The proof is my solemn word," replied Djambek.

"And you call that proof!"

"Do you deny that you demanded twenty thousand
piasters to bribe the judges with?"

"I deny it."

"And you did not specify to me the several sums
which would be required for each of the members
of the court?"

"No."

Artschil suddenly arose.

"I waive my office as judge for to-day in order that
I may appear as a witness. Djambek came to me in
great anger directly after his interview with Serop-
Effendi and said he would not accept his services as
attorney because he had declared the court to be open
to bribery, and in fact had demanded the sum just
spoken of."

A tumult broke forth in the court room. Specta-
tors, witnesses, and officers of the court shouted and
gesticulated in wildest confusion and there were loud
cries of execration against Serop. At this critical moment when Djambek was filled with hope, Cherif-Pasha
unexpectedly entered. He was accompanied by Totia.
At his entrance quiet was restored, and Serop-Effendi
hurried forward to tell him what had occurred.

Cherif-Pasha hesitated for a moment, when Totia

whispered something to him. The high official turned
to the judges and said :

"It is not my wont to interfere in court proceedings, but to-day I am obliged to express my astonishment that a mere spectator should be allowed to act in
the *rôle* of an attorney."

"He has not even announced himself as a witness
and yet has been allowed to speak," suggested Serop-
Effendi in a low voice.

"That is contrary to the provisions of law," continued the pasha. "If every one present was allowed
to express his opinion in a case, there would never be
an end to the trial.—I regret, Emin Bey," addressing
the president of the tribunal, "that I am obliged to
speak of this, but you are as well aware as I am that
the law must be followed implicitly. Furthermore,
I have to say that this troubler of the peace is known
as a restless, and as I have recently had occasion to
know, a revolutionary character. I warn you to-day
for the last time," he said to Djambek in a harsh
tone "that my patience will soon be at an end, and
that you will have cause to regret mixing yourself in
matters that do not concern you and which you
make your own simply to stir up strife and dissatisfaction. Go now! you have nothing further to do
here."

"It is the right of every free man to be present
here if he chooses."

"If you talk much more you will cease to be a free
man."

Djambek's friends crowded forward to make an
end of the dangerous colloquy, and almost by force
obliged him to leave the room.

He scarcely knew how he reached the street, his brain was in such a tumult.

"Come," said Artschil, taking him by the arm. "The case is lost. You can do no good, and will only get into serious difficulties yourself by remaining."

Djambek followed his relative mechanically. He looked about him absently, and it was only after he had lain for some time as if stunned on the divan at Artschil's house that all that oppressed his heart burst forth in expressions of passionate indignation and anger.

Artschil thought it best to let him go on without interruption, and when he had ceased his tirade, through very exhaustion, his uncle proposed that they go out for a sail.

"Come," he said, "the sea air will do you good."

Djambek made no objection. They hired a boat and directed the sailor to go in a northerly direction, toward the ruins of the castle of the great queen. Djambek remained silent, absorbed in the wild thoughts that possessed him, until they came in sight of the mighty ruins, when he let his eyes rest upon the massive masonry which once bade defiance to the enemy and was thought to be invincible, but which now lay shattered and crumbled. Bushes and fig trees had planted their roots between the blocks of stone and helped on the work of destruction by widening the crevices, as if seeking to break their chains of stone and to obtain room to breathe.

"Do you not believe that those olden times were better, when the mighty hand of the great queen was stretched in protection over our poor land?" said Djambek, at last breaking the silence.

Artschil shook his head.

"History leaves to us only what is good, and is silent on the evil. The chroniclers of events dared not write down what those above them would not like to hear. Injustice, treachery, corruption, were not rare in those days."

"And yet the records of that time speak so often of a man's word being something holy; and of how lying and hypocrisy were execrated and severely punished."

"Just as to-day perjury is punished when it is proved," rejoined the other. "But how many lies go about under the cloak of honesty simply because no one can, or no one will tear off the disguise. The whole world, I tell you, is but a mighty lie!"

"You are perhaps right. With a few exceptions all men prefer attaching themselves to the evil rather than to the good."

The boat reached the land. The two sprang out. They slowly walked up the path thick grown with weeds and shrubs, which led to the ruined castle on the height above. There they sat down under a fig tree, whose wide-spreading branches threw a grateful shade, so that there the grass grew thick and green.

The evening star had just appeared, and the clouds which had been blood red were slowly changing their color. At first they glowed with a dark crimson, then took on tints of bronze and copper, broken here and there by lines of lilac and light blue, until the whole horizon changed to a fading rose color. Then long yellow rays stretched across the heavens, while a white mist, half-transparent and gleaming here and there like mother-of-pearl, enshrouded the city in the distance. The rays became paler and paler, until finally they lost themselves in the downfalling darkness, while far in the background, a few stars began to twinkle.

The two friends had silently watched this approach of night. Finally Artschil arose.

"The world may be ever so bad, but it remains ever beautiful," he said musingly.

As they rowed back to the city a fine boat met them and some one waved his hand to them.

"That is one of Murza-Khan's boats and there he is himself," said Artschil returning the greeting.

The boat passed close to them.

"May your night be pleasant!" cried the owner, saluting Djambek with an elaborate *temena*. "I still think my way of seeking justice the better!"

"What did he mean by that," asked Artschil.

"That money is the best means of obtaining everything—even justice," Djambek replied with a bitter smile.

CHAPTER VIII.

OUTLAWED.

THE trial ended the same day; the sentence was ten years' imprisonment.

As the defendant was still at large the court ordered that it be proclaimed throughout all parts of the province that Elisba was granted a term of three weeks within which to surrender himself; should he fail to present himself within that time all his property would escheat to the government, while every subject would be bound in duty to make him prisoner, or, in case he resisted capture, to shoot him down.

This harsh sentence aroused a bitter indignation throughout all Adjaria. Many of the people loudly expressed their opinions, and cared little that the caimacam's petty officers noted down their names to be reported; while others spoke their dissatisfaction only among themselves, but were agreed with their lands-people in thinking that the cup was now full. While formerly they had bowed to the yoke, and in outward appearance had accepted the provisions of the Mohammedan law in its relation to the affairs of daily life, many now took special pains to glorify their ancient Georgian descent, and to declare openly that they had nothing in common with the followers of the Prophet.

All this, of course, came to the ears of the authorities, but they paid little attention to it. The times had gone when the Adjarians would risk their lives and property to defend their old inherited rights against the oppressor; their weapons were now carried only for show, and only in most exceptional cases, as recently, drawn for action.

The rage of Yordane and Elisba's other people knew no bounds. They knew that their patron was, in any case, a lost man. Ten years in prison, in the best part of a man's life, was no better than a sentence of death—and the doubtful freedom which he now enjoyed must continually be imbittered by the knowledge that some day a traitor would betray him to the enemy, or send a bullet to his heart.

All were agreed that Elisba would not surrender himself. Even if he entertained the idea, the people would not permit him to carry it out. In this they were firmly agreed, though many would suffer through him, for if his estates were confiscated Ali Bey would see to it that none but those who were his obedient subjects should obtain leases. Yordane expected this too, and withdrew to relatives in the mountain to await events.

Elisba and his wife had escaped to Georgian territory. The flight over the highlands and the Achalzich Mountains had been a wearisome and difficult one, so that Eka fell ill from long-continued anxiety and hardships. Fortunately, they found relatives who welcomed them gladly, and little by little Elisba accustomed himself to the idea of not seeing his home again.

His chief anxiety was from his wife's illness. The fever had lasted two weeks, and her situation was a

critical one. There was no physician to be had, and
they had to do their best with what medicine and advice their neighbors could give them. But these did
not avail, and after the third week there was no longer
hope that she would recover.

Djambek had determined to visit his friend, to counsel with him as to their plans for the future. He was
accompanied by a number of Elisba's people, to whom
it was highly important that they should know what
their patron intended to do.

Weary with their hard journey over the mountains
they arrived finally at the place where Elisba had found
refuge. As they approached the house, cries of mourn-
ing were suddenly heard.

"Those are death lamentations," exclaimed Djambek, and he put spurs to his horse, fearing that some
of the police had ventured over the boundary to murder the fugitive. He knew nothing of Eka's illness,
as he had received no reply to his letter, telling Elisba
of the result of the trial. As he was about to throw
himself from his horse, Elisba rushed out, his face distorted like a madman's.

"Elisba! Elisba! What has happened?"

Elisba recognized his friend, and with a sobbing
cry staggered toward him.

"Speak, Elisba! What misfortune has happened?
Where is Eka?"

The loud lamentations heard in the house was the
answer.

"My poor, poor friend!" he cried in a broken
voice.

Elisba sobbed, unable to speak.

"Take courage," said Djambek. "Fate has, in-

deed, dealt you blow upon blow, but it becomes a man
to stand firm, and, with all his powers well in hand,
resist all that Fate can do." He dismounted from his
horse, and taking his friend by the hand, said: "Come,
we will go into the forest, and you shall tell me all
that has befallen you." Djambek remained with him
until after the funeral. He sought to comfort him,
and change the gloomy current of his thoughts, but
Elisba could talk only of the dead, and his grief only
gave way to boundless anger—to oaths of vengeance
on the author of all the misfortune that had so mer-
cilessly overwhelmed him. Homeless, alone in the
world, what had he now to hope for? He felt as if he
were not worth the shot that any betrayer might at
any moment fire upon him; and yet he wished to live
—he felt he must live. He had sworn a solemn oath
which must be kept. He would not attack from behind the man whom he hated as his bitterest foe, his
destroyer, but openly, face to face, he would meet him,
give him every opportunity to defend himself, that it
might not be said that Elisba was an assassin, and
then—one must die! "He or I!" he would repeat
whenever Djambek sought to dissuade him from his
plans for vengeance. "I swore it as I kneeled by her
dead body—by her, of whose death he is guilty, and I
swear it to you, Djambek, a hundred, a thousand times
over. My resolution is fixed; nothing can prevent
my carrying it out."

Djambek returned home full of sorrow and anxiety.
He was accompanied only by his two servants, Yordane
and the others having preferred to stay near their patron. In them, too, the feeling of hatred had extin-
guished all others. They gladly promised to stand by

him and assist him in whatever he might resolve to
do. He alone had the right of dealing vengeance—
vengeance for the blood of the one nearest to him—
and this old law, long fallen into disuse, suddenly lived
again in their hearts. But they would assist in so far
as his enemy might not be met alone but under guard
of his escort and then they would have to do with
them.

The thought of Thamar kept Djambek's anger and
bitterness of heart within bounds. Were it not for this
he would have turned his back upon the land and gone
to the neighboring state where the members of his race
lived under more peaceful and better ordered conditions. But the quieting thought that he was near her,
the knowledge that her thoughts were often lovingly
with him, made all appear to him less bitter, less unbear-
able, and had Cherif-Pasha to-day sought to undo his
injustice toward him, Djambek would have been the
first to have implored Elisba to abandon his thoughts
of vengeance.

The term having expired, Elisba's property was
formally confiscated. As his house was one of the
best in that neighborhood, Ali Bey took it for his own
residence. As he had received numerous reports of
threatening talk among the peasants, he thought it
best only to show himself when accompanied by his
armed escort, and then he felt courage enough to conduct himself toward individual residents in a harsh,
overbearing manner. He thought in this way that he
would command more fear and respect.

In former years, when the harvest had been bad,
the authorities had often acted indulgently and allowed
the tax-payers to carry over their indebtedness to a

more favorable year. Now, on the contrary, there was no mercy shown. Whoever could not pay had property taken from him, and if he had no other property was driven from house and home. It was as if an effort was being made to drive the people to a revolt.

The caimacam made a visit one day to a distant estate, a small farm which stood in some dependent relation to Elisba's property. The tenant, living there in the hills, quite shut out from the rest of the district, had only recently heard of what had taken place. The caimacam demanded of him immediate payment of a large sum and threatened that if it was not paid at once he would be prosecuted. On hearing this the man rushed out of the house and wandered among the hills like one distracted. Suddenly, as if sprung from the ground, Elisba stood before him.

" What is the matter, Stephanik? " asked his former landlord.

The man broke out in tears and told the other his misfortunes.

" When do you say they will come to arrest you? "

" In three days."

" Do you know which of the officials is coming? "

" The caimacam himself."

" The caimacam? " cried Elisba almost joyfully. " Are you sure? "

" It is so, master ; he said it himself."

" Go home quietly, Stephanik ; perhaps I may be able to get you an extension of the time. But, mark well! tell no one that you have seen me. Remember that they are hunting me to the death."

Stephanik went home with a more quiet heart,

though afterward he bethought himself that little aid could be hoped for from a fugitive and exile.

Just before sunrise of the dreaded day which was to him of the same import as the end of the world, he was awakened from his uneasy sleep by the clatter of horses' hoofs, and a few minutes later there was a loud knocking. He went trembling to the door.

"Who is there?" he asked with chattering teeth.

"It is I, Stephanik—Elisba."

In glad astonishment he threw open the door.

"Is it possible? Is it really you, master?"

"Did I not give you my word?"

Stephanik stuttered a few phrases and then ran back into the house.

"Quick, Maiko," he called to his wife, "Elisba is here. He has brought us help. Hurry, old woman, and see what you can get him for breakfast."

The woman now ran out too, but started back in terror as she saw behind Elisba a number of dark figures.

"You are not alone."

"I fear that I should be of little assistance alone. For what I have in view I need the help of my trusted friends. But we have no time to lose. At what hour do you expect the caimacam, and from where is he coming?"

"He is coming from your house, where, as I have heard, he lives now."

"From my house? So much the better. He will have to pass Bear Rock, then."

"There is no other way, except the narrow foot-path along the Sturz, which he could hardly make use of."

"Good! Quick, now, man, we have no objections to a morsel of breakfast, but we must have it quickly, for time presses. We must go farther, for there are preparations to make."

"So you will not meet him here," said Stephanik in surprise.

"Oh, no. It would be doing you an ill service to arrange the affair in your house."

Elisba and his companions took a hasty refreshment, and then the leader turned to Stephanik.

"You will take our horses, and bring them to the dead oak tree in the forest; remain quietly with them until you hear from us. Now, then, my friends, let us be off," he said to his followers.

Bear Rock was an enormous block of stone, which long ago had been loosened from the face of the mountain and rolled down until stopped by a clump of trees directly overhanging the road. Here it had become firmly fixed, and out of its crevices had grown a thicket of shrubs and small trees, completely covering its top and effectually hiding any one who might be concealed there from those coming along the road. As the stone was smaller at the bottom, and was thickly overhung with vines, there was a place there too where several persons could be effectually concealed. It only needed to cut a passage through the thick growth of vines and bushes toward the road to prepare a most excellent place for a sudden attack.

This was soon done, and the bushes laid so as to conceal the opening. Then a part of the little troop placed themselves on the side from which the caimacam would approach, as it was probable that when his escort saw the horsemen in front they would turn to

flee. Elisba and the others placed themselves on the
other side of the rock. In this way the caimacam's
party would be completely surrounded—on the right,
the wall of stone, on the left, a steep precipice, and
before and behind, Elisba's company.

In order that the attack might not be made too
soon, a man was stationed on the road a few hundred
paces from the rock, in the direction from which the
caimacam would come. He was directed to sit by the
roadside until he heard the approach of the horsemen, and then slowly walk back as if he were a weary
traveler, but in such a way that they should overtake
him near the rock. When they were come to the point
where the attack was intended to be made, the man
was to say in a loud voice, " That is Bear Rock."

Elisba and his followers were fully armed. Each
had a dagger and a pair of pistols in his girdle and a
gun over his shoulder. Elisba carried, in addition, as
he was entitled to by right of his rank, a broad,
curved sword at his side.

They had waited about an hour, when the sound of
horses' hoofs was heard. All took their guns from
the shoulder, and held them ready to fire. Soon voices
were heard approaching nearer and nearer, and soon
it seemed as if the riders must be directly in front of
the ambush, and Elisba began to fear that his out-
guard had in some way been prevented from giving
the appointed signal. In breathless excitement he
whispered to his men to dash out as soon as the first
horse's head came in sight. At the same moment he
heard Ali Bey's voice.

" How did this rock get here, fellow? "

" I don't know, master. It is called Bear Rock,"

replied the man in a loud voice, and the horsemen suddenly pulled back their horses in consternation, for there in front of them stood a band of armed men, with guns ready to fire. Their first impulse was to turn backward and escape, but there, too, was a second band, with guns aimed at them.

"Surrender! Throw down your weapons, or I give the order to fire," cried Elisba.

Ali Bey's escort consisted of six men, while their opponents numbered four times as many. Besides, the riders carried their guns carelessly slung over their backs, so that they could not make use of them before the others could fire. After a moment's consideration, they obeyed Elisba's demand, seeing that their only hope was in not seeking to defend themselves.

Ali Bey had for his only weapon the curved saber at his side. He drew it, but seeing that his escort had surrendered, he too abandoned the idea of resistance.

Sorrow and trouble had so changed Elisba's looks that his enemy did not recognize him at first, but when the young man stepped nearer, the caimacam started back in terror and a death-like pallor overspread his countenance.

"You have taken from me my home!" cried Elisba, fixing his blazing eyes on Ali Bey. "I have to thank you that I am hunted like a wild beast, and it is through you I have lost my wife. The cup of your wickedness, vile wretch, is full—full of the blood and sweat of those you have oppressed—so full of shameful villainy that it would be no more than you deserve if one should tie a rope around your neck and throttle

8

you like a mad dog, for you are not worthy of a bullet in your vile heart. And yet it shall not be said
that Elisba was a murderer—that a stronger force fell
upon you to do the hangman's duty." He drew his
saber. " Defend yourself—it is for life or death ! "

The weapons flashed. Ali Bey fought like a madman. But soon he felt that his arm was weakening,
that he could not follow the rapid movements of his opponent. With a quick, desperate movement he caught
hold of Elisba's sword with one hand, that he might
give him a deadly blow with his own in the other.
But like a flash of lightning Elisba tore his dagger
from his girdle and buried it to the hilt in the caimacam's breast.

" Then—take that, coward ! " he cried hoarsely as his
opponent sank dead upon the ground. " You have
chosen to fight unfairly."

Ali Bey's sword had also reached its mark and
wounded Elisba on the shoulder; but the wound was
not a serious one, and a tightly bound handkerchief
sufficed to stop the bleeding.

" Take away the corpse of your vile master," said
he, turning to the terrified guard—" take him back to
where he came from—to my house, for all I care now,
since his foot can no longer shame the threshold.
But remember one thing," he added sternly, " and
that is to give a true report to your superiors. Do
not dare, in your cowardice, to make up a story of his
being overpowered by a superior force of murderers. I
shall know it if you do, and we shall remember each
of your faces, and woe to you if you spread abroad a
slanderous account of this day's doings.—One shall
pay for all with his life, and all for one ! "

Elisba's men took the weapons of the guard as their rightful booty, and while the soldiers in trembling haste, glad to have escaped with their lives, prepared a stretcher of boughs, the band of avengers silently took their way toward the mountains.

CHAPTER IX.

THE MUEZZIN.

"WHAT do I say to all this, friend Djambek?"
Murza-Khan puffed contentedly at his nargile and
blew a cloud of smoke into the air. "To speak frankly, I am rather pleased. I paid a visit to Cherif-Pasha
yesterday for the sole purpose of mitigating his anger.
He is fairly raving over your neighbor's little escapade,
and has given orders to have a price set on the murderer's head."

"The murderer! Elisba killed his opponent in a
fair duel."

"I know that. And I was greatly surprised to
hear the trembling report that Ali Bey's brave escort
gave of the matter. They did not even seek to excuse
their cowardice, as Elisba had threatened to strip
the skin from their bones if they failed to speak the
exact truth. That made the pasha even more angry
than did the news that his officer had been killed.
Astounding! his own men driven into a corner and
threatened as if the land had no rulers and no garrison! It is a shame that you could not see him, Djambek. His veins swelled so that it looked as if somebody had put a net of thick cords over his face."

"And you, what did you say?"

"I let him roar himself out first, because I knew it is always best to let a man's anger have free play for a while. Then I said; 'Go carefully. If one thrusts into a hornet's nest he must have fire near at hand or there will be plenty of boils and blisters.' He threw his pipe on the ground so that it smashed, and yelled out: 'Fire! I'll give them fire! I have got a successor to Ali Bey who will turn this nest upside down, and every third village shall be garrisoned.' 'In that way you may do something,' I answered"

"You would have done better to dissuade him from such a step."

"I? Am I his counselor. He has enough other people for that. How would it look for me to say to him, 'Do this and leave that undone'! I should not like it much myself if any one interfered in my business—told me to raise flax instead of silk, for example. No, I raise what I choose, and he may do as he pleases."

"And yet you seem to anticipate that the matter will end badly. Otherwise, you would not have warned him of hornet stings. Do you not believe that if the oppressed province rises in rebellion the movement will find an echo here in your district?"

"I do not believe it will go as far as that. Your hot-blooded nature makes you see things ahead which only exist in your imagination. The times are past when such a united movement could take place. Nowadays each thinks for himself, and not for the common good."

"You think so. You speak as one who is blessed with goods, and who finds it easy to purchase his ease and peace by a yearly tribute. But do not forget that the poor are in the majority, and have not much to lose—compared to what they may gain."

The veranda on which they sat overlooked the edge of the cliff which projected over the sea. Everything here breathed quietness and prosperity. No other sound came to them but the low murmur of the blue sea, where, in the little bay, a half-dozen graceful sloops and cutters rocked, the property of the owner of the estate.

Thick carpets from Teheran and Smyrna, of wonderful combinations of colors, covered the stone floor, and might make one imagine he was treading the soft turf below. Costly pillars of many colored marble supported the vaulted roof, and numerous plants and flowers filled the air with perfume. Coffee, in delicately worked silver cups, stood in reach of the hand, and with them crystal goblets of water cooled with snow from the mountain and blood-red sherbet of pomegranates. Murza-Khan, with half-shut eyes, reclined luxuriously on the cushioned divan, and drew the smoke from his costly water-pipe in slow, comfortable puffs—the picture of a man to whom personal enjoyment is the only condition and the only object of life.

"I tell you," said Djambek, resuming his conversation after a long pause, "the end may be a very serious one. 'But a single spark is needed to start a blaze —and you know well how a fire spreads. First, they will satisfy their revenge on their oppressors; but then, when the masses have once tasted blood, if they once meet with success, their moderation will be lost, and any one who possesses riches, and lives in luxury, will be counted an enemy who must be destroyed. Therefore, measures of prevention must be taken in time, and one in your position, especially, should do all that lies in his power."

"Your picture is a vivid one; but still it is only a picture. The land will never be aroused to that pitch. I know my people better. And even if it were otherwise, do you suppose a crowd, or say even an army, of badly armed, poorly disciplined rebels could, in these days, offer any serious resistance to well-armed, highly disciplined troops?"

"We see many things carried out where at first it seemed impossible. But, aside from all that, who assures you that if the people, in their desperation should call on the neighboring states for help—"

"The Russian?" interrupted Murza-Khan, rising excitedly. "You mean that? Then know this; that at the first sign of such a movement, I put all my property in hazard and use my utmost influence to crush it at its birth; and the first traitor that came in my way I would lay his head at his feet!"

"That would not make the others harmless that stood behind him."

"Pah!" rejoined Murza derisively, "the people are but a herd, to be driven by one who has the longest whip and who can crack it the loudest; and I know how to drive them, be assured— But let us drop the subject. They are but imaginary specters—green fruit that will drop before it is ripe. The visionaries who cast glances toward our neighboring state only know it by hearsay; they do not know that over there things are as bad, if not worse, than they are with us."

"I hardly think that is so. You know I received a part of my education in Odessa; and I always no-

ticed that every effort was being made to introduce the
benefits of Western culture."

Murza-Khan laughed. " What do you understand
by Western culture? Heavier taxes and less personal
freedom? I went to Marseilles once to sell some of
my silk. You should have heard the sighs and groans
of these ' Western culture ' people! At that time the
nephew of the great robber Napoleon had seized the
supreme power; behind every man stood a spy, to
listen and report every word he said; they were driven
to prison in herds; every man that had two sound
arms had to stick them into a soldier's coat, and risk
his life for the benefit of the throne robber. I was glad
when I succeeded in getting through with my business
and on board a ship bound for home. And I thought
to myself : With us things are better ; there no one
obliges me to make a target of myself for matters I care
nothing about; and with a handful of dirty piasters I
can make the tax gatherer bow to the ground. If I
want to carry on some business matter without the
officials sticking their noses into it, I have only to slip
a piece of shining metal into the caimacam's hands.
Therefore, I say again, Elisba was a fool; he could
have arranged matters with the caimacam much more
cheaply than by seeking to get so-called justice—which
I do not expect to find in perfection even at the side
of the Prophet in paradise. What has he got now to
offset the loss of his wife and his property, and that
men are always on his track, trying to earn the five
thousand piasters reward for putting a bullet through
his head?"

" If all thought as you do, matters would soon be
worse than they are now. And as I said before, few

are in a position where they can buy peace and friendship with the officials as you can."

"Fortune opens the door to every one, and it is so much the worse for him who stumbles over the threshold and cracks his skull!"

Dusk had settled down so rapidly and suddenly that the sea was but a gray cloud uniting with the horizon. Murza-Khan had left his divan, and was walking thoughtfully up and down. Suddenly there was heard a long drawn out whistle, which made him stop to listen. In a few moments it was repeated, and he walked to the railing and peered into the darkness until far out on the sea a red light could be seen.. The color of the light changed to green, and then to white. He threw a stolen glance at his visitor, and walked restlessly up and down again a few times, and then, stopping in front of Djambek, said:

"Will you spend the night with me? You will be welcome, only I must beg you to excuse me for a couple of hours. I have promised to see a tenant to-night on business, and he lives at some distance."

"I thank you for your hospitality, but I must go back to the city, as I intend taking a boat for home that leaves at midnight. As you have business I will not detain you longer. Farewell, I am sorry that you are not to be won to the side of justice."

As Djambek slowly took his way back to the city, his mind was busy with what had passed between himself and Murza-Khan. He had had strong hopes of gaining over the rich, influential nabob, but he had now to admit that with so selfish a nature it was impossible. One who thought only of himself was not the man who could be made the leader of a movement

which had for its object the common good of all.   And
yet it would be so easy for him to do the land a great
service.   It was not by force of arms that Djambek
hoped to bring about a reformation—then at least,
that thought was far from him—but if Murza-Khan
would make an attempt to work upon Cherif-Pasha
with words and advice, there were many others who
would not indeed venture alone, but who would join
him, and their influence all together might suffice to
bring the governor to take a different course.

As matters now stood, Djambek saw to his sorrow
that there was no possibility of a redress of existing
grievances.   He felt himself to be too young for a
leader.   He felt certain that his own people and many
others would be true to him.   But to what end?   He
no longer had admission to Cherif-Pasha, so that there
was no possibility of mediation there.   He thought of
Artschil, but abandoned the idea almost as soon as it
was formed.   Artschil was a brave, honorable man,
but he was in the service of the authorities.   He ate
their bread, and for that reason could not appear as
their opponent.   The old Georgian feeling, too, had
long slumbered in his heart, and at his age one can not
be aroused for such things.   "He lived among the
wolves, and must howl with them."

Djambek saw that there was nothing to be done
but to endure; to look quietly on while rascality, injustice, and avarice won the battle.   And perhaps,
after long years, when he should be an old man, he too
might sit in the sun and take things as calmly as
Murza-Khan did, and smile at the enthusiasm of youths
who believed they could alone successfully oppose established power.

Arriving in the city, he went to Ahmed's house to pass the evening.

The muezzin was a pious Mohammedan. All that related to his faith he looked upon as holy and unquestionable. In this respect, therefore, he could be deemed a most loyal subject of the Sultan, in whom he recognized a semi-supernatural being. But for the Sultan's representative he had less reverence, and in his heart he felt a righteous indignation over the many wrongs that were to be traced to the pasha's door. Toward Djambek's family he felt the greatest attachment. He owed to Djambek's father the position he now held, as well as many obligations for help in time of need. The kindnesses, too, which his sister had received he considered as done to himself. In his eyes the son of his benefactor was a young man of great promise, who one day might be called on to play a great *rôle* in the land. He saw in him a sort of reformer of the future, who, when the time should come, would bring about a better order of things. The thought came to him often of how fine it would be if the prophet should in a dream open the eyes of the mighty ruler in Stamboul, and say to him: "Beyond the sea dwells a young man whose wisdom is the wisdom of age; who loves only righteousness, and seeks only justice. I have chosen him to bring fortune and peace to his country. I charge thee, therefore, call him to thee, and give him power in thy name."

To this day dream Ahmed often gave himself, and so when Djambek spoke of the state of the land and complained of the wrongs done in high places, the muezzin nodded smilingly and said: "Keep thy pa-

tience, Djambek, I see the day coming when thou shalt
be called to rescue the land."

Djambek's hopes did not go as far as that; he had
no dreams of playing a prominent part. If he could in
some way assist in putting down bribery and official
corruption all his hopes would be realized.

But the two did not speak of these matters to-night,
for the old man had a note for Djambek which he had
intended sending to him by messenger. When the
young man had read and reread it, he turned toward
Ahmed and, under its influence, poured out his whole
soul to him. Ahmed listened to him good-naturedly,
with only now and then a remark. He felt a sympathy also for Thamar, not alone because she was the
queen of Djambek's heart, but for her own sake too.

"See," he said, indicating a small closet behind
whose glass doors he kept his valuables, "she always
brings something to please me," and he brought out
the little presents she had given him. "Once she
wanted to give me a string of amber beads, but I would
not allow it. It would look as if I wished to be paid
for the little services I did. When she offered me a
silk handkerchief for my sister I could not resist, but
I made her promise not to bring anything more that
cost much money."

"You are too sensitive, Ahmed. The services you
have done can not be paid for with amber beads.
Take what she gives you; I know her heart, and she
will feel badly if you refuse."

"Do you know, "said the muezzin after a pause,
"at first I felt some scruples about this business? It
did not seem right for a man in my position to be acting as a go-between. But afterward, when she came

and smiled so winningly and, at the same time, so imploringly, I said to myself: Ei! the prophet never said that love was forbidden, and why should I be more strict than the embassador of Allah. But the prophet insisted on repaying kindness with kindness. It would have been a shame, therefore, if I did not serve you when I could. And the oftener she came the gladder I was to think to myself, This good, handsome couple is made happy partly through me."

Djambek gave him his hand. "You are a good man, Ahmed. If the prophet had only such servants, he might well be content."

"I do not think it is so hard for one to do his duty. There are verily many temptations to every man to do some wrong; but if he only thinks, 'Shall I break the commands of Allah to enjoy a brief pleasure and forget that he will severely punish all unfaithfulness?' then it is not hard to withstand."

"I fear Allah overlooks some things here and there. How else could wickedness prosper as it sometimes does?"

Ahmed raised his hand warningly. "Speak not so, Djambek, perhaps he hears us now."

"You think so?" Djambek was about to add something further, but the reverent tone in which the other had spoken restrained him, and he changed the subject by telling the muezzin of his sister, how well she carried on the household, and how faithfully she served him. "Bachelors usually keep house but poorly" he said, "but they should see mine. And then she seems so contented. One would never think from her cheerfulness that she has suffered so much."

Ahmed smiled with pleasure. "True, and this

cheerfulness and content she owes to you. Often has she told me how you treat her, not as a master treats his servant, but rather as a son his mother."

"But there is no question of master and servant between us."

"Strictly speaking, there is, of course. Does she not eat your bread? But there is no humiliation in service when one does his duty."

"That is to say, when both sides do their duty. There you are right, Ahmed. I feel more respect for the humblest servant who does his work faithfully and conscientiously than for those in high position who are, indeed, servants too, but act as if they were the masters, and rob, cheat, and betray those whose bread they eat. But I must go now." .

"Wait one moment. Lazar is coming to let us know when he is ready to start. And, in the mean time, I beg you will partake of some refreshment."

Ahmed hastened to the closet and brought out some decorated plates and a fork and knife, which he placed before his guest with evident pride. Then he brought from another room a basket of fruit and white bread. Just as they had finished the frugal meal Lazar appeared and informed Djambek that he was ready to start.

CHAPTER X.

A CRY FOR HELP.

CHERIF-PASHA had partly carried out the threat he had made to Murza-Khan. The man whom he appointed as Ali Bey's successor had served with the military since his sixteenth year, and was a type of those "iron-eaters" who think everything must march according to the drum. The military force under the pasha's command was not indeed large enough to allow him to place a garrison in every third village, but a number of new posts were established, to be at the caimacam's disposal.

The first thing that Redjeb Bey, the new official, did was to summon all the village elders before him; those who failed to come were punished with heavy fines. To those who came he announced his programme. He told them he should follow up severely the slightest infraction of law; that as the representative of the government he would make no concessions, but would see to it that every requirement was strictly lived up to. In conclusion, he spoke of "that rebel and outlaw" Elisba, for whose arrest all subjects must do their utmost. Should he find that, either from fear or from pity, any one had given the fugitive a place of shelter, he swore that he would level his house to the

ground and have the faithless subject shot without
mercy.

After this friendly announcement he dismissed the
elders with the command to appear before him twice a
month to receive any new directions he might have to
give, and to render an account of all their doings.

The people went away shaking their heads. They
had never been spoken to like that before. It was just
as if the new caimacam had been the commander of a
hostile army, who gave the conquered people his directions as to what they should do during the term of his
occupation of the country.

It was the most bitter for those who had failed to
obey the summons, and who now found themselves,
according to their wealth, condemned to heavy fines
or to imprisonment. The positions they held as village elders they considered as posts of honor conferred
upon them by their fellow-villagers; they received no
pay, and therefore felt that no one had a right to treat
them as dependent officials.

From this time every one objected to taking these
offices, but the caimacam, on his own authority simply,
named as elders the oldest inhabitants. No objections were listened to. It was "either accept or go to
prison."

Such measures were not calculated to make things
move smoothly again. On the contrary, the discon-
tent soon became general, and if no one ventured to
speak his dissatisfaction aloud, the fire smoldered the
more fiercely under the ashes.

Redjeb Bey conducted himself toward the higher
classes with harshness and rudeness. As he had come
up from the ranks, and had often suffered as a scape-

goat for his superiors, he now took advantage of his position of authority to have his revenge on those who had stood over the people from birth. In this respect he was very democratic; he found it to be very unjust that certain people should be counted higher than others because they had happened to inherit property and titles; he would only grant such right to one person—the Padishah—all others should like himself climb by hard labor to the top of the hierarchical ladder.

Many of the large land owners did not feel constrained to pay their humble respects to the caimacam, and among them was Djambek. If Redjeb Bey had called on him he would have fulfilled the duties of hospitality, but he considered it superfluous for him to humbly appear before the representative of a government for which he had more reason every day to feel contempt. The caimacam took notice of this, and took occasion more than once to speak of "these great lords who think themselves of more importance than His Majesty in Stamboul."

The ill-feeling between the people and the government thus grew greater every day. There was, to be sure, no talk of bribery, but every one suffered under the iron rule and brutal strictness which the caimacam thought necessary for the safety of the state. To make matters still worse, the crops this year were a failure, so that the small land holders found it as much as they could do to support themselves, to say nothing of promptly meeting the demands for taxes. As Redjeb Bey would listen to no sort of compromise, it was finally determined to send a delegation to the city to represent to Cherif-Pasha how matters stood, and induce him to use his power to ameliorate the heavy conditions.

Totia, who received the deputation, closed one eye and laid his finger along his hawk-like nose.

" My dear people, this is a ticklish matter," he said. " Cherif-Pasha is still much incensed over the recent occurrences, and I fear he will not even consent to see you."

This time Totia had not exaggerated matters, as he usually did, in order to increase the importance of his services. The pasha had sworn vengeance on the province where his representative had been so severely dealt with.

A present to Totia, a little purse of silver pieces, on which hung so many drops of the poverty-stricken people's sweat, induced that worthy to make an attempt to get an audience with the pasha for the delegation, and he succeeded in so far as obtaining permission for the people to enter. Their reception was certainly not a cordial one. The governor asked them gruffly what they wanted, and as their spokesman made known their requests, the pasha scowled.

" What ! After having murdered one of my best officials, you dare to come and ask for favors !" he said harshly.

" We, your Excellency, did not murder Ali Bey."

" I hold you all responsible, for at least in your hearts you all consented to the shameful deed."

The spokesman was silent for a moment, then he said :

" We had naught to do with it, Excellency, but that we do not mourn the caimacam's death is not our fault. He was not the man to gain our special affection."

"Perhaps his successor will know better how to win your hearts," replied the pasha sarcastically.

The spokesman shook his head. "It is said," he replied, "that dogs love the hand that beats them. But we are not dogs. And therefore, Excellency, we pray you speak a word in our favor. We will go to our work with redoubled energy to meet our obligations as soon as possible. Only grant us a delay, for if they take from us the little that we have, there is naught left us but to die of hunger."

"I will tell you something," returned the pasha, after a few moments' thought. "The possibility of your re-establishing yourselves in the favor of your rightful masters shall not be taken from you. By right, each and all of you deserve punishment, for if you had done your duty as obedient subjects the rebel and murderer would have long since been given up to justice. And yet I will show you that the government is inclined to mercy, if you will but do your part in restoring matters to their proper condition. Hear, then! In case the villain Elisba is delivered up within one month, not only shall those engaged in his capture receive the promised reward, but their villages, be it one or many, shall receive a present of this year's dues, and the whole province receive an extension of one year for payment of taxes. You can not certainly ask more. One service for another. You know now what you have to do. Go!"

When the delegation were again in the ante-room, Totia rubbed his hands in satisfaction.

"Na! my people, you did not expect anything so good as that!"

They sorrowfully shook their heads. "We would have preferred simply an extension of six months."

"You are fools!" ejaculated Totia, "a higher reward for a simple piece of work could not be thought of."

The delegation returned home and made their report to a meeting of the people. The first results were bitter complaints that Cherif-Pasha's conditions simply amounted to an absolute refusal of their request. Afterward, however, single voices were heard, at first hesitatingly, and then more confidently, intimating that it was a matter to be taken into consideration. Especially one who had had differences with Elisba, spoke in this way. It was the duty of every one to look out for himself. If Elisba had sacrificed himself for the good of the others, it would be different. But he had fought for his own interests and satisfied his own vengeance. If one considered only that by it a whole land was to be saved; that many who would otherwise have to take their beggar's staff in hand might retain their little property—then possibly it was going to an extreme, not to take the proposition into consideration, when the good of one was opposed to the welfare of the many.

These arguments were not without effect on a part of the assembly. The majority indeed opposed the idea, and declared themselves against sacrificing one of their lands-people, who had always stood by them. But a minority agreed with the speaker referred to, and the assembly broke up in dissatisfaction and dispute. Otia, the leader of the minority, discussed the matter at length on the way home, and ridiculed the others for having such tender feelings, when, in fact, he said, they would grin with pleasure if they heard one day that their requests had been granted as a special mark of the pasha's favor.

Among those who attended the meeting was the elder of the village of Skalta. When he returned home he told Djambek of what had been done. He did not neglect to speak of Otia's speech, and how he and a number of others were in favor of accepting the pasha's conditions. This made Djambek feel great anxiety for the safety of his friend. He lost no time in sending a warning to Elisba, in order that he might at least avoid setting foot on his native territory. Otherwise, he could not assist him.

One day a boy coming in great haste brought him a message saying that Ahmed could not wait for Lazar this time as the message was urgent.

Djambek tore open the letter and read as follows:

" Beloved : I am driven nearly to desperation. After my uncle had been silent for a long time on the hated subject, he called me to him to inform me that he had positively promised my hand to Hassan Bey. I answered with a positive ' No,' and tried to leave the room, when he barred the way and said he would force me to follow his wishes. Then I threw myself at his feet and confessed that my heart belonged to you. I beseeched him to remember that my life's happiness was concerned; I sought to show how superior you were to the other, but he only laughed scornfully at all I said, and called me insane to think he would give his relative to a fool. Then I poured out all that was in my heart; I declared I would never give my-

self as the price of his manœuvres; that I was ready
to throw myself into the sea rather than bind myself
for life to a man for whom I felt only hatred and
comtempt. Thereupon he got furiously angry. He
denounced me as ungrateful, common, low—and swore
an oath that within a few weeks I should be the wife
of this hated man.

"We are to leave the city in a week. My uncle is
going to Artwin, and I am to accompany him as far
as Murgal where I am to remain under Russudan's care.
My only friend and confidante, Daria, remains here.
A change of air is necessary for me as the heat in Batoum appears to be dangerous for me. I know very
well what this change means. They mean to separate
me from all my friends and keep me in solitude, in
order to force me to consent to the will of my jailer
and be chained for life to this man to whom I will
never belong.

"Rescue me, my friend. I am ready for anything;
only save me from this frightful position!

"THAMAR."

Djambek had become deadly pale, and his hand
trembled so that he could scarcely read the letter to its
end. After brooding over it for a long time he read it
through again, and then grinding his teeth in impotent
rage strode up and down the room like one possessed,
clinching his fists as if he would destroy an enemy
that stood before him. It was a long time before his
fierce excitement subsided so that he could think con-
nectedly of what was to be done.

Rescue her! how could he? And yet why should
he not place his life upon it and make the attempt?

At first he could see no hope of success, but as he dwelt more upon it he saw a possibility of its being done. He had in former years often traveled up the Tchoroch, and had frequently gone farther than Artwin. He had often, too, landed in Murgal, and believed he could still remember its principal features. He determined to go there at once to make himself better acquainted with the locality. If he wished to gain time he must start without delay, as the voyage up stream was difficult and slow.

Quickly making up his mind, he at once set about making the necessary preparations. Putting together what he needed for the voyage he sent it by his servant to the boat. Then he called his old housekeeper.

"Take this," he said, handing her a large sum of money. "I am going on a journey, and may be gone for some time. This will serve for your living until I return."

The woman clasped her hands in surprise. "You are not going into any danger, are you?" she cried imploringly. "Oh, be careful. Stay quietly and peacefully at home. Oh, do not—"

"Be still! My happiness depends on this trip. My duty, too, calls me. I shall see Ahmed in any event, and you will hear of me through him. If any one inquires for me, say that I have been called away on urgent business."

He hurriedly left the house, while the old woman in tears made numerous mystic signs behind him which, to her mind, were calculated to avert all evil from his head. He and his servant plied the oars so vigorously that in four hours they were in Batoum. Here he gave the man some money and directed him to return.

"I shall remain here some days," he said, "and perhaps shall have to go farther on business—but you will hear from me in eight or ten days at the farthest."

Then he left his servant and took his way into the city alone.

"I thought you would come to-day," said Ahmed, as Djambek entered. "This time it was her friend who brought the note, and she seemed so sad and anxious that I feared something was wrong."

"Yes, Ahmed, her future and mine depend upon it," said Djambek, in an excited tone. "I must tear her from the claws of her jailer."

"What! Will they try to—" exclaimed Ahmed.

"They will make her and me unhappy for life. Her uncle has reasons for wishing her to marry a man whom she hates. I must risk everything to prevent it. I have no secrets from you, and you shall know all," and he imparted to him his plan, which was to go at once to Murgal, and there make arrangements for an abduction.

"And after that?" asked Ahmed gravely. "Have you thought of what is to follow? What will become of you then? Do you suppose you will be allowed to quietly settle down in your home again?"

"No. I know too well that they will place every obstacle in our path. We must fly where their arms can not reach us."

"And never again place your foot upon the paternal threshold?"

"I think Cherif-Pasha will finally be reconciled when he sees that there is no help for it. I have friends and relatives who will use their influence to mitigate his anger, and make him see that I am not a husband for his niece who is to be despised."

"I fear you take too hopeful a view. You take it for granted, too, that you will be successful in your purpose; there are many things that may cause a failure. What then?"

"Then? I have told you that the matter is decisive of my future. If my project succeeds, then I will patiently endure banishment, though it last longer than I now hope. If my project fails, then life has no further value to me, and I shall know how to make an end of sorrow."

The muezzin raised his hand reprovingly.

"You will then be presumptuous enough to throw away the life that Allah has given you? Do you forget that you have duties to your fellow-men? that you are perhaps called for a great work in behalf of your fatherland? Do you believe that a clear head and strong arms were given you for nothing? No, Djambek, under such conditions I will know nothing of the matter. Your first project is a violation of human laws; against that, because of my friendship and love for you, I have nothing to say. Your second resolution, however, is a heavy transgression against the laws of Allah, and therefore I can not, as a humble servant of the Almighty, have aught to do with your project."

"If, however, I solemnly promise you not to be guilty of this transgression?" said Djambek.

"You say that as indifferently as you made the threat a minute ago," replied Ahmed sternly.

"Tell me this. May I count on your help if I will take a solemn oath to bear all ill-success with resignation?" continued the young man.

"Yes," said Ahmed, after a little thought.

"Good, then! here is my hand. I swear by the memory of my parents, and by the dearest thing I possess—her love—that I will not let my courage fail. I will never give up hope. If not now, then perhaps at some future time we may be united. But I am confident of success. I ask but two things of you."

He drew a packet from his pocket.

"These papers," he continued, "show that I have all my ready money with a business friend in the city. He is an honorable man. I leave these papers with you, and shall go to him at once and notify him that in a few days a friend will come and take the money. You see this ring? I will show it to him, and leave an impression of it with him. To the bearer of this ring he is to give the money, and you will be the bearer."

Ahmed threw out his hands in the Oriental sign of assent.

"It will be time enough," Djambek continued, "if you get the money in a week from now, when I shall come through here with her. My second request is that you will procure me a bark, a good sea-going vessel, and have it ready for me at the point where the Adjaria and the Tchoroch join. From there on we must have a large vessel, so that we can continue our flight across the sea."

"But will your business friend not be suspicious? Is the sum you leave with him a large one?" asked Ahmed.

"Yes, it is considerable, but I will reassure him in regard to that. Do you know the man? His name is on the envelope."

Ahmed looked at the name.

"No," he replied. "I have heard the name, but can not remember ever having seen him."

"You can let him think you are one of my tenants in case he asks. I will give him to understand that I am about to buy a new estate, which will, indeed, be the truth, if I am forced to turn my back forever upon my native land. I must go now. Do not forget, my dear Ahmed, that perhaps my whole fate hangs upon your punctuality. I will return for a moment to bring you back the ring."

Djambek found his business agent at home, and arranged with him to have the money ready within a few days. Leaving with him the impression of his signet ring, he returned to Ahmed, gave him the ring, and, with a warm embrace, bade him farewell.

CHAPTER XI.

AN ORIENTAL ELOPEMENT.

DJAMBEK used the week in making observations in the locality where his plan was to be carried out. Taking the route by land, a steep path over lofty mountains, as being less traveled than that by the river, he reached his destination in three days.

At Murgal the river flows through a wide valley. It is a charming village, noted for the salubrity of its climate, which is considered especially good for those whose health has suffered from the fever common in Batoum. Djambek chose an isolated house close by the river, on the outskirts of the town, as his stopping place. An old man lived there whose support was raising fruit and vegetables. Djambek represented himself to him as a business man engaged in the wholesale fruit trade, and desirous of seeing whether arrangements could be made for direct trade between Batoum and Murgal. Under this pretense he soon made the acquaintance of many of the inhabitants, and easily discovered which house was intended as the residence of the pasha's niece. It was the best house in the vicinity. It, too, lay apart from others, on a slight eminence. In front was a thick grove extending to the river, and behind it were extensive fruit orchards. The grove had several clumps of trees, which were almost impassable, so thick were they, and here Djambek found a favorable place for making observations of the house. From what he knew of Thamar, he felt sure that she would walk here in the cool of the evening, and would especially frequent the spot where a clearing afforded a beautiful view of the river. Here he accordingly prepared his arrangements for carrying out his project.

At first he had intended to make his flight with Thamar by the land route; but after experiencing its difficulties himself he was unwilling to expose her to its hardships and dangers. It was therefore necessary for him to inform himself thoroughly as to the water route, which also was not without its dangers. There were places where piles of rock left only the narrowest of passages and sudden turns on whose sharp, rocky edges a light boat might easily come to grief unless there was an experienced hand at the helm. These particulars he learned from the old man with whom he lived; and he determined to engage him for the voyage. His boat was small and very light, so that if they were followed there was the more hope of eluding the pursuers.

He therefore asked the old man carelessly if he could take him to the city in the course of the next few days, in case he should want to go; to which the old man assented.

While Djambek was thus making preparations for the release of his beloved one, she was passing anxious days in Batoum. She was treated as a prisoner, and could not even associate with Daria. She could, therefore, hear nothing from Djambek, and did not even know whether he had received her letter, still less whether he would make the attempt to rescue her. Russudan followed her every step, and Cherif-Pasha only showed himself to speak harsh words or mutter dark threats.

At last, one morning—Russudan had left her room just before—Thamar heard a rattling in the chimney, and thought she saw a stone fall on the ashes in the fireplace. It was apparently a white pebble with black lines; but when she picked it up, she saw that the black lines were letters. In happy surprise she read these words, written in French :

"Your lover has prepared everything for your release."

This, doubtless, had come from Daria, and Thamar blessed the ingenuity of her friend, which had taken such a weight of suspense from her heart. She had remained standing by the fireplace, and now started involuntarily as she heard her name called.

"Thamar, Thamar, how are you?" she heard again in a few seconds.

"Where are you?" she asked, looking around the room.

"I don't understand you. Speak more into the chimney."

Now she understood. "You are there, Daria?"

"Yes." A low titter came down; then: "I am on the roof. Russudan has gone into the servants' quarters, so I thought I would take the opportunity of making you a chimney call."

"How good you are, Daria !"

"You found the stone?"

"Certainly. If you only knew how happy the message has made me!"

"She is coming! I must go. Farewell!"

Russudan was astonished to find her charge smiling and apparently happy, when she had left her in tears.

"You are surprised?" said Thamar. "I have come to the conclusion that it is foolish to show people who ill-treat you that their ill-treatment troubles you seriously. From this time I shall only laugh at you, and all your ill-treatment will be unable to draw a tear from me."

Russudan shrugged her shoulders indifferently.

"You seem to think," she said, "I am put here solely to annoy you. My only duty is to see that you do not again commit grave offenses against our customs and laws, and I shall prevent you, as far as my power lies, you may be sure."

"Really? I recognize only the laws and customs of the land my mother belonged to. I fear neither you nor my uncle, and you will never be able to carry out your plans."

"Perhaps in the solitude of Murgal you will speak less daringly."

"Do you think so? You will perhaps be disappointed, for I have determined to treat all your annoyances with indifference."

Russudan faithfully reported all this to her relative, but the pasha only shrugged his shoulders, and said that Thamar would see that he fulfilled his oath.

The day for the departure was fixed, and the boats engaged. Cherif-Pasha was to stay a week in Artwin, and then return to Murgal, where Thamar was to re-

main in the mean time, to be joined a few days later
by Hassan Bey, who was coming to take his bride.
The indispensable Totia, of course, accompanied the
pasha.

Djambek, not knowing on what day the party was
to arrive, spent most of his time in the grove, whence
he had a good view down the river, anxiously watching
for the approach of the boats. Several days passed,
when, at length, one evening toward sundown, a large
boat was seen coming up the river, carrying a numerous company. The boat came slowly and with difficulty against the current, and Djambek soon made out
the figure of the pasha standing with Totia at the bow.
No female figures were to be seen. The aft part of
the boat was occupied by the pasha's armed escort.

From Djambek's place of observation he could see
a good portion of the river in both directions. The
boat turned toward the land, and soon drew up to the
shore. A part of the escort hurried back and forth,
loading packages and boxes on their shoulders, while
others hastened to put planks together to serve as a
landing stage. Then a veiled figure was assisted ashore,
followed by another whom Djambek recognized as Russudan, and the little procession moved toward the house
which had been prepared for Thamar. Totia was con-
versing eagerly with Cherif-Pasha. Then they shook
hands, and Totia sprang ashore and followed the others.
The boat was shoved off, and continued the journey up
stream.

Totia was then left behind with a guard! This
was not a surprise, for it was to be expected that the
pasha's confidant would keep a close watch over his
charge.

Djambek waited until it was dark, and then went home to pass a restless night. He arose before daybreak and betook himself to the grove, though it must be many hours before Thamar would be likely to go out. His impatience would allow him no rest.

Hour after hour passed with no sign of her coming. He regretted now that he had not sent her a message. Perhaps she would not come to the grove at all. He thought of all sorts of plans, and in his feverish anxiety debated whether he should not attempt to enter the house under some disguise. But he could not hit on any scheme that promised success, and so waited with a weary, anxious heart, as the forenoon passed. When the heated hours of the day came he left his place of concealment, knowing that there was now no chance of her coming out until the cool of the evening. After sunset he came again, and waited until it was fully dark, but no one came.

Thus passed the first day. His impatience increased until it was hardly bearable. It was so hard to know that his beloved one was near him, and yet to be obliged to wait concealed like a criminal until some chance should bring about a meeting!

As he returned to the house the old man was sitting at the door engaged in packing fruit into baskets. An idea came to Djambek.

" Do you sell your fruit at the houses about here ? " he asked, as if greatly interested in his worthy landlord's business.

" Oh, no. The people here have enough fruit of their own."

" But I have heard that some strangers arrived today. They might like to get such fine fruit as that."

10

"Strangers? That would be possible, then; though I don't believe they would pay much, for rich people don't often come to Murgal."

"You are wrong. I have heard that these people are rich and distinguished."

"Ah? Then I'll try my luck to-morrow."

"I would," said Djambek encouragingly. "I know from experience that strangers pay well, especially if it is for something really excellent."

"I will take a basket there to-morrow," said the old man.

"They are living in the house of Platon, the rich merchant," suggested Djambek.

"*Tchekuraderim.* I thank you, effendi."

Djambek considered how he might use this to advantage. After long thought, he said:

"They say there is a handsome young girl in the party."

The old man nodded indifferently. His only interest was whether they would buy his fruit. It mattered nothing to him whether the buyer was old or young, good-looking or ugly.

This indifference somewhat embarassed Djambek. Should he intrust a message to the old man or not?

"You know—young people are very fond of nice fruit" he said at last, in an attack of indecision and helplessness.

"Yes, yes," said the other, nodding his head.

"And it is easier to sell to young people than to old. One only has to know how to talk and get their good favor. You see I understand the business."

"You understand, I see. If you went you could

easily get their good favor, but how can an old man like
me talk to a young thing ? "

An adventurous idea passed through Djambek's
mind. Suppose he should disguise himself and go
in the old man's stead ? But no, the danger of detec-
tion was too great.

" Well, you might say to her," he continued, after a
moment's pause, " that the air is very fine here ; that
there are some beautiful views to be had, and fine, cool
places under the trees. I found a beautiful place quite
near the house. In the grove there it is delightfully
cool, and one gets a beautiful view of the river, too."

" Yes, that is so."

" You may be sure she will be thankful for the information."

" I will follow your advice." He had now finished
his work and arose. " A peaceful night to you, effendi," he said courteously.

" *Gedjeler khayr olsun,*" said Djambek, returning
the salutation.

The next forenoon Thamar heard a voice in the
court calling out : " Fruit, melons, figs, peaches, buy !
buy ! " She looked out of the window and saw an old
man with a basket of fine fruit on his head. She
hurried down. At the entrance she met Russudan,
and together they went out to the fruit seller.

The old man took down the basket from his head
and spread out his fruit temptingly. As he answered
Russudan's inquiry as to the price of a melon, she
clapped her hands together :

" What ! are you out of your senses ? " she exclaimed.
" One can buy a melon for a quarter of that price in
Batoum."

"Not so fine and fresh as this mistress," he said,
and then remembering Djambek's advice, he added,
turning smilingly to the young girl: "Fair lady, see
these peaches. Have you such as these in the city?
Try one, and you will not be able to let them go. It
will do you good. You are a little pale, fair mistress,
but be patient a few days ; the air of Murgal will bring
the roses back to your cheeks. Only you must go out—
there in the grove it is beautiful ; one can see down the
river and over to the mountains, and the fresh air on
the water—"

"You are an old gossip," interrupted Russudan
harshly. "You are mistaken if you think we will pay
dearer for your fruit for that."

"You will buy my basket?" he said to Thamar.
"If you knew how pleasant it is there in the shade
and how good fruit tastes there. A fine young man
who is stopping with me goes there almost every day
and can't say enough about the beauty of the place
and the fineness of my fruit. He is a handsome—"

"Be still, you fool," said Russudan angrily, while
Thamar's cheeks flushed red. "Do you know whom
you are speaking to?"

"He told me you were distinguished people from
Batoum."

"He? Who?"

"Why the young man—"

"Give me the peaches," said Thamar hastily, for
she thought she understood at whose suggestion the
old man had come. "And don't you want the melons,
Russudan? The figs, too, look good."

"No, they are too dear for me," replied Russudan coldly.

" Leave your basket here," said Thamar, " you can come and get it to-morrow. Here is your money." The old man took the money, touched his breast, lips, and forehead with his right hand in salutation and went his way.

Russudan's suspicions were awakened, and she resolved to be on her guard. Had not Thamar betrayed herself, the old man's words might have passed unnoticed, but the girl's evident embarrassment when the young man was spoken of gave her watchful guardian something to think about, though she was by no means certain what the danger was. She determined to watch Thamar more closely than ever, and when the latter that evening left the house, she followed her at a safe distance.

Thamar wandered through the grove in all directions, carefully followed by Russudan, who hid behind a tree whenever the girl was likely to see her. Suddenly the latter saw the girl stop and listen for an instant, and then swiftly pass behind a thicket. Carefully gliding from tree to tree, the elder woman followed until she came to where Thamar had so suddenly stopped. No sound disturbed the quiet of the grove. But when she had gone a little distance farther she heard the sound of soft whispering. The thicket here was so closely grown that a bird could hardly have passed through ; crouching close to the ground, she listened with all her ears.

The whispers were so low that she could only now and then catch a syllable, but there was no doubt but that Thamar was with some second person. Russudan kept her place, patiently waiting until the others should show themselves.

But after a while this trial of patience became too much for her. The occasional words she caught showed that the two had much to tell each other, and she found little satisfaction in taking so unsatisfactory a part in the affair. She crept forward carefully to make no noise, and at last found an opening through which one might with some difficulty pass. Like a cat creeping upon its prey, she slowly, carefully crept through the opening until she was stopped by a huge rock that stood in the way. She tried for some time in vain to pass around the obstruction when, suddenly overhearing words, she made the pleasing discovery that the pair were seated directly behind the rock. An opening at one side, she discovered, would enable her to hear quite distinctly all that was said. She laid her ear close to the opening and listened.

"All sorrow shall now be at an end, dearest; to-morrow at this time we shall be far beyond the reach of our enemies."

"Are you not afraid they will overtake us?"

"No. At sunrise all in the house will still be sleeping. By the time they discover your flight we shall be far on our way. I would have preferred going to-night, but the nights are dark now, and there are some dangerous places in the river. So we must have patience until morning. We can reach Batoum in six hours—four hours more and we are in Poti—then over the boundary into safety!"

"How happy I shall be there, my beloved!"

Russudan knew enough. There was nothing more to be gained by listening, and she had no time to lose if she would defeat their plans. Carefully leaving her hiding-place, she glided through the thicket and ran to the house, as fast as she could go.

Totia, who was walking up and down in the court, started with astonishment as she came panting in.

"Quick! come to my room. Important news!" she exclaimed breathlessly. Arrived in her room, she locked the door and told him all she had heard.

"So then the pretty pair intend running away, do they?" said Totia with an evil smile. He let his companion go on in excited talk, while he thoughtfully considered matters with himself. Then he motioned to Russudan to be silent. "It would be easy," he said, "to fall upon the fellow and capture him."

"Yes," assented Russudan. "I know where he lives."

"I do not think, however, that that would be the best way. It would be better to catch him in a net."

"The simplest way would be to make him harmless on the spot."

"If we surprise them now, they can deny everything, while proof will be beyond question if we catch them in the act. Will you allow me to manage it? Cherif-Pasha will be under obligations to us both."

"I do not see what good their denial would do them, since I heard with my own ears."

"Yes, yes! but your evidence alone is not sufficient to make me safe in seizing the would-be abductor."

Totia had a plan in his mind which he wished to keep to himself. He lied certainly in saying he would not have the right to seize Djambek. But in that case Russudan would get all the credit, while on the other hand, he wished to play the chief *rôle* himself.

"You may be sure I will do what is best," he said. "I know you will," replied Russudan. "Only I thought the simplest and safest way would be to place the audacious robber in chains, and keep the girl in the house under lock and key."

"That they might use the next opportunity? I could certainly remove him from here by force; but in no case could I imprison him."

"Very well, you know best."

"Yes, believe me. We must let them put their plan into execution, and then we shall have caught them in a trap. Cherif-Pasha can then use his power to make the young man forever harmless."

Russudan nodded in assent, and seemed only waiting to hear the particulars of his plan. But he showed no inclination to disclose them. "I will set out to-day for Batoum," he said, "and to-morrow the messenger will start to bring you the news of the capture. But not a syllable must she hear; we must act as if we had not the slightest suspicion of their plans."

"But tell me what—"

"Hush! She is coming."

Thamar appeared at the entrance to the house, and Totia hurried toward her.

"Have you any message for Cherif - Pasha?" he asked. "I have just learned that he needs my services in Artwin."

"And when are you going to leave?" she asked in pleased surprise, for his absence would be very favorable to their plans.

"In an hour," he replied.

"I have no message. A pleasant journey!" and

she hastened into the house, fearing lest he would notice her pleasure at his going away.

Totia threw a meaning look at Russudan. " Now, be cautious," he said in a low tone ; " do not let her see that we know their plans, and we are sure of them."

CHAPTER XII.

THE stars were still shining when Djambek awakened his landlord.

"It is time to go," he said; "get your boat ready, and manage to be to the black rocks before it is light. I will meet you there. I have important business, and must be in Batoum before noon. Look!" he added, drawing a purse from his pocket and jingling the coins; "this shall be yours as soon as we are away from shore."

The next morning the old man had been waiting some little time at the black rocks when Djambek appeared. Before the man could say a word, Djambek sprang into the boat, and assisted in a closely veiled female figure who had followed him.

"Stop! that is contrary to our agreement," said the boatman. "I will have nothing to do with this business. There is something wrong in it."

"Fool! why need you worry about it? I have hired your boat, and it belongs to me until you land me at my destination, and no one can deny my right to take some one with me if I choose."

"I will not be mixed up in the business," persisted the boatman. "Here! take back your money."

Djambek, with a sudden movement, grasped an oar, and with a vigorous push sent the boat flying into midstream like an arrow.

"Now, we will talk further," he said, pushing the man away from the tiller, and grasping it firmly. "Do not be a fool! how can my affairs concern you? And, at any rate, I am doing nothing unlawful."

"You must first prove that to me before the authorities."

"And lose valuable time on your account! You try my patience too far. It will soon be at an end."

"But I will have nothing to do with a matter that—"

"Whether you will or not concerns me very little. I am master of the boat now, and mean to remain so."

Thamar had anxiously listened to the dispute in silence, but now she summoned up her courage, and spoke to the man.

"Be reasonable! My—husband has told you that a loss of time would greatly injure us. You are a business man yourself, and know that there are times when one must keep an appointment at any cost. Your trouble will be well paid for. She raised her arm, on which sparkled a heavy gold band. "Besides what you have been promised, you shall have this in addition," she said.

"Why do so?" cried Djambek reproachfully, to arouse the man's cupidity. "As the idiot appears to regret our bargain, he may carry us back to shore and pay back the money I have given him. Somebody else will be glad enough to let us have a boat. Go back," he commanded the old man.

The artifice succeeded. The old man had suspected at once that this was a case of elopement, but the heavy reward silenced his scruples. "As far as I am concerned, I am willing to take you to your destination, though I am very sure there is something wrong in the matter."

The boat had swiftly floated with the current during the dispute. The man laid his hand on the tiller. "Allow me, master, there are some bad places soon."

There was no need of rowing. The current carried the boat along as if driven by steam. The valley became narrower, and the shores steep and rocky, until finally they rose like walls on either side, so high in places as to almost shut out the daylight. Beyond mountains rose to the sky, and here and there streams dashed thundering down the cliffs. The boat dashed rapidly on, tossed from one wave to another, and the boatman had to use his utmost skill to avoid the huge rocks that here and there showed above the surface.

Thamar was silent, anxiously holding her companion's hand and pressing it involuntarily in alarm when they approached a specially dangerous place. The river curved in places so suddenly that they held their breath as the boat seemed headed directly on the rocky banks; it seemed as if the next instant there would be a crash, and their frail boat be dashed into a thousand pieces, but in the same moment the bow would turn at a sharp angle and avoid the danger as by a hair. It required continually a sharp eye and a strong arm at the helm to prevent them from being wrecked. As the river became narrower the stream thundered, foamed, and dashed the more. Coming up stream the passage had not seemed to Thamar so dreadful; they had come in a large, heavy boat, on which the water dashed with little power, while the bark they were in now was small and of the frailest construction.

Djambek, too, had become silent. Although the boatman seemed to have grown up to his work, there were times when the slightest accident would have brought about a catastrophe; times when, if the rudder failed to work, or, indeed, broke, as might easily happen, all skill would be in vain, and it was doubtful in such a case, whether they could by swimming have escaped from the seething waves. Djambek constantly held himself in readiness to attempt Thamar's rescue should the necessity come for it.

Gradually the stream widened, and they finally came into still water. Djambek breathed easier.

"That was a bad piece," he said to the old man at the rudder. "You did bravely."

"The worst is still to come," he returned, lighting his pipe. "Not far from where the two streams meet is the worst place."

"Then we will land sooner," said Djambek. "Near the Adjaria there will be a sail boat, which we shall take for the rest of the journey."

"Then I need not go with you to Batoum?"

"No."

"So much the better. But you should have had your other boat come farther. The bad part commences above the Adjaria, and if I land you there, you will have a good half-day's walk before you come to your boat."

"Unfortunately, I did not know that. We shall then have to rely on your skill, and hope that you will safely bring us through."

"Have no fear. When one has made the trip once

a week for twenty years, as I have, he knows the dangerous places well enough to avoid them."

The water here being less confined flowed more smoothly and slowly, and their course was not so rapid. But soon they came again into narrow places, and in addition there suddenly burst upon them a violent storm. The lightning flashed almost continuously, lighting up the dark passes, and the thunder rolled like a cannonade, echoing among the rocky heights. The wind howled and whistled through the narrow passes, and drove the water into high waves, which tossed the boat dangerously. Djambek had wrapped Thamar in his cloak to shield her from the rain, which came in torrents.

"I shall remember this as long as I live," he said, as a pale-blue flash glided down the rocks, like a huge, fiery serpent, not far from them, followed instantly by a peal of thunder which made their boat tremble.

Thamar could not speak. She had covered her face with her hands, frightened at the blinding flash of the lightning, and pressed close to Djambek, who, with his arm about her, tried to reassure her. Even the old man could not repress exclamations of alarm, for the rain dashing in his face blinded him, and should they at such a moment run against a rock, destruction was sure. The clouds, too, had settled down so thickly that, except when the lightning lighted up the surroundings for an instant, it was difficult to see what was ahead. Creaking and tossing, the boat dashed on.

At last there came a pause in the storm, and the sky began to grow brighter. A heavy sound like that of far-off cannon could be heard in the direction they were going.

"That is the Adjaria," cried the boatman, pointing to a towering mass of rock directly in their course. With all his strength he threw himself on the rudder, and in a wide curve the boat shot around the reef. They now had an open view, and Djambek noticed a large sailing boat lying some five hundred yards away.

"Is that your boat?" asked the old man.

Djambek nodded. "I suppose it is," he answered.

There was another place to pass where the leaping, foaming waves showed that there were many rocks beneath the surface, and the boatman had to use his utmost skill to avoid the danger. The boat swung now to the right, then to the left, then turned sharply toward the shore. At this instant there was a crash, and the boatman, who had been holding the tiller with all his strength, was hurled into the stream.

At first Djambek only saw that their companion had disappeared. But he instantly recovered his self-possession, and leaped to the stern of the boat to give the unfortunate man assistance, but there was no sign of him to be seen. The boat in the mean time was driven rudderless through the tossing waters, but with extraordinary good fortune escaped striking the rocks. But presently it was carried directly toward the large boat they had seen in a current so strong that it tossed them as if mad and hurried them on at a rate that almost took away their breath. Djambek saw that a great danger threatened them. If the boat with this terrible momentum were dashed against the other, both would undoubtedly be shattered in pieces. He threw a swift glance to right and left, and saw that the roughest part was behind them. In an in-

stant he saw that their only hope of escape was to
throw himself with Thamar into the water and swim
to the other boat. There was no time for consideration, for they were approaching with terrible swiftness.
He grasped Thamar firmly around the waist.

"Come, darling!" he said gently, but firmly.

She obeyed without a word, and both slowly let
themselves over the side of the boat, and for a few
moments clung to it. Then Djambek let go his hold,
and with all his strength strove to keep himself and
Thamar above water.

The accident had been seen from the larger boat,
and a number of people stood ready with ropes to help
them at the right moment. Djambek, holding Thamar with one arm, was now carried by the swift current
close by the boat, and fortunately succeeded in grasping one of the ropes that was thrown to him. A few
minutes later both were drawn into the boat.

Djambek's first thought as soon as he had recovered
his breath was to look for Ahmed, but he saw only
strangers about him, who stared at him curiously.
Then one of them motioned to him to follow him to
the tent on the forward deck, where Thamar had been
carried. As he reached the entrance, the folds were
thrown back, and there stood Hassan Bey, while over
his shoulder the face of Totia grinned maliciously.

"An unexpected meeting, is it not?" said Hassan
Bey, an angry fire flashing from his eyes.

"Unexpected and unwished," said Djambek grimly.

"Young man, your plan has miscarried. Your
little game with us was not so easily won as you
thought it would be," said the other.

"What have you to do with my affairs?" said

Djambek fiercely. "What right have you to address me in such a tone? Am I your subject?"

"Just now you are simply my prisoner," returned the other, and before Djambek could defend himself, they had seized him from behind, bound his hands and feet, and carried him to the stern of the vessel, where they left him lying on the deck.

Djambek ground his teeth in rage, and cursed the fortune that had brought him into the hands of his enemies. There could be no self-delusion as to the seriousness of his position. What he had done was a double crime, since he had dared to abduct a relative of the ruler of the land. His fate hung on Cherif-Pasha's will alone. There was Artschil, but the best he could hope to do would be to prevent his being put to death. He could raise no protest against a long, perhaps life-long, term of imprisonment.

And now another thought tortured the prisoner; should he ascribe it simply to misfortune that he had fallen into the hands of his enemies, or had he been betrayed? And if betrayed, by whom? A single person came into his thoughts—Ahmed. The thought that a man who had received only kindness at his hands could so requite him, brought tears of pain and anger to his eyes, and he struggled with the chains that bound him, as if he thought he could break them like cords.

In the mean time the vessel glided rapidly down stream, and soon passed a large sloop lying in a little bay. Djambek's glance mechanically fell upon it. He saw a well-known face which for an instant looked at the passing vessel, and then anxiously gazed in the direction from which they had come. Ahmed! The

11

muezzin shaded his eyes with his hand, and looked earnestly up the river, paying no more attention to Hassan Bey's boat. He was then waiting for the fugitives. Had his anxiety led him to come further than the appointed place, or was it, perhaps, merely a comedy to avoid the appearance of treachery? Djambek could not decide.

Soon the minarets and domes of Batoum came in sight, and the vessel turned toward the shore, where a number of vehicles and a small body of armed men were waiting. The prisoner had hoped to see Thamar, but he was disappointed. A number of men seized him and carried him to a wagon. The armed men ranged themselves on each side, and then all proceeded to the city at a sharp trot. He looked back in vain. There was no sign of Thamar to be seen.

When the company in charge of the prisoner had got out of sight, Hassan Bey and Totia left the vessel. Thamar was placed in a carriage, and by another route taken to Cherif-Pasha's house.

CHAPTER XIII.

A FRIEND IN NEED.

THE city prison was in an old building which a speculator had planned on a large scale for an inn, but who, failing in business, had been glad to dispose of it half finished to the government. The better part of the building was occupied by the police. At the end of one of the wings were a few cells for prisoners. In one of these sat Djambek, awaiting the return of Cherif-Pasha, who, without doubt, would dispose of his case summarily.

The prisoner was in a most dejected state. The catastrophe which had ruined all his plans was ever in his thoughts, and he always came to the conclusion that Ahmed had played the part of a traitor. Had he been more composed in mind, the fact of Totia's presence at the time of his capture would have impressed him more, as he had seen him leave Murgal, and Thamar had repeatedly expressed her relief at his intended absence. But in the moment when Djambek so unexpectedly found himself face to face with his rival, he had been so startled at the unlooked for meeting, that he had hardly noticed the other's presence, and he was now so occupied with the thought of Ahmed's treachery that Totia was put quite in the background.

When now and then by a strong effort of the will
he succeeded in putting aside these gloomy thoughts,
it was only to look into the future with despair—a
future that was veiled in black clouds. In five or six
days the governor would return, and Djambek could
easily guess what his fate then would be.

The affair made a great sensation in the city, and
Artschil of course heard of it. He had endeavored to
obtain an interview with the prisoner, but his request
to see him was refused. The pasha must decide the
matter, and in the mean time Hassan Bey thought it
proper to keep the prisoner in solitary confinement.
To satisfy his personal vengeance, Hassan Bey had
ordered that no food or drink should be given him.
This would bring him to a proper state of mind, he
said grimly, and prepare him for what was shortly to
come.

Djambek suffered greatly under these hard conditions. His cell was a close, narrow room. He had
little desire for food, but thirst caused him endless tor-
ments. Had there been any guard to be seen, Djambek would have attempted to bribe him to give him a
few drops of water. To be sure, he had nothing of
value with him, as he had thrown away his weapons
when he sprang into the water, and what money and
jewelry he had had with him had been taken away by
Hassan Bey's people. Still he might perhaps have
made a bargain with his silk girdle or richly embroidered jacket. But no one came, and he had to abandon this hope. His cell had two small barred windows,
one looking on to a court, and the other on a small
grass-plot on the border of a swamp.

Two days and nights passed thus, and he felt a

deadly lethargy coming over him. His power of consecutive thought weakened, and the remembrance of what had happened was mingled with various fantastic pictures. The old man who had guided the boat and who had found his death beneath the rushing waters, now occupied his mind almost exclusively, and it seemed to him as if the drowned man sat by his side and demanded recompense for his death. As the day waned it seemed to him as if the old boatman became more importunate, saying that he had to go home that night, as he had agreed with Cherif-Pasha that he would be drowned again before his eyes.

Finally Djambek sprang up and ran up and down the cell like a tiger in his cage. He muttered disconnected words, clinched his fists, and at last began to tear at the bars of his window. It had become quite dark, but in spite of the darkness, he thought he saw the old man's face before the window. "Djambek! Djambek!" he heard his name called, and sprang back in terror to avoid the old boatman, who doubtless now, he thought, intended to insist upon his reward. At that moment something fell upon the floor of his cell. What was that? He had heard something chink like a piece of money. Had then the old boatman in his anger thrown down at his feet the purse he had given him? His nerves were so shaken that he did not dare to feel for it. He crept to his bench and threw himself down. At last he fell into an uneasy slumber, and when he awoke it was broad day. He had entirely forgotten the incident of the night before, and was astonished to see upon the floor a little packet done up in some gray material. In the instant as he bent over to pick it up his remembrance came back to him. But it was no purse thrown by a ghostly hand. Quickly he loosed the string and unrolled the package. It contained a number of iron instruments, and Djambek saw at once that some friend was helping him. He now had a means of escape. It was not a difficult task, for when he inspected the window bars closely, he found that each was fastened separately in the wood-work. The distance from the ground was inconsiderable.

The prospect of regaining his freedom gave him back his strength. He felt no longer hunger or thirst. The hallucinations of yesterday vanished, and he counted with impatience the hours until dusk. Then he commenced, and when darkness fully came, his work was nearly finished. He waited a while until those in the building should be asleep. He threw himself on his bench to consider how he might best escape the pursuit of his enemies. At first he thought of going directly to Murza-Khan and asking him to let him have one of his boats. But after further consideration, he abandoned the plan. Murza-Khan was not the man to be trusted in such a case. Not that he would openly act as his enemy, but he might refuse giving help that would bring him into conflict with the authorities.

Where, then, should he go? To go to his home, and thence to the mountain, would be too hazardous. The route up stream was slow, and as soon as his flight was discovered his enemies would doubtless suspect at once that he had fled thither, and he would soon find them on his track.

While he was thus considering one plan after

another, he suddenly thought he heard a light knock near the window. Was it his friend of yesterday?

Now he heard his name called softly. He sprang to the window to peer into the darkness, and asked in a whisper who was there.

"Are you ready?"

"Who speaks?" he asked, to make sure that it was not a spy.

"It is I. Ahmed!"

"Ahmed!" How could that be? Could the man have betrayed him when he now sought to rescue him? Why not? He might, perhaps, feel remorse, and seek to partly, at least, undo his shameful work. But was it the time now to hesitate? No! First liberty, then he would see. "I am ready" he said, and finished tearing away the bars. Then he swung himself through the window and sprang to the ground. Some one grasped his arm and whispered:

"Be silent! Not a word until we are in a safe place."

Making a long detour, they reached Ahmed's house.

"Water!" was Djambek's first word. "I am perishing with thirst?"

The muezzin brought him food and drink, and while the other eagerly devoured them, gave him an account of what he had done.

"I waited there for you all that day and the following night," he said. "Whenever a vessel came in sight I thought it was yours, but my hope was always in vain. Finally I determined to return here after directing the boatman to remain there with the boat until I should send him word. Here I first learned of the catastrophe which had befallen you, and only to-day I had my suspicions confirmed that you had been overheard and betrayed."

"From whom do you know that?"

"From her."

"From—Thamar?"

"No. From her friend, who came to me to-day and left a letter for you."

He handed Djambek a letter, which he opened in feverish haste.

"Russudan overheard your plans," it said. "I heard it from Totia, who hurried to Batoum to inform Hassan Bey. Unfortunately, he has succeeded, and we can do nothing. Thamar is suffering from the excitement she has undergone. She has a fever, but I hope no serious sickness will result. Indeed, we must consider this as fortunate, for Russudan declares that Thamar has become insane, as none of her appeals or threats have any effect upon her. I let her think so, as she will undoubtedly so advise Cherif-Pasha, who will then leave my poor friend in peace for a time, and much will be gained by that.

"You must now be sensible and obedient, friend Djambek. You can not help us here, and must remember that Thamar's life will be placed in jeopardy if she learns that you are exposed to the vengeance of your enemies. Away, then! Try to get beyond the boundary. You shall hear of Thamar through Ahmed, and I hope it will be good news.

DARIA."

Djambek folded the letter together and took the muezzin's hand.

"I am deep in your debt, my friend! How can I ever repay you?"

It shamed him to think he had ever doubted his friend, and he earnestly begged his forgiveness.

" Let us speak of more important matters," interposed Ahmed. " You must leave the city instantly. It will be easy to do so under cover of the darkness."

" But whither ? "

" Beyond the sea," said Ahmed. " Everything is ready. The same vessel that waited for you on the river is now in the harbor. I gave directions to the boatman as soon as I heard of what had happened. He is waiting for you not far from here in a spot where there are no other vessels, so that he can sail out of the harbor without being noticed. Now, in regard to money. I got your money as you told me to do, and you can use it now to advantage." Ahmed went to a locked case and took out a package of considerable size. Here is your money—or rather drafts which you can use to better advantage abroad. They amount to two thousand purses,* and there is besides fifteen thousand piasters in coin. The boatman has agreed on two purses for taking you to the nearest Russian port."

Djambek took the package and opened it to take out some of the drafts.

" Before I leave the country, perhaps forever," he said, "I must provide for the care of a few who are dear to me. It is probable that the authorities will deal with my possessions as they did with Elisba's, so I must make provision that those who have shown their loyalty to me shall not be breadless. In the first place, your sister. You can not refuse to take this for her. It is a simple duty that I fulfill. Your services

---

* A purse equals five hundred piasters = $22.50.

are not paid for by it. In case they do not disturb her where she now is, keep the money as a provision for evil times. But if, as I fear, they drive her from house and home, then she can come and be near you. That will be pleasant for both of you. The rest of what I leave with you, divide equally among my servants. Let them know, too, that as soon as is possible I shall join Elisba, and then we will advise together as to what it is best to do for the future. Should any of them wish to see me they will find me there or hear of me from Elisba."

"You are giving me too much for my sister," objected the muezzin; "she is not accustomed to such a way of life that she will need so large a sum. Let me, therefore, give you back a part of it."

"You do not wish to offend me, Ahmed? I know your sister is always satisfied with a little, but that need not prevent her living more comfortably if she have the means of doing so. So please say nothing more about it. And be assured again, my best of friends, that I have no intention that this should be in payment of your services. What you have done for me can not be paid for with money."

"Your will shall be done, Djambek. I thank you for your kind thoughtfulness for my sister. I thank you in her name and in mine. Have you any further wishes? I think I can be of service to you in a matter that is near your heart."

"You mean Thamar?"

"Yes, in your exile you will feel doubly lonely, for your heart will remain here."

Djambek bowed his head sorrowfully. "And how lonely! I fear there will be times when separation will drive me to hopelessness—to despair!"

"No! That must not be," interposed Ahmed earnestly. "What would man be without hope? You must never give up hoping for brighter days. It will sustain you and bring you yet to victory. Think on what I say to you, and may it give you strength in time of despondency! As for Thamar, I will see that you often receive news of her. Depend on it, that as soon as I know where you are I will find ways of sending you messages. But it is time now for you to depart. In a few hours it will be dawn."

Djambek arose and followed his friend. They walked in silence through the unoccupied part of the city which lies southerly toward the sea, and in a few minutes they could hear the murmur of the waves. As soon as they had climbed the slight elevation which separated them from the sea, Djambek saw the gleam of a green light.

"There is your boat," said Ahmed in a whisper. They descended to the shore, and going a few paces farther, Ahmed blew a whistle. When he had repeated the signal, they heard the splash of oars, and soon a row-boat appeared before them. Ahmed exchanged a few words with the boatman, and then said to Djambek: "This is the master of the ship himself. You are now secure."

Djambek's heart was so full of sorrow that he could speak no word of parting. His whole life seemed to pass before him like pictures seen in the clouds. He saw the paternal mansion, the people joined to him by ties of friendship, the loved one. The remembrance of little events that had long slumbered in his memory suddenly came vividly before him and increased the pain that filled his heart.

"Farewell!" said Ahmed, struggling to repress a sob. "Farewell, and may Allah have you in his keeping!"

Djambek could not speak a word, try as he would. He pressed his friend's hand and drew him to his breast, and then with an effort sprang into the boat.

The muezzin remained standing on the beach. He saw the green light begin to waver, then to rise and fall, then become smaller and smaller, until it suddenly disappeared.

A light breeze drove the cutter out to sea. Djambek stood leaning over the side and, with dim eyes, watched the receding lights of the city until they had vanished.

A world of thoughts crowded upon him as he waved his hand in farewell to his country. A multitude of fears and hopes, confidence and despair. The lot was cast, the arrow shot from the bow. There was no turning back. Even should a most unlooked for change take place in the government of the country, would he be able to return? What could happen that would permit him, the exile, the outlaw, to go back in safety? The death of his enemy? Then new enemies would instantly arise, for his crime was not such as is wiped out by the death of certain individuals. He had sinned against the whole system of laws and customs, and for that there was no forgiveness or forgetfulness.

And Thamar? Was she not now in the absolute power of an angry man, who would use his utmost endeavor to make her bend to his will? What were the ties of blood to him, when he sought to bind her from motives of his own self-interest to a man she hated?

Was it not to be feared that he would torment her to death, now that in her supposed state of insanity he could make no use of her to further his corrupt ends?

These gloomy thoughts were interrupted by a sudden call.

" What boat is that? "

The ship-master sprang forward and gave the steersman a sign. Then making a trumpet of his hands, he called back.

" A fishing sloop."

" Halt ! " was the answer.

The command was not obeyed, however. The vessel followed quickly the steersman's change of wheel, and turning flew toward the open sea.

" It was a revenue cutter," explained the sailor. " It would probably have been unpleasant for you to have met him."

He was silent about the contraband goods which he had on board, and which he intended landing at the next port.

CHAPTER XIV.

IN THE MOUNTAINS.

TOWARD evening the fugitive arrived in Nicholaja, after having fallen in with Murza-Khan on the way. The boat had suddenly changed its course, as the captain had declared that in that region there was no danger of meeting revenue officers. Soon after a three-colored light was seen, such as Djambek had noticed when sitting on Murza-Khan's veranda. The captain came to tell his passenger that he intended stopping here for a short time. The morning broke as they approached the shore, but Djambek could not make out where they were, as there was a thick fog overhanging the land. Suddenly they heard the splash of oars, a boat came alongside, and a number of men climbed on board. The first that approached the fugitive was Murza-Khan.

"You here!" he exclaimed in surprise. "I thought you were under double chains and behind thick walls."

"I am obliged to you for your friendly anxiety," returned Djambek, half pleased and half displeased at the meeting.

"Well, I am glad you played them a trick. Has Cherif-Pasha come back?"

"Not yet."

"That's a pity. I would like to see him rave."

"You may soon have that pleasure. He is to return in a day or two."

"So? Then I must look him up, and tell him that I met his dear nephew—you have become one of his relatives, have you not?—and that he was looking especially well. He will fairly foam with rage!"

"And curse you for not having taking me prisoner."

"Am I his bailiff? And do I need to have known anything about the business? Things which do not concern one one need not notice. For that reason, I beg to ask you to look the other way until we finish our business here. It can have no sort of interest for you to see what we are doing."

"Certainly not. I would prefer not to look deeper into your affairs, as they are purely personal. If you would be as active in certain other lines, it would be a fine thing!"

"'Everything for one's self, nothing for others.' That is the motto surest to bring success. There is no such appreciating and grateful creature to work for as the 'I'! But it strikes me that you, too, have had your own interests pretty well in mind—or was this abduction of a fair lady perhaps conducive to the general good? Now don't be offended, Djambek, I meant nothing ill-natured, and in my heart I am quite with you, though I myself should hardly have plunged into such a sea of difficulties on account of a pair of black eyes. But that is a matter of taste. And perhaps Cherif-Pasha's heart will melt and he will clasp you to his heart in a flood of repentant tears!"

" I hardly consider that probable, unless you should succeed in convincing him of the error of his ways," returned Djambek, good-naturedly.

" He is likely to listen to me! He paid so much attention to me before!" said Murza-Khan sarcastically. " No, my friend, you must seek a better mediator than me. I have no faculty in that line. My specialty lies in working him up to the boiling-point. I shall tell him I met you, that you were looking finely, that you seemed in excellent spirits, and that you told me you intended taking a little pleasure trip before your marriage! Possibly it would be doing you a service, for it is very likely that it would result in his having a stroke of apoplexy—he would be in such a rage! But they are waiting for me, and I must bid you farewell."

Murza-Khan joined his men, and having taken their wares on board, the sloop proceeded to Nicholaja.

Djambek intended first of all to find Elisba. He wanted much to see his friend and learn what plans he had for the future. He would not have disliked stopping there permanently, as he would be in more or less frequent communication with his home. Villagers from Skalta often came there, and could keep him informed of what was going on at Batoum. Should he not find it advisable to stay there, he could go on to Tiflis, where he had friends of his school days, and where he felt sure he would receive a hearty welcome.

He hired horses and servants, and took the road which led by way of Ozurgethi and Aschalzich to the region where Elisba made his headquarters. He arrived in Aschalzich on the fourth day, and determined to take a short rest there, as the rest of the journey over the Perangage Mountains was a very difficult one.

To his agreeable surprise he met a young man whom he had known well in Tiflis, and who now held an important official position there. This meeting gave much pleasure to both, and as Djambek had no hesitation in telling his friend that he had left his native country on account of difficulties with the authorities, the young Russian official earnestly advised him to accept a position under the government.

" They will be glad to give you a place," he said, " especially as preparations are going on which are likely to lead to important changes. The relations between us and our neighbors are strained—less here than over there in Europe—and you will see that, sooner or later, there will be a war. In such case, you would be a valuable acquisition for us, and you may depend on getting a good position. Think it over. I believe I am advising you for your good."

" Yes. I will consider your advice," returned Djambek, "though at present I hardly think I could accept it."

They spent the day together, and the next morning Djambek took the road again, and toward evening arrived at his destination.

· Elisba's joy was great as he saw his friend. Embracing him warmly he drew him into his house, and set before him all manner of refreshments. He had no suspicion of what had happened, and Djambek was the first to inform him.

" So, then, my fellow in misfortune," said Elisba bitterly, " they have driven you too away from home and country. Curses upon this villainous crew with hearts of stone, that have eyes and ears only for their own profit! "

12

Then Elisba told him how complaints were every day becoming louder, how the present caimacam oppressed and maltreated the people, and how many declared themselves ready to oppose the authorities with weapons in their hands.

Thereupon Djambek thought of the conversation he had had with his friend at Aschalzich, and he told Elisba of it.

"Do you know," said the latter, "I have often thought that it would be a good fortune for the country if war should break out. I would not hesitate a minute, then, to offer my services to the Russians."

Djambek looked his friend searchingly in the face.

"Do you mean it?" he asked. "Do you forget that you would be called a traitor to your country?"

"Traitor to my country!" exclaimed the other. "My country is the homestead where I grew up—my people are those who, like me, have been robbed and oppressed—but those who hold power there have no claim upon me. I cut myself loose from them when they obliged me to meet force with force. I feel myself under no obligations toward them, but I do feel it my duty to help free my countrymen from the yoke that lies so heavily upon them. What allegiance do I owe to these shameless tyrants, creatures who would suck the very blood from our veins? None! They are strangers to us; a race to which we do not belong; a band of robbers who have seized our country to plunder it. Here, where we stand, is our mother-soil. We are of Georgian blood, and have nothing in common with the oppressors over there. And therefore I would feel myself rather a patriot than a traitor if I placed myself by the side of our brothers in a struggle for the freeing of my land from a hated yoke."

"But remember," said Djambek, "that these here of our own race stand themselves under a foreign yoke, and that you would be helping the rulers of the land, rather than our brothers."

"I have thought of that, too, and have come to the conclusion that my land would be better off under Russian rule—much better. Here there is not that absolute power of the individual over the life and property of those under his jurisdiction, without responsibility to any one. No one, not even the ruler of Tiflis, dares do an injustice on his own responsibility. If he do it, he knows he will be called to a strict account. No, Djambek, the old kingdom can not rise again, because the great queen can not be born the second time; but the old customs, privileges, laws, can be revived, and we must be grateful to those who have the will to do it. Should the favorable opportunity come and Russia take up our cause, I swear that I would set my life in hazard without a moment's hesitation to aid in carrying out the project. But, I am sorry to say, that time appears a long way off, and so I have resolved to use my best powers now on behalf of my oppressed people. Many have left their homes— some forced, others willingly—and these will join me, and for every hair of ours that is unjustly touched, there shall follow swift and bloody revenge."

"Do you speak in earnest?" asked Djambek. "Have you fully decided?"

"Absolutely," replied Elisba firmly.

"And are you sure that you will thus do your land a service? Have you not heard that there are

many who look longingly at the price set upon your
head?"

"Everywhere there are base creatures. Tell me of
a land in which there grow no weeds. But that shall
not hinder me in my purpose. I know how the majority feel and how they sigh for relief. Shall I hold
back because of a miserable few, who would soil their
hands with the price of treachery and seek the favor
of their enemies through treason?"

"You know, then, what Cherif-Pasha has promised
the people if they will betray you?"

"I know."

"Elisba, I fear you will run blindly into destruction."

"Blindly? No! I see plainly what lies before
me. I know the danger that confronts me, and if I
defy it it will be because I can not do otherwise.
What is my life to me? For whose sake should I try
to preserve it? They have murdered my wife and
driven me from my home. What have I to look forward to?"

"Do not speak so," said Djambek. "Would you
listen to such words from me who shares your fate?"

"Hope remains with you, my friend," returned
Elisba quietly. "It has left me forever. Fortune
may yet permit you to join Thamar, though you are
now separated. She lives, she thinks lovingly of you
—her heart will always be yours. But the dead—the
dead we can not bring back. No, Djambek," he
continued after a pause, "I have fully determined
to devote myself to the freeing of my country. I
can, perhaps, do little, but I can at least do something toward that end. We will meet violence

with violence, and perhaps we may convince those in power that the practice of injustice is not the most profitable way of ruling a people. Here in the mountains we are masters. A little band in these passes can defy an army. The advantage is therefore on our side. But enough of this for the present. Let us talk of your affairs. What do you propose to do? You might, I suppose, through the influence of others, bring about a reconciliation with the authorities. Or, if you went to Stamboul yourself—"

"That would be a useless journey," interrupted Djambek. "I know for a certainty that there is no hope of a reconciliation on the part of Cherif-Pasha. He has special reasons for wishing to form an alliance with Hassan Bey. Do you know what my present plan is? It is to stay here with you and wait to see what the immediate future will bring."

"But do you know what the result will be if they learn that you have joined company with an outlaw?" asked Elisba.

"Am not I one myself?" returned Djambek.

"Not yet," replied Elisba.

"But I soon shall be," continued Djambek. "I do not deceive myself in the slightest as to the steps Cherif-Pasha will take. In his eyes I am a worse criminal than you, since I have insulted him, the representative of the Padishah. Hassan Bey and my other enemies will do their part, too, to keep his anger alive. I expect that the first thing he will do will be to confiscate my estates, and I should not be at all surprised if he set a price on my head, too. I shall wait here for all this, and I expect soon to receive news by a messenger. I shall then know what to

do. But tell me frankly : Shall I be a burden to you
here ? "

" Why, you know nothing would please me more
than to have you near me," replied Elisba warmly.
" You will soon be able to tell for yourself whether I
am right in my conclusions. You shall see for yourself how the people come with their complaints, how
they swear vengeance against their oppressors, and
your blood will boil in your veins. Only to-day a
poor, persecuted family arrived—a man, wife, and four
children, the fifth had died from the hardships of the
journey. Such blood cries to heaven, my friend, and
we will not wait until the Prophet appears with a flam-
ing sword, as some of the poor people expect he will.
We will teach these bandits that right and might are
two different things."

Djambek soon had an opportunity of seeing that
Elisba's indignation had good grounds. Day after
day came dissatisfied or unfortunate people, and their
complaints increased more and more. The caimacam
sought to enforce a policy of crushing severity upon
the people, and thought he had discovered therein the
true system of government. The people whom he drove
from their homes would serve as a terrifying example to
others ; and he purposed thus to free his district of the
rebellious element. In this he received support from
a few who preferred their own interests to those of the
community at large, and who hoped by servility to gain
the good will of the rulers. Many of these were not
disappointed. Their policy bore the expected fruit.
But not all; for Redjeb Bey thought it politic to have
most of the confiscated lands occupied by those who
had more identified themselves with the governing

race, and to this end he brought in people from places on the coast, where the Mohammedans were in the majority.

Elisba was kept fully informed of all this.

"Do you see?" he said to Djambek, "they are trying to force the old race out of the land and replace it with their own. It is absurd. By the way, I have sent the caimacam a letter."

"You—to the caimacam!" exclaimed Djambek. "What did you say to him?"

"I gave him notice that he would meet with the same fate as did his predecessor if these complaints continued."

"A declaration of war, then!" cried Djambek, not without a touch of irony in his tone.

"Certainly. Does that appear to you to be ridiculous?"

"No; terribly earnest, on the contrary, and—don't be offended—very audacious."

Elisba shrugged his shoulders.

"It is certainly in earnest. Whether it be audacious, time will show," he answered quietly. "You are like many others," he continued, after a pause, "who earnestly desire a better order of things, but would prefer that the change come direct from Heaven; who have a dislike for the old order of things, but can not shake off their superstitious reverence for whatever is old and established."

"You do not judge me correctly," returned Djambek. "I certainly do not advocate sitting with our hands in our laps, but I would first seek to bring about a reform through the weapons of reason, not with gun and sword. If I had a dispute with you about a matter, I would lay my reasons before you and try to bring you to my side. Would it help my case any, if, instead of that, I should draw my dagger, and one of us should be killed?"

"You forget," said Elisba, "that such people as these can not be reached by argument. Would you go to the caimacam and say to him: 'Sir, you have not taken the correct view of the case; you can attain nothing by cruelty and severity'? Don't you suppose the good man would at once clap you behind lock and key?"

"You and me—yes. But if a man who enjoyed a special distinction in the land took hold of the matter, a man who had the right to be heard by those in power—"

"Can you name such a man?" asked the other.

Djambek hesitated. Then he said:

"At the moment I can not."

"Well, then, must we lay our hands in our laps and wait for the Prophet?" asked Elisba scornfully.

There was no reply to be made, and Djambek remained silent.

The next morning, as he came out of the house, he was surprised to see his servant there.

"Is it really you, Mamukia?"

"Yes, master."

"Did you receive a message from Ahmed?"

The man nodded. "Lazar came," he said, "just as I was getting ready to leave."

"You intended, then, to flee?"

"Yes, for I had heard that an order had come from Batoum to surround your house and throw all the occupants into prison."

"It is not possible!" exclaimed Djambek. "And where is Ahmed's sister?"

"I warned her and tried to persuade her to escape with me to the mountains. But she refused—said she had nothing to fear, as she had done no harm. I had done no harm either; but from what has been going on of late, it appears that there is very little protection in being innocent, and when they began telling all sorts of things about you, I thought I had better be going while I could. Spiridon and Josse have come with me. We have brought your horse and the best of the weapons. I wanted to bring away everything of value, but Ahmed's sister objected and said she was responsible, and then there was very little time."

"You have done quite right," said Djambek. "I am only much troubled about the poor woman. Not that they can have anything against her, but she will try to prevent their entering the house, and that will get her into trouble."

A few days later others arrived, and among them several of Djambek's tenants. They brought bad news. The house had been taken possession of by Redjeb Bey, and all who were in it had been thrown into prison. The tenants had been notified that they must give up their land, as it had been promised to other people.

Djambek's anger was now fully aroused.

"The villains!" he shouted, shaking his fist. "The cowardly villains! Because I have escaped them they wreak their vengeance on the innocent." And he hurried to tell Elisba.

"You wonder at that?" said Elisba quietly. "Have I not told you of enough other similar cases.

What do you think now? Is this the proper time to
visit the caimacam and argue with him that he has
acted unjustly? Perhaps you might convince him of
his error! Well, what do you think?" he urged, as
the other stared before him in silence.

"I think," said Djambek slowly, "I think that it
is the proper time for me to go over to your side.
With such rascals one must act otherwise than by
peaceful representations. Will you accept me as a
member of your band? I devote myself to your cause,
and will support you with all my strength."

Elisba grasped his hand.

"Welcome, my friend, and our first work shall be
to free your people from prison."

CHAPTER XV.

A PLOT AND ITS FAILURE.

As Murza-Khan had prophesied, Cherif-Pasha fairly foamed with rage when he heard what had occurred. He immediatly set out for Batoum. There he first learned the full particulars. At first his people did not dare tell him of Djambek's escape. This was reserved for Murza-Khan, who came to call on the governor as if casually.

"A fine affair this, is it not?" said the pasha, almost immediately on his entering.

"What do you refer to?" asked Murza-Khan, pretending ignorance.

"You must have heard. This miserable wretch, Djambek—"

"Djambek! I am glad you remind me of him! for I had almost forgotten to give you his message. I met him a few days ago as he was taking a little pleasure trip. He looked finely and in excellent spirits. I was to give you his special salutations and—"

Cherif-Pasha sprang into the air like a jumping-jack.

"He! he — on a pleasure trip! Have you lost your senses? The villain is here under lock and key waiting the just punishment of his crimes."

"Then he must have been captured yesterday or the day before, for I assure you I saw him myself three days ago. He charged me to convey to you his special salaams, and to say that he would come soon to take away your niece as his bride."

Cherif-Pasha could only shout out inarticulate sounds while Murza-Khan chuckled to himself in the highest gratification. The governor ran up and down the room, stamped upon the floor, tore at his beard, and finally rushed out of the door to call Hassan Bey. The latter soon appeared.

"Tell me," said the pasha, "is Murza-Khan out of his senses, or does he speak the truth? Where is that wretch you captured?"

"I regret to say he has escaped," replied Hassan Bey with downcast eyes.

"Escaped! Oh! oh!" and again he went into a frenzy of wrath. "Who let him escape? Why was he not watched? What sort of a police have we got that can not even keep a prisoner after he is caught! Give orders at once that Yaver-Aga be put in chains. I will teach these people to neglect their duty!"

"Has Djambek been doing something he ought not to?" asked Murza-Khan blandly.

The pasha stared at him as if he was some surprising natural curiosity. "I beg you, my friend," he said, "go with Hassan Bey. He will tell you. I find myself incapable of saying another word about it or even thinking of it."

As soon as the governor had become a little more calm, he gave orders to take possession of Djambek's house and to arrest all the occupants. He also offered a reward for Djambek's capture.

He reserved a visit to Thamar for the last. When Daria told him with many tears that Thamar, after a severe fever, had fallen into a state of delirium, he shook his fist and swore he would bring back her senses with a whip. But when he saw her he started back in surprise. Her senses seemed really bewildered. Her lips murmured unintelligible sentences. Then she gave a sudden cry, and this so frightened the pasha that he hastily left the room. There was no doubt but that she had lost her senses. With the Orientals the insane are looked upon as peculiarly dangerous creatures, whom it is best to avoid, if one would himself escape their malady.

So all his plans for the future were crossed! Hassan Bey would, of course, never agree to such a marriage, even if she in time recovered. And who was responsible for all this misfortune? Who but that thief, that crafty villain, Djambek? And instead of being able to strangle him here with his own hands, Cherif-Pasha must hear that he is in safety, and that he even dares to send him a taunting message. "But he shall pay for it!" swore the pasha, "by the beard of the Prophet! If it takes the whole military strength of the land, even if it be necessary to go into foreign territory for him, this shame shall be washed out with the blood of the presumptuous villain!"

But first he poured forth his anger on Djambek's property and his people. Even Artschil did not escape. He was removed from office. This was well as far as it went; if now the cause of all was once more in his power, the pasha felt that he would in a measure be satisfied.

But instead of this wish being fulfilled, Cherif-

Pasha soon received news of a very different import.
An armed band had attacked the prison and freed
the prisoners. They had even seized the caimacam,
dragged him with them for some distance, and threatened him with death in case he again gave grounds for
dissatisfaction.

Redjeb Bey came himself to inform the pasha of
the circumstances. He complained that they had
beaten and mishandled him, and that the leader of the
band, Elisba, had placed a gun at his head and would
have killed him, had not Djambek sprung forward to
prevent the murder.

" Well, let him go this time, but woe to him if he
again does injustice—his death-warrant will then be
sealed ! " had been Elisba's words.

Cherif-Pasha was dumb with wrath and fear. He
brandished his hands in the air, threw fierce looks at
the caimacam, but could not utter a word.

"I know of but one way " said Redjeb Bey, " to
make an end of this matter. We must get the rebels
into an ambush and then mow them down. To be
prepared for all their attacks would require an army
in each section to be constantly on the watch. I have
no fear for myself. I know that my life belongs to the
Padishah and his representative, but what good end
will it serve if I fall a sacrifice to these murderers ?
My successor would fare as ill, and one or two suc-
cesses of that kind would set the whole land in a blaze
of rebellion."

"Very true," interposed Hassan Bey, who had entered while the other was speaking. "The only thing
to be done is to smother the insurrection at its birth.
I am ready to assist Redjeb Bey with a strong body of

troops. He may take command, as he is acquainted with the localities better than I am, and it will be strange if we do not succeed in crushing this brood of rebels."

"Do what you think best," said Cherif-Pasha finally. "Matters are unquestionably in a bad position, and worse, in that, as I may tell you in confidence, our Russian neighbor begins to bestir himself uncomfortably. It appears that he has the intention of intermeddling in our affairs in the west, and I see no way of a friendly solution of the difficulties. Should hostilities once break out, the position would be a critical one if we had troubles of our own to look after, too. I therefore give you full authority to prepare an expedition against the outlaws. And I think it will be well to use the utmost severity in crushing the rebellion before it spreads further. You will do well, then, to get in motion as soon as possible with all the troops you have at your disposal."

"I am ready," replied Hassan Bey; "I only wish first to arrange a plan of operations with Redjeb Bey. The rebels ought to receive no warning of our movements. They doubtless have friends enough, however, to keep them well informed. It would be well, therefore, to draw them on as far as possible into this district, so that they may be cut off as much as possible from their supporters."

"Good! I quite agree with you," assented the Pasha. "I rely on you and Redjeb Bey to make a quick end of the matter. You need not spare Elisba, but his associate, the boy who has dared to defy and insult me, I would like to have delivered alive into my own hands, that I may show him what it means to defy the representative of the Padishah.

Hassan Bey and the caimacam at once set about making their preparations. The simplest plan seemed to be to drive one of the land-owners to make resistance. He could then be imprisoned, and Elisba would probably feel it his duty to attempt his release. Hassan Bey would then see to it that the attempt did not succeed. It only remained to commence the affair, and to bring the troops to the neighborhood where the attack of the enemy was to be expected.

The carrying out of the plan did not seem a difficult one to the caimacam. Near the village of Kedi lived a distant relative of Elisba's who had already attracted Redjeb Bey's attention by the sympathy he had expressed for the rebels. It was only necessary to summon him and question him harshly to make him compromise himself. Then, when he had been imprisoned, the caimacam would send one of his dependents to Elisba to play the part of a complainant, and in the name of the prisoner implore him to release him by force.

"That is the most comfortable way of bringing on a war," said Redjeb Bey, laughing. "In great affairs it is not much different, so it ought to succeed in our lesser ones."

As Hassan Bey agreed with him, there was no need to lose any time in putting the plan into operation. Redjeb Bey went to Kedi on the pretense of looking up taxes that were in default. In looking over the books which the village elder showed, he found that the person he had in mind as a victim was in a dispute with the authorities relative to the payment of his taxes. He claimed to have paid them to the late caimacam, Ali Bey, but failed to take a receipt. Relying on his word, the village elder had let the matter rest. But now the caimacam showed himself greatly displeased, rated the village official severely for his neglect of duty, and threatened him with heavy punishment if the matter was not at once put in order. Greatly frightened, the village official sent at once for the man that he might make his personal explanations.

The caimacam's stratagem worked well. When the land owner appeared, there arose a dispute between them, which grew warmer and warmer, until Redjeb Bey cut the matter short by having the man thrown into prison.

He then immediately sent a swift messenger to Hassan Bey, at the same time sending one of his creatures to Elisba to make a complaint in the name of the prisoner. Otia, as this spy was called, reached his destination in a few days, and was immediately led to Elisba. He was the same man who after the interview between the villagers and the pasha had taken part against Elisba. As Redjeb Bey had assured him that Cherif-Pasha's promises should be carried out in case he succeeded in enticing the enemy within reach of the troops, he entered on his mission very zealously, and gave a horrifying account of the injustice done the tax payer. He spoke of cruel treatment, the despair of the wife and children now without means of support or a roof to cover their heads, and worked upon Elisba's feelings so effectively that he felt sure the latter would make an attempt to rescue the man. He wished to accompany the band, thinking he could easily leave them at a favorable moment and go ahead to warn the caimacam of the enemy's approach.

13

Djambek noticed the overzealousness with which Otia championed the cause of another. He had, too, a dim, indefinite remembrance of something that had prejudiced him against the man. But he could not remember what it was, and so let it go, thinking that it was only an instinctive dislike.

Elisba called his followers together for a council. He related the man's story, and spoke earnestly of the necessity of putting an end to such tyranny by energetic measures, and expressed the hope that they would yet accomplish this if they acted boldly and punished every such act of injustice upon the spot.

All agreed with him, and announced their willingness to take part in an attempt at rescuing the prisoner. Many were in favor of starting at once, but Elisba thought it better to wait a day or two, as he expected a new accession to his ranks shortly.

Otia's patience was severely tried, but he avoided saying too much, lest he should arouse suspicion.

Finally it was announced that they would start that evening. The people came together from all sides, and toward noon there was encamped in the field before Elisba's house a little army of several hundreds.

The leader was consulting with a few of the men when suddenly Yordane came hurrying up with a stranger who had just arrived, and who said he had important news for Djambek.

Elisba took the letter and went into the house to find his friend.

"An important letter for you," he said, handing it to his associate.

Djambek opened it and read the few lines from Ahmed, inclosing another from Daria:

"Thamar's friend has just been here, and charged me to send you the inclosed without a moment's delay. There is danger threatened."

Then he read aloud Daria's note:

"Be on your guard. They are trying to draw you into a trap. I know from a reliable source that Hassan Bey leaves here to-night with a large force to join the caimacam in Kedi. They seem to expect you there to make an attack on the prison. Your lives are in hazard, so do not permit yourself under any pretense to go near that place.   DARIA."

Elisba stood a long time in silence, his eyes upon the ground.

"Then there is a traitor among us," he said finally.

"Without doubt," said Djambek.

"Are we to believe that Otia—"

"Yes, he has been sent to lead us into a net," Djambek interposed, the whole matter becoming clear to him. "I remember now a circumstance that speaks strongly against the man." And he told his friend of the part Otia had taken at the conference. .

"And who is the person who has sent you the warning?" asked Elisba.

"You know her. She was in our company when we took part in your wedding—Thamar's friend."

"Ah! I remember her. We are deeply indebted to her, Djambek."

"Yes, our lives were in her hands."

"Do you think this Otia invented the whole story, or is a part of it true?"

"That is hard to tell. What do you think of doing now?"

"First of all, we will try this man. If it be shown that he is guilty of this shameful treachery, to deliver his own countrymen to the enemy, a severe example must be made. Yordane," he said to his former tenant, who just then entered, "tell Otia that we wish to speak to him."

In a few minutes Yordane returned accompanied by Otia.

"Stay," said Elisba to the former as he was about to go out again. "You shall be a witness of our interview." Then, looking Otia sharply in the face, he said to him:

"You are of the opinion that the prisoner can be easily rescued?"

"I think so," he answered. "The prison is an old building, and the caimacam has only a handful of soldiers with him."

"Only a handful! Perhaps some twenty or thirty, eh?"

"Certainly not more."

"Then it would suffice if I sent Yordane with a part of our men. Why should we all make the long, hard journey?"

"You forget, sir, that the people of the place may assist the caimacam."

"Pah! they would be more likely to assist us than him. No, you have forgotten a part of your message."

"What!"

"Yes, and the most important part, too. Why did you not tell us that the caimacam expects a strong armed force from Batoum to assist him."

Otia became pale.

"From Batoum?" he stammered. "I knew nothing about that."

"Your memory appears to be very short, or did you, perhaps, have some particular reason for withholding that important information?"

"I don't know what you mean, sir." Otia's voice trembled and his eyes looked toward the door as if calculating the chances for escape.

"Your face and your voice betray you, miserable wretch," cried Elisba, at the same time springing to the door and drawing his pistol. "You knew very well that Hassan Bey had planned with the others to draw us into a net, and you offered your services for the price of blood to deliver us into their hands."

The man could do nothing else but fall upon his knees and beg for mercy.

"They forced me to do it—they threatened my life if I did not do as they wished."

"You lie! It was for a reward that you agreed to betray your countrymen. The glitter of gold confused your eyes and stifled the voice of your heart. For a vile reward you lent yourself to the betrayal of hundreds of your own people to the headsman. That is the truth, man. Do you think your tale has even the appearance of truth? Who could be forced to such a deed? Had you been an honorable man and they threatened you as you say, you would have said: 'They have threatened my life and my property if I do not do their bidding. I will abandon my goods and join my own people in fighting for their rights.' Yordane! bind his hands, and you, don't you stir, or I will put a bullet through your head!"

Yordane having quickly taken off his girdle and
with it tied the man's hands behind him, Elisba threw
open the door.

"Take him out," he said, "that I may accuse him
publicly."

He went out, and waving his hand, called his followers together. They came and formed a half-circle
about him. Then he said in a loud voice:

"I do not feel justified in acting alone the part of
a judge. We are here all equal, and all sworn to fight
for the good cause. Where it is necessary to meet the
enemy with weapons in our hands, one must be the
leader, and you have chosen me. But in the present
case each one has the right to express his personal
opinion. The decision must rest with you." Then
he related how Otia, under the mask of friendship, had
crept in among them to betray his countrymen to
death. "Now speak, all of you. What punishment
does he deserve?"

"Death! Death!" was the unanimous answer.

"You have heard your sentence." said Elisba,
turning with a look of contempt to the prisoner, who
in his terror had sunk upon the ground.

"Permit me to say a word," said Djambek, who
stood by Elisba's side; and at a nod from the leader,
he proceeded. "There is no question but that treachery is one of the most shameful of crimes, perhaps
the most shameful. Only a coward is capable of it,
and I agree fully with your verdict; but on the other
hand, it does not seem to me to be fitting that we
should play the *rôle* of the hangman. We do not fight
against such worthless, contemptible creatures. Our
cause is a noble one—to fight for the rights which are

ours by the inheritance of ages. Our cause is too holy that we should allow it to be said of us, They have taken the pretense of freeing the people as a cloak to hide deeds of murder. Until now we are free from this reproach. Elisba slew his enemy in honorable fight. He risked his life for his vengeance. But in this case, the circumstances are different. We are a hundred against one. Do you not believe that when this is known, hundreds who are now secretly in sympathy with us will reproach us with having put to death one of our own blood? Do you not believe that our enemies will spread the news as far and as quickly as they can that we are a band of murderers to be avoided by every lover of peace and justice? And do you not know that when such statements are often repeated they will come to be accepted as truths by the masses? Until now our fellow-countrymen yonder know that they will find in us help and protection; but if this deed is spread abroad they will hereafter look upon our acts with distrust and suspicion. Let us go against our enemies and offer them open battle, but let us not stain our cause with a deed of revenge for which neither courage nor strength is required. Let those play the *rôle* of hangman whom we despise and hate because they use their power for the oppression of the weak. And one thing more. I owe it to an accident that I was enabled to warn Elisba of this treachery. I do not claim that as a service, but I feel sure that you are thankful to the good fortune that saved us from certain destruction, and will therefore feel more merciful toward this poor, cowardly wretch who kneels trembling before you. I do not wish to be stained with the blood of the wretched creature. I

should consider it an insult if I were charged with
wishing to punish him otherwise than by driving him
with whips out of our midst. And now do what you
think is right. What do you say, Elisba? Do you
agree with me?"

While Djambek had been speaking Elisba kept his
eyes grimly fixed upon the ground. His friend's words
had awakened a responsive feeling in his mind, but,
on the other hand, he felt that a stern example was
necessary to prevent others from playing the same
rôle.

"You interfered once before," he said in a low tone.
"Had we at that time disposed of the caimacam this
could not have happened."

"And his successor?" said Djambek. "Do you
think he would have sat with his hands in his lap?"

"Very well; we will not dispute about the matter.
We have to thank you for the discovery of the danger,
and therefore I will not oppose your wishes." He raised
his voice. "Have you considered Djambek's words?"
he asked, addressing the circle about him.

"We have."

"What is your decision?"

Some cried, "Death!" others, "Let him go!"
others, "Whip him out!"

Elisba raised his hand and motioned them to be
silent.

"We can not arrive at any decision in this way,"
he cried. "I will divide you into groups, and then
one from each group can announce how many voices
are for death and how many for mercy."

They quickly understood, and the half-circle was
quickly divided into three groups.

"Who are in favor of death?" asked Elisba, after a few moments.

A man stepped forward from one of the groups.

"We are," he said.

"How many?"

"Ninety-five."

"Who are for whipping him?"

Another man stepped forward.

"One hundred and thirty-two," he said.

"How many are for letting him go without punishment?"

A third stepped forward. "Five hundred and ninety-six," he said.

"Very well; that decides the matter." Elisba turned to Yordane. "Loose him. He is free."

Otia sprang forward and attempted to kiss Djambek's feet, then Elisba's, but they thrust him aside with contempt.

"Go, wretch!" exclaimed Djambek, "and let this be a warning to you for life."

In the mean time a murmur of dissatisfaction had arisen among the men. Those who had been in favor of death were dissatisfied that the man should escape without any punishment, and Bessarion, Elisba's servant, came forward to remonstrate with his master.

"It is decided," said the latter coldly: "the majority wished it."

Otia was sensible enough to use the moment while the company were excitedly discussing the matter to get away. As soon as he reached the forest he broke into a run.

He did not see that Bessarion and a few others had

separated from the rest and were following on his track.

"And now," said Elisba, "we must find out whether that villain did not in part tell the truth. I will select two trustworthy men, and send them to Kedi to learn how matters stand."

CHAPTER XVI.

A LUCKLESS EMBASSADOR.

HASSAN BEY arrived with his troops and waited several days without hearing anything from the messenger. A part of the force was quartered in the prisoner's house, the rest in the village and on the surrounding farms. A strong guard had been placed around the prison.

As the days went by without any news from Otia, Hassan Bey became impatient.

"Suppose your messenger is a partisan of Elisba's, and has betrayed our whole plan to him?" he said to Redjeb Bey.

"That is not likely. He is one of those who look to their own profit before anything else ; and he knows he can get no compensation there if we confiscate his property here. He must come soon. Let us go out for a little while. The cool evening air will be a pleasant change from the closeness of the room."

Dusk was approaching, and deep shadows covered the valley. The small room in which they sat was already almost dark.

Hassan Bey arose to follow the camiacam, who had stepped to the door and was about going out.

"What is that?" said the latter, suddenly stopping.
"Who put that there?"

The twilight was still sufficient to show the object
distinctly, and Redjeb Bey saw a package wrapped up
in cloth lying before the threshold.

Hassan Bey stepped nearer.

"Perhaps it is some delicate present, the gift of some
one who requires your protection," he said jokingly.

The caimacam called his servant, who was just then
passing.

"Do you know who brought this?" he asked.

The man assured him he had seen no one.

"See what it is?"

The servant commenced to unroll the package, but
suddenly dropped it with a cry of horror, as the re-
moval of the last fold disclosed a human face.

"What is it?" asked Hassan Bey, stepping closer.
But he, too, started back. "Here is the messenger
you were waiting for!" he cried to the caimacam.
"They have cut off your ambassador's head and sent
it to you as a present!"

Redjeb Bey stared at the ghastly head, unable to
say a word, while Hassan Bey, muttering curses, strode
up and down before the house.

"We have to do with a desperate enemy!" said
Hassan Bey at length. "Believe me! These desperate
peasants have nothing to lose, and so shrink from nothing. I confess I am for the moment helpless and do
not know how to begin. Shall we hunt them out of
their den? In that case I must have not hundreds,
but thousands of men behind me, and even then it
would be easy for them to massacre us while we were
climbing up those cursed rocks."

"Very true," replied the caimacam; "but now that we have gone thus far, are we to stop and let the outlaws have their way?"

"That we must not do, or all Adjaria will blaze with rebellion. We must proceed with firmness and severity. But our force is not large enough. We must get troops from Trebizonde, and then strike a decisive blow. In the mean time, I will remain here. They may be presumptuous enough to make an attack, after all. You had best go to Batoum and arrange matters with the pasha."

Redjeb Bey agreed, and said he would start the next morning. His departure, however, was hastened by his receiving late that evening a message from Tibeti, where he usually resided, saying that Elisba with his band had attacked the place, taken most of the guard prisoners, and burned the government building. There was not a minute to lose. The caimacam ordered his boat to be got ready immediately and started at once for the city to advise Cherif-Pasha that a regular campaign must be begun against the rebels.

The news of these occurrences reached Batoum before Redjeb Bey's arrival. There was even more known there than the caimacam had to announce. He found great excitement prevailing, as the day before there had come reports that the rebels would attack Batoum itself, and that morning Cherif - Pasha had received a note wherein Elisba announced his coming in the next few days.

Cherif-Pasha sought refuge for himself and his household under the pretense of a visit to Murza-Khan. He hoped to find safety under that hospitable roof from the dangers that immediately threatened. His flight, as every one considered this sudden visit, gave rise to the wildest rumors. The political news of the day was mixed up with these rumors, and it was even said that Elisba had encamped near the city with several thousand men, intending to form the advance guard of a Russian army corps, which was ready on the frontier to invade the country immediately on the declaration of war. It needed but little to bring about a panic. The merchants prepared to place their goods on board of vessels, while the rest of the inhabitants were divided into two parties, according to their nationality, the one preparing also to remove their goods, while the other was ready with glad hearts to welcome the deliverers who were to free them by fire and sword from a long oppression.

Artschil used the opportunity for going by ship directly to Constantinople. He had many friends there in influential circles, and it seemed to him to be a good time to attempt making an end of Cherif-Pasha's rule by giving in the proper quarter a true account of the existing circumstances.

Cherif-Pasha had entirely lost his head. As he saw his capital deprived of defense by the withdrawal of the troops under Hassan Bey into the mountains, and hearing every day fresh news of the rebel's actions, he trembled for his life, and even thought of resigning his position to escape the fury of the storm that he saw approaching.

The caimacam was, therefore, no little surprised when he saw what unexpected changes the events of the past few days, unimportant in themselves, had brought about. All whom he met spoke in sarcastic and contemptuous tones of Cherif-Pasha, and all laid on him the blame for the dangers that now threatened them.

There were many voices, too, who spoke openly in favor of Elisba's party. He had been forced, they said, into his present position, and it was but a just punishment that was now overtaking those who for years had piled up riches wrung from the hands of the poor and defenseless. It was thought by many that Elisba had been induced by the Russian Government to bring about a general uprising at the proper moment, and this was so confidently believed by many that they made no scruple of openly declaring their adherence to the new movement. It was now suddenly brought to their minds that the authorities here were but foreigners, and that beyond the mountains lived those of their own race, and that matters went much better under Russian dominion. The question of nationality blossomed in a night and constantly gained new adherents; and while heretofore one had heard on the streets little else but Turkish spoken, now the Georgian language was the most prominent. One even heard many Russian phrases. It was as if at a single stroke the city had changed its inhabitants.

Redjeb Bey had opportunity to hear all this during the few hours he spent in Batoum, and it was almost with despair that he started for Kardjeti-Tziche, to confer with Cherif-Pasha on the steps to be taken.

Murza-Khan had been no little surprised at the advent of the pasha with his extensive following. He had indeed heard some of the prevailing rumors, but paid them little attention. But he learned from Totia in confidence that matters were undoubtedly in a bad

way, the pasha's factotum not considering it necessary
to keep silence as to the real cause for their visit to
their influential neighbor.

Murza-Khan could not suppress a sarcastic smile
as he again met his guest.

"One hears all sorts of stories," he said, "but I
will not believe they are true."

Cherif-Pasha felt the necessity of speaking frankly
to his host, in whom he hoped to find a protector for
the time being.

"I do not know what you have heard," he said,
with a sigh, "but I may say to you, as a particular
friend, that things have taken a turn for the worst."

He then began to complain of the failure of Hassan Bey's enterprise, and expressed the fear that his
strength was not equal to that of the insurgents.

"What!" exclaimed Murza-Khan, "does the government feel powerless before a gang of crazy adventurers?"

"Not exactly powerless," replied the pasha, seeing
the bad effect of his confidential avowal. "No, certainly not powerless, but for the moment there are
unpleasant complications. Of course the rebellion will
be crushed in a moment as soon as our troops can face
them, but these bandits know every hole in the mountains, so that we have as yet been unable to find them.
Let us once get at them, and you will see that the
government is by no means powerless."

Murza-Khan's face again showed traces of a sarcastic smile, as he nodded his head and said:

"Yes, the old proverb says: 'If you will hang a
man you must first get his head into a noose.' Tell
me, is it true that Elisba sent you a message say-

ing that he intended to make you a visit in Batoum shortly?"

"Pah! that is—I believe—yes, I remember now, some one did bring me a writing signed with his name. I presume it was the work of some practical joker."

"Who knows? He undoubtedly is aware that the troops are busy elsewhere, and it would be quite like him to make the venture. It would be a fine chance for him."

"What do you mean? You don't suppose he would have the audacity?"

"You forget that Djambek is with him, and that when I saw the young man, he spoke of making you a visit before long. Perhaps the present rumor, or, still more, the letter, is connected with that. Is it true that Djambek intends to marry your niece?"

"What are you thinking of? Aside from the fact that I would strangle him with my own hands if I met him, it is hardly probable he would care to marry an insane girl."

"That is strange. I had an opportunity recently to overhear your niece talking with her friend Daria. It was quite by accident, and they had no suspicion that I overheard them—and she appeared to me anything but insane."

Cherif-Pasha looked at the other distrustfully. Was he making sport of him in his misfortunes, or did he speak the truth? What if Thamar had been pretending in order to avoid the marriage he wished her to make, and suppose Elisba really meditated an attack in order that his friend might carry off his bride? His head became suddenly so confused that he felt

14

giddy, and he tottered toward the divan and sank down upon it. At that moment Redjeb Bey entered.

"All is lost!" he cried. "Every hour the enemy is expected to appear in Batoum!"

This news aroused the pasha, and he found strength enough to stagger to his feet. Then he tottered back and forth for an instant like a drunken man, and fell heavily back on the divan, and from there rolled upon the floor, where he lay senseless.

"It appears that your news has somewhat affected our friend," said Murza-Khan indifferently. "We will send him to the women to be nursed. Come, I would like to know how much truth there is in these reports."

Redjeb Bey followed his friend out of doors, and there answered his repeated questioning.

"The truth of the matter?" he said. "I fear it is very much what is reported. In Batoum there is perfect confusion and worse feeling. It is asserted that Elisba is near the city ready to make an attack. That may be prevented. I, of course, immediately sent word to Hassan Bey. But what is worse, war is at the door, and it is asserted positively that Elisba has arranged with the Russians to prepare for them a way into the country, and to call on all the inhabitants of Adjaria to rise in rebellion."

At this, Murza-Khan's eyebrows drew darkly together, and he laid his hand mechanically on his dagger.

"If I knew that was the fact, I would not be long in giving Elisba something to think about. The Russians! Does the fool think he will be any better off if the Russians get the country? I could tell him how my father fared with them, and how he just had time to sell his property and come here, or they would not have left him a nail. And now these idiots expect to invite over here these hungry wolves! Never!" he cried wildly. "Never! And I remember now how that dreamer Djambek talked about some such thing until I told him that I would strike such a traitor dead with my dagger without a minute's hesitation. There may be truth in these reports, and we will do well to provide for our safety."

"What! will you flee, too?"

"Did I speak of fleeing?"

"I thought perhaps you meant it would be safer to load your valuables on a vessel, and then—"

"Undoubtedly," interposed the other, "but there is no hurry. For the present the whole affair is but child's play. Has war been declared? No. Then why vacate the premises for them before they have even knocked at the door? First of all, we must put an end to this child's play of Elisba's. We are a peace-loving people here, but if any one disturbs us, we must, for good or for evil, break the peace and exchange our tools for weapons."

"Very true," said Redjeb Bey. "It would be a shame if a handful of adventurers could for any length of time disturb an industrious people and threaten them with serious danger."

"That they shall not. If they have any quarrel with you let them fight it out in your district, and not come to harrass us. We always got along well with you, and we want no change at present."

"You shall be remembered for this. When we have brought these robbers to terms, you may depend

on your manly behavior being made known in high
circles, I promise you."

"It is not necessary," said Murza-Khan, with a
gesture of refusal. "I am not one of those who strive
for honors and feel themselves something great because
they can wear a star on their breasts. What I want is
peace and quiet. I have always known how to get
along well enough with the authorities and with my
neighbors, who are all more or less dependent on me.
I have only to say to the people : 'Over there in the
mountains is a band of idlers, fellows who think they
know more than anybody else, and want to bring
about a change. Arm yourselves! We will show them
we don't want their help, and we will root them out,
for they are joined with a covetous enemy of ours who
has long had his eyes on our property. Over there
the people are so burdened with taxes that they don't
know where to get anything to eat, and so want to
come and take what we have got.' If I talk so to the
people, you will see how they will come together in a
minute to clean out the place. I am sure that in less
than three days I can get a little army together, and
then—Elisba, may the Prophet be merciful to you!"

Redjeb Bey saw at once that he had gained a valuable ally. If Murza-Khan would undertake to harass
the enemy from this side, the safety of the city would
be assured. Hassan Bey would need no re-enforcements, and he himself could play a *rôle* that would
bring him much credit.

The thought had already occurred to him that he
might possibly replace Cherif-Pasha, who, in his present weak, broken state, would doubtless be glad to re-
sign. Murza-Khan had expressly said that he wished

no reward. But some one must reap the fruits if matters were brought to a satisfactory conclusion, and why should it not be he as well as another. The prize was, at any rate, worth the attempt, and he determined to keep on the best terms with Murza-Khan. He had noticed that a reference to the Russians had greatly excited the latter.

" You would do quite right to speak thus to the people," he said, " and I admire your sagacity." Then lowering his voice to a whisper, he continued : " I can confide in you as a true comrade. It is actually true, what I just intimated. In Stamboul they are expecting a declaration of war every day, and large bodies of troops are already massed near the frontier. I know it from most reliable sources. Unfortunately, Cherif-Pasha has been very indolent of late, and has paid little or no attention to this. Now, in his present condition, I fear very much that he is incapable of calling up the requisite energy, and I think it proper to take all precautionary measures. Hassan Bey is an active, brave man. With his assistance, I could assure the safety of Batoum, and also make a movement against the rebels which would prevent their acquiring any power before the outbreak of war. If this movement is not crushed in time, we shall have an enemy before us both within and without the frontier."

Murza-Khan was silent for some time. Then he said, with a sudden determination :

" Cherif-Pasha is not become indolent recently ; he always was so. Do you know what, Redjeb-Bey ? You must act in his place. He is incapable, at this critical moment, of taking the direction of affairs. I will persuade him to make you his representative, and

then, if our undertaking meets with success, his place
will naturally fall to you.   I believe you would be the
right man for the place."

The camiacam's looks brightened.   He took the
other's hand.

" Murza-Khan should in that case be the absolute
lord of his domain, and the government would make
no claims of any sort upon him.   You understand?"

" Good!   To-morrow I will send out a summons to
my people."

CHAPTER XVII.

FOR FRIENDSHIP'S SAKE.

CHERIF-PASHA was seriously ill. His sudden indisposition was the result of a stroke of apoplexy—not a severe one, indeed, but severe enough to make him for the time incapable of mental or physical exertion. He regained consciousness the next day, but perfect rest and quiet were necessary for him. He therefore made no objections when Murza-Khan proposed to him that Redjeb-Bey be intrusted with the temporary management of affairs. As he expressed the wish to remain as Murza-Khan's guest for the present, the latter hospitably gave up his house to him and withdrew to a small farm near by, where he could arrange his plans with his people undisturbed. These had so far fallen in with his wishes as to declare themselves willing to keep a sharp lookout, and prevent any incursion of the rebels into the district. But his proposal that in case of war with the neighboring state they should take up arms found no response.

Hassan Bey was directed to return with his troops to Batoum, the pasha's representative considering that the safety of the city was the first thing to be considered.

Since Elisba had sent his message to Cherif-Pasha nothing had been heard of him. Redjeb Bey took every

means of obtaining information in regard to his movements, but could learn nothing reliable. The sentiment throughout the district was so inimical to the
government that no native could be found to offer his
services to obtain the required information. Some
would indeed go, under pressure of threats, but after
spending a few days with friends in the mountains,
they would return and say there was nothing to be
seen or heard of Elisba; or else they would really find
his stopping place in order to inform him of what the
Government was doing, and then would make entirely
false reports to Hassan Bey regarding the rebel leader.

In this way, too, Djambek learned that Murza-Khan
had taken sides with the government, and that Cherif-
Pasha with his whole household was enjoying his hospitality. This news caused him much anxiety. If so
influential a man as Murza-Khan joined that side, it
was to be feared that many of his countrymen would
abandon the good cause, and once more willingly assume the yoke of oppression.

He thought of the future, and often asked himself
what he was to do under these circumstances. To
remain for years among the hills and act the avenger
when one of their countrymen had been outraged was
not what he wished for—especially if it should come
about that the oppressed did not wish for help. He
often talked with Elisba, but he, too, could say but
little as to future plans.

"For the present," he said, "I shall remain here
and await events. Should the present quiet become
permanent, I might buy a small estate and settle down
until there was again something for me to do. But
you may be sure they will not grant our people a long

term of peace. As soon as they feel themselves
stronger, they will begin again. But as for you, Djambek, I again advise you to go to Tiflis. If it really
comes to blows between the two countries, your presence there will be of great service to us."

After considering the matter a few days, Djambek
concluded that it would be best for him to follow his
friend's advice, and he determined to start the following morning.

Elisba accompanied him a part of the way and
Djambek arranged with him to forward any messages
that might come for him. Should any letters come
from Ahmed, Elisba was to open and read them, as
they might concern his safety and interests as much
as Djambek's.

Arrived in Aschalzich, Djambek at once sought
out his old school friend, the young Russian official.
The latter showed himself much pleased to see his
friend, and assured him that his chief, the general,
was greatly interested in the efforts of the Adjarians
to throw off their yoke of oppression. This greatly
pleased Djambek, and he gladly accepted the invita-
tion of his friend Kapanidze to be presented to his
chief. He found General Tasafioff a cultivated, agreeable gentleman who knew at once how to adopt a
tone pleasing to the ears of an Adjarian.

"We are here in a position to see easily what is
going on in the neighboring state," said the general,
in the course of conversation. "I know from my own
observation that the government there is not such as
can satisfy a people who have brilliant traditions
behind them. Were you but savages, you might, perhaps, rest satisfied with existing conditions; but being

a people who hundreds of years ago stood on a higher plan than your present rulers now occupy, I can well understand the dissatisfaction that you must feel. I know that those of you who dare avow your sentiments are but few comparatively, but in their hearts the great majority of all the people are with you. And your opportunity will come. With our neighbor sick in body and spirit we shall soon have vigorous dealing, and then your opportunity will stand at the door."

"I think so, too," said Kapanidze. "I spoke to my friend some time ago about it, but he appeared afraid, lest he should be thought playing the part of a traitor to his country."

"I have grown old in honor," replied the general, "and would be the last to advise an equivocal action. Did Djambek come to me to-day as a born Mussulman and the leader of a rebel troop, I would at once arrest him and deliver him to the Turkish authorities. But that is not the case. He belongs to that same race who once before called on us for aid to free them from the cruelty of these same oppressors, and I find it quite natural and indeed patriotic if he now feels a desire to free his country from its cruel masters."

"Yes," said Kapanidze, "it is my honest opinion that Djambek belongs to us in a double sense. His name alone is sufficient to show his Georgian origin, and besides that he received his education in Tiflis and Odessa. What do you think of it yourself, Djambek? Am I not right?"

"I believe you are. I tried honorably for a long time to bear patiently the injustice that weighed upon us heavier and heavier from day to day. I was on friendly terms then with the Vali-Pasha, and I used every means to convince him that his subordinates were pillaging the land under disguise of their official duties, but all was in vain."

"Even the abduction of his niece!" added the general with a quizzical smile.

"You know of that, too?"

"I told you that we keep a sharp lookout on what is going on across the boundary."

"But you must not think that I took part against the pasha because I failed in my attempt to withdraw my bride from his control. Perhaps that was the turning-point—I will not deny that—but it was not the ground on which I declared myself an enemy of the pasha. I was inspired above all by my love of my country, and by the recollection of its glorious past, to bid defiance to a man who deemed himself above other mortals."

"I believe you," replied the general. "I did not mean to insinuate otherwise. And I could tell you a story, too, of what occurred many years ago. My wife was a Georgian, and in Georgia it is still quite in order for a young man to carry off his bride."

He paused a moment and seemed lost in reverie. Then he continued:

"No, my young friend, I only meant to say that I could very easily imagine myself in your place at your years, and I know from experience how grand it is to fly through the night on a swift steed with your love in your arms!"

"Yes, if you reach your goal," said Djambek dejectedly.

"True! But one must try until he succeeds. But

to return to our subject. Let us come to the point. Will you join us?"

Djambek hesitated but for a second, then he said firmly:

"I will!"

"And do you think your friends will approve the step?"

"I know they will. It was Elisba who persuaded me to go to Tiflis and see if any aid for our cause was to be got there."

"Honestly spoken! and you shall have an honest answer. There is much interest taken in your cause, and it will be put in action sooner than you think for. More I am not at liberty to say, but you will learn the particulars at Tiflis. But of this I can assure you, I welcome you most gladly as a comrade."

"And I can say to you," returned Djambek earnestly, "that my highest wish would be to fight at your side for the liberation of my land."

"That wish may be fulfilled, for if at the proper time you can organize a corps of volunteers you will be of great service to us here on the frontier. But you will learn of all that at Tiflis. I will add this good news to my report and you shall carry it yourself to Tiflis."

The second day Djambek continued his journey to the Georgian capital.

. . . .

Three days had passed since the parting of the friends, when a messenger brought a letter from Ahmed. Thinking that it perhaps might concern himself as well as Djambek, he opened it. The letter was from Daria, and read thus:

"FRIEND DJAMBEK: If Thamar is not soon released from her desperate position a misfortune will happen. She is here in the power of a wretch who uses the weakness of her uncle to persecute her with his addresses. Hassan Bey had at least the decency to remain away when she gave him to understand that his attentions were distasteful to her, but not so this Murza-Khan. He met her one evening while she was walking alone, took hold of her, and told her he knew that her illness was only pretense. She was so surprised and agitated at his manner that she forgot her *rôle* and half admitted what he said, hoping he might be induced to take her part.

"He said she was quite right not to accept Hassan Bey, and she was feeling very hopeful of his assistance when he suddenly told her that he loved her and that he would persuade her uncle to favor him.

"Notwithstanding the aversion that she then showed toward him, he has followed her persistently since, and I fear has some evil project in view. What shall we do? How save her from these merciless men? We plan all kinds of adventurous projects, but when the moment comes find we can not carry them out. Once we were already in a boat out at sea when a storm came up, and had not a vessel come to our aid (one of his vessels, too!) we should have perished. She is near despair, and I know nothing to do but to send you word and perhaps you can help us.

"She has no suspicion that I have written you. I have not told her lest her anxiety should increase her troubles.

"There is the possibility of a rescue. North of here I have found a good place, a little cove where a boat might be hidden. No one ever goes near there. Will you make the attempt?

"I count on your getting this in four days. You will need two days to reach here. After that time I will go with her to the place every day. Perhaps fortune will favor us.

"I warn you and your friend against Murza-Khan. Next week the people he has called together here are to go with Hassan Bey to hunt you out if possible and attack you. He has sworn your destruction. Be on your guard.

DARIA."

In a moment Elisba had made his decision. He would attempt a rescue without letting Djambek know anything about it. This was an opportunity to pay for all his friend had done for him. If he succeeded— well; if he failed, he would only lose a life which seemed to him almost valueless.

"You come from Ahmed, do you not?" he asked the man who had knelt down by the fire and was warming his hands.

"Yes, from Ahmed."

"It is well. Let them give you something to eat. I shall start this evening. You may go with me, if you wish."

Elisba started at dusk In spite of the increased danger in taking that route, he determined to go by the river as time was of greatest importance. He took with him only Yordane, a servant, and the man who had brought the letter. "The fewer the better," he had said to his trusted companion, after informing him of his plans, and the other agreed with him. Four persons in a boat were not likely to attract special attention.

They arrived safely in the neighborhood of Batoum where they remained in hiding until evening. Then they made a *détour* and reached the harbor, where Elisba soon found a fisherman who gave him the use of his boat.

.   .   .   .

It was nearly noon the next day when they came in sight of Kardjeti-Tziche. Elisba turned the rudder that they might not go too near the shore, where they could see a number of Murza-Khan's boats at anchor. Then, when the castle was hidden behind a bend of the shore, they turned their boat toward the land that they might not pass by the cove of which Daria had spoken.

Finally Elisba concluded that they had found the place, and he told his companions to take in the sail. "That must be it," he said, pointing to a little cove bordered by trees and thick bushes. They pulled in to the miniature harbor and landed at a point comparatively free from bushes, where they could see some distance landward. Elisba and Yordane sprang ashore while the servant hid the boat under some overhanging trees. At that moment they heard voices.

"They are coming," whispered Yordane.

But it was not those they were looking for, but some children carrying fishing nets.

Elisba and his friend had no time to conceal themselves, and as the children saw the two armed men, they turned and fled with loud cries.

"That is unfortunate," said Elisba. "The little rascals will alarm the whole neighborhood and spoil our plan. What shall we do?"

" Let us get away as soon as possible and find a place to conceal ourselves and wait."

" That is easily said, but Murza-Khan has a whole fleet at his command, and could soon search every *pik* of the coast."

" Then we had better escape as we can. We have failed, and it would be mere foolishness to expose ourselves to being captured, which amounts to the same as being killed. You owe it to your people to avoid that danger."

" There is nothing left us but flight, I am sorry to say. I do it with a heavy heart, but—" he stopped suddenly and pointed landward—" I see two women— If it should be they ! "

" Come ! " said Yordane, taking him by the arm. " I hear a noise in the bushes. The ground burns under our feet ! There is danger ! "

He had dragged Elisba but a step or two with him, when a number of armed men sprang out of the thicket on their left.

" Halt, traitor ! robber ! murderer ! " cried the one in advance, springing on Elisba, who in a flash had drawn his pistol. " Surrender, or you shall pay for your rashness with your life ! "

Elisba fired, and Murza-Khan fell headlong. Elisba and Yordane took advantage of the confusion which followed to spring to their boat. But a volley followed them, and they fell into the water dead.

" What can that mean? " asked Thamar in terror, as, following her friend, she saw from a distance the tragic scene. " Are those people fighting in earnest, or is it only sport? "

Daria, pale as death, took her friend by the arm

and pulled her away. "Fly! for heaven's sake, fly! It is a shameful murder!" she exclaimed.

She could not say more. She drew her trembling, sobbing companion with her by force. She thought, "My friend's lover is killed, and I am the cause of his death!"

CHAPTER XVIII.

WAR AND CHIVALRY.

DJAMBEK became very anxious on not hearing from his friend for a long time. With increasing impatience, he waited from one day to another, hoping for news. At length he determined to send his servant to make inquiries, and then waited in feverish impatience for his return.

Finally the man came back and reported that Elisba had left his house a few days after Djambek's departure without saying where he was going. Since then nothing had been heard from him, and his people were in the greatest anxiety.

Had there not been important business which detained him, Djambek would have immediately started to see what had become of Elisba; but just at that time he could not leave Tiflis without hazarding the success of the whole undertaking. General Tasafioff had said truly that his government had a great interest in the fate of Adjaria. Djambek received proof of this in Tiflis, where he was very cordially received, and was invited by officials in high quarters to lay before them the fullest details in order that a decision might be quickly arrived at. He had accordingly had confidential interviews with a number of influential persons, and was now waiting for the plans to be approved by the Czar, in order that binding stipulations might be entered into on both sides. While waiting news from St. Petersburg he must remain in Tiflis. Should he leave now he would be looked on as merely an irresponsible adventurer, and the whole plan might fall to the ground.

A few days went by thus, when one morning he received a summons from the commander-in-chief. There he was told that important news had come from St. Petersburg. War was declared and the authorities in Tiflis were commanded to at once enter into negotiations with the two leaders of the Adjarians.

As the commander-in-chief had full authority to act, there was no reason for further delay, and the terms of a compact were at once agreed upon, by which Elisba and Djambek were at once to call together their forces and place themselves under the orders of the Governor of Aschalzich.

There was now nothing further to do here, and Djambek made his arrangements for starting the next morning.

On his return journey he stopped at Aschalzich to see General Tasafioff and get his advice as to the formation of the volunteer corps. He himself was very far from claiming the right to be commander of the corps. He would leave that to his friend, who had made it the object of his life to free his land from the Turkish yoke. Did he find taking arms unavoidable, he would join the ranks of his countrymen, though he felt no great desire to take part in the killing of those who must suffer for the deeds of their rulers.

Djambek informed the general that he considered

himself as Elisba's embassador only, and that as soon
as his friend returned he should send him to make
the further arrangements with the governor.

After his interview with General Tasafioff, Djambek continued his journey, hoping that he would find
Elisba already returned to his post.

But in this he was disappointed. The people were
in great excitement, and feared that Elisba had fallen
into the hands of the enemy. Where or why he had
gone no one could tell. They only knew that one day
a messenger had brought him a letter, and that he left
the same evening in company with Yordane and a servant.

In accordance with the promise he had given the
general, Djambek selected a company of men and
sent them over the frontier to announce to all their
partisans that war had been declared, and that all were
to meet at a certain place to begin in earnest the work
of freeing the land.

The news spread rapidly, and everywhere was received with enthusiasm. While before no one had ever
thought of a united action against their oppressors, now
every one wondered that they had not long since put an
end by force to the cruelties of these vampires. It was
as if the scales had fallen from the eyes of all at once,
and the authorities found themselves helpless before
the sudden uprising. But against which foe should
they proceed, the enemy within or the enemy without?

It was too late now to seek to pacify the country
with soft words and mild measures. The people asked
no favors now, and those who but a little while before
would have bowed in the dust before an angry word
of the caimacam now shook their fists in his face muttering curses and vows of vengeance. The few who

still took sides with Stamboul kept a discreet silence, and many packed up their valuables to remove them to some place where the earth did not tremble and rumble so threateningly as here.

In Batoum there was so great a panic that they paid but little attention to affairs in this comparatively distant region.

All the troops that could. be spared in Armenia were forwarded to the port to garrison it and the important fortress of Tzichis-tzeri.

Every day brought new companies of volunteers to Djambek's camp, and the place was soon filled with an imposing corps of well-armed and well-mounted men. Djambek was fully occupied in getting this little army into some sort of order and discipline, a task for which he had little taste, but executed it to the best of his ability.

A pressing inquiry had once come from Aschalzich as to whether Elisba had not yet returned, as the order to march was expected every day, and on his sending an answer in the negative, Djambek had received a message from General Tasafioff, saying that he should expect him to take command of the corps in case Elisba failed to return before the expected orders were received.

A few days afterward Djambek was awakened from sleep by his servant.

"Bad news, sir!" cried Mamukia in excited tones. "Giurgi, the man who went with Elisba and Yordane, has returned."

"Has a misfortune happened?" asked Djambek of Giurgi, who just then entered.

"Yes," he replied, and told in a few words the results of the ill-fated expedition. When he saw that

he could be of no help to his companions, he used the
opportunity while Murza-Khan's people were busy with
their wounded leader to escape. After undergoing
numerous perils and hardships he had at last reached
Batoum half dead and found an asylum with Ahmed.
When he had sufficiently recovered he started for the
mountains, and after a long and wearisome journey
had arrived at the camp.

Djambek was dumb with grief and excitement.
To serve him, his friend had risked and had sacrificed
his life! Something extraordinary must have happened to have led Elisba to so suddenly leave all else
and go to the rescue of Thamar. Had he perhaps received a message which was so pressing that nothing
remained but immediate action?

Djambek sat sunk in troubled thought trying to
unravel the tangled threads, but his thoughts were so
confused that he hardly knew whether he was awake
or dreaming. Was it not all perhaps the hideous
creation of a dream? He opened wide his eyes and
stared at the two servants.

"Ahmed gave me a message for you," said Giurgi
in a troubled tone, noticing the other's grief.

That brought Djambek again to himself. "Quick!
give it to me," he exclaimed and took the letter with
trembling hands, while Mamukia set a pine knot in
flames to give him light.

Ahmed's letter explained matters. On hearing
Giurgi's story he saw at once that on receiving Daria's
letter which he had forwarded Elisba had gone in
place of his absent friend to Thamar's rescue.

"And now I will act for you," wrote the brave
muezzin; "I am, indeed, but a messenger of peace,

and you can not expect me to appear with weapons in my hands before the villains who hold your bride a captive; but it will be a comfort to you and to her to have me near her. My plan is made. In the midst of the panic which reigns in the city my services are not needed. Who thinks of the muezzin's prayers now! I will therefore get into the enemy's camp under some disguise. Perhaps I can obtain employment of some kind there. If I do, you may depend on my watching over her faithfully. Furthermore, the man who brings you this says that Murza-Khan is severely wounded. If so, the poor girl may be allowed some peace from the importunities of the man who has so basely sought to tear her from you. Take courage, my friend! Do nothing rashly. Tame thy impatience, lest an evil befall thee. I adjure thee to be careful in the name of her who trembles more for thy life than for her own."

Djambek sighed deeply and rose from the couch. "It is well," he said listlessly. "Leave me now." When the others had gone he gave way to his grief. In thought he went to the spot where his friend had shed his heart's blood for him, and his eyes overflowed with tears as he thought that just now, just when his fondest hopes were about to be realized, when he was called to bring to his country its longed-for freedom, he lay silent and powerless forever.

And Thamar! What oppressions must she suffer under in the power of this shameless enemy! The thought aroused him. Now to action! Not rashly, not alone, now, but with the power that stood at his command, with comrades eager and impatient for the hour when they might spring upon their oppressors.

Yes, he would take as a legacy the object his dead friend ever had had before his eyes. They would rush forth like an angry torrent against an enemy who from each one of them had forced tears of blood. And he also shall suffer, he whose life-object it has been to deny himself no pleasure, even though it be bought with the ruin of his nearest friend! He was ready. While heretofore he had always hoped that Elisba would return and relieve him from the weight of this undertaking, now he burned with fierce impatience for the moment when he might cry, "Up, comrades! the hour has struck!"

No time was to be lost in informing the Russian authorities of what had happened. He hurried out of the house and sprang upon his horse to go himself as the bearer of the tidings that his friend was dead, and to announce himself as his representative. On the way the fever which had seized him moderated, and he could think of the future more calmly. In his excited fantasy, he had seen himself with his troops dashing through the land, ever pressing toward one goal—the place·where Thamar was held captive. But how would it be should he receive orders to go in a wholly different direction? It was true that an expedition against Tzichis-tzeri, which lay not far from Kardjeti-Tziche, was of great importance, but at the same time it would doubtless be considered of first importance to make secure against an attack from the south. It was therefore more than probable that his corps would receive orders to hold some point in that direction. These thoughts troubled him all the way, and it was with an anxious heart that he entered the door of the commandant's headquarters.

But this time his fondest hopes were to be realized. The general, after hearing his news and expressing his sorrow and sympathy, informed him that the Russian troops in Armenia had won a brilliant victory, and that he was all ready to march to join them in an attack on the fortress.

"You will go with us. We need all the strength we can get," he said to Djambek. He paused a moment and examined the map, and then continued: "We shall have to take measures to guard against an attack from the south, and right in that direction lies a place in which you are doubtless interested. You guess, of course, that I mean Kardjeti-Tziche."

Djambek started in pleased surprise, and could only stammer a confused answer.

The general smiled. "This is hardly the time to think of adventures which smack of the days of chivalry," he said, "but if they can be had with a double advantage, why not undertake them? Between Murza-Khan's castle and Tzichis-tzeri the enemy has thrown up earthworks. If I should send you to take Kardjeti-Tziche, and place there a small garrison, we should have these earthworks between us, and after you have rescued the—enchanted princess—you might give your cardiac emotions a little rest and go and capture them. How would that suit you?

"Good!" he continued, cutting short Djambek's expressions of gratitude; "let it be so then. As soon as you receive word from me, march directly over the mountains toward Kardjeti-Tziche. But before descending into the valley wait for orders from me. I wish you much success, and send my best compliments to your bride!"

CHAPTER XIX.

DJAMBEK and his men marched rapidly over the mountain. They wished to show their allies that if they were not brought up to war they could at least obey orders promptly. They met with no obstacles, except the difficulties of the road, and these were overcome in good spirits. In the few villages they passed through much sympathy was shown them, and all seemed to rejoice that the existing order of things was about to be changed.

The march over the Peranga Mountains was finally concluded, and they arrived upon the plain which joined the last range of hills between them and the sea. Here they rested on the banks of the Tchuruk-Su, to take a few hours of needed rest.

Djambek could scarcely control his impatience. There, beyond those hills, lay the place which drew him mightily, the place where his bride lay captive, little thinking that her rescuer was so near.

A few hours more and the longed-for moment would come! But how endlessly long seemed these hours! They must wait here until they received word from the main body, then they were to proceed to Kardjeti-Tziche, and hold the place until re-enforcements came

from the northeast, when they would proceed to the
reduction of the earthworks of which the general had
spoken.

Djambek's chief anxiety was lest his presence
here should be known too soon. Kardjeti-Tziche
was not more than five hours distant, and he knew
that Murza-Khan had connections with all the surrounding country. Djambek had indeed chosen a
retired place for their camp, but an accident might
bring some one there, and thus greatly interfere with
the success of his plans. He took what measures he
could to guard against this danger by posting sentinels and by strict orders to his men not to leave the
camp, and to arrest any one who might approach.

The next morning the pickets brought in a peasant
they had taken. The man admitted that he came
from Kardjeti-Tziche and had been directed to find
out whether the enemy was near, the news of the advance having already reached Murza-Khan. After a
good deal of pressing, the man was induced to give
some particulars. Nearly all the able-bodied men of
Kardjeti-Tziche had been pressed into the service, to
defend the fortress of Tzichi-tzeri. Murza-Khan being
therefore left without any guard, had made ready a
number of vessels, and was prepared at the first sign
of the enemy's approach to go aboard with all his
household and sail to Trebizonde for safety. The
man further said that Cherif-Pasha a few days before
had died from a second stroke of paralysis. Djambek
tried to get some information from him in regard to
Thamar, but he persisted in saying that he did not
know that there were any women there.

Having got from him all the information they

could, Djambek ordered that he be given some refreshment, telling him, however, that he would be held as a prisoner.

This matter was hardly ended when some of the sentinels again appeared, bringing two horsemen with them. They wore the Russian uniform. At last! Djambek hurried to them, and to his great joy recognized one of them as Kapanidze.

"Here I am!" he cried as Djambek approached. "I see you have lost no time. We had some doubt, whether you could accomplish the march in the time the general gave you."

"We did it in less time," returned Djambek, shaking his friend's hand. "We have been here since yesterday."

"Indeed! You must have had wings. So much the better. We can make the attack all the sooner. Three battalions are camped directly north of here, ready to march as soon as you do." He looked at his watch. "If I start at once I can reach them again by twelve o'clock. So at midday you will start, and the faster you go the better. You go directly toward Kardjeti-Tziche, while we have to bend a little to the north to cut off any re-enforcements they may send from the earthworks. Murza-Khan's house is not garrisoned, as we hear. In that case you can join us with the larger part of your force. If you leave two hundred men there, it will be sufficient. In case, which is not likely, that you find the place fortified, you must storm it. We must, under no circumstances leave any of the enemy in our rear."

"I understand."

"Good. Now a glass of wine—I am dying of

thirst—and then farewell until I see you again yonder!"

He hastily drank off the wine and sprang away at a gallop.

Djambek gave orders to break camp, and in an hour they were ready to march.

As soon as the sun reached the meridian they were in motion. Their pace was a rapid one, but not too fast, as they intended to make the last part at a double-quick, to give the enemy no time to escape.

After three hours of uninterrupted march, they halted by a little stream for a short rest. Then they went on again, until they came to the last wooded hills, which gently descended to the sea. Here they again halted and formed a wide half-circle, Djambek placing himself at the extremity of the left wing. Then the word was given, and the line moved forward with a rush.

They were within five hundred paces of the house when Djambek saw a boat suddenly put out toward the open sea. If they should escape him at last! he thought, and putting spurs to his horse, he dashed forward followed by the others. A number of boats lay upon the beach. Djambek sprang from his horse. Calling on some to push off the boats, he directed the others to occupy the house, which was undefended. In a few moments his orders were carried out. As soon as he saw one of the boats ready, he sprang into it.

"Row for your lives!" he cried. "We must overtake that boat there."

There was not a breath of wind. The sail flapped idly on the mast. This was favorable for Djambek, as now the strength of the rowers would decide the victory.

The men laid to the oars with all their might, and the boat shot forward, while a couple of others put off from shore to join them in the pursuit.

The space between them rapidly lessened, and soon those in the cutter could be distinguished. Djambek recognized Murza-Khan, who was excitedly urging on his rowers. The cutter was a small, slender boat, chosen doubtless for its speed.

They approached a couple of lengths nearer, and now Djambek could distinguish two female figures, who leaned over the side, extending their arms as if imploring help. He tore his white turban from his head and waved it as a signal of encouragement to the girls.

The other boats which had followed Djambek now approached and divided to the right and left so as to form a half circle around the fugitives.

" There is a large vessel yonder," suddenly cried one of the men, and looking in the direction indicated Djambek saw a little cloud of smoke on the horizon. That was unfortunate! Doubtless there was a Turkish man-of-war there who might yet give them a stiff piece of work to do.

" Forward! forward!" cried Djambek to the oarsmen. " We must at all hazards capture that boat before the stronger enemy comes down on us."

The men laid to the oars with increased vigor, and in a few minutes they were alongside the other. Then, to his horror, Djambek saw Murza-Khan throw his oar into the sea, draw his dagger, and spring toward Thamar.

" A foot nearer, and she will be a corpse!" he yelled, seizing the girl in an iron grasp. " Dare approach, dog, and I will throw you a lifeless booty!"

Djambek was dumb with horror. Mechanically he cried to his men to stop rowing, for he knew the savage was in earnest. At that instant, one of Murza-Khan's men sprang up and with a mighty leap over the other oarsmen, fell upon him, tore the dagger from his grasp, and hurled him to the bottom of the boat.

"Quick, men! quick!" cried Djambek, and in a moment he had sprung into the other boat and was holding Murza-Khan down with all his weight and strength. His dagger gleamed in the air—but a commanding voice bade him hold.

"He is my prisoner," said a well-known voice in his ear, and now for the first time he knew who it was who had brought help in so urgent need. "Ahmed!" he cried in astonishment, "you, the hero?"

"Silence!" said the muezzin casting down his eyes as if ashamed. "Do not remind me that I have forgotten the *rôle* of a man of peace."

During this scene the other oarsmen had remained perfectly quiet. What interest had they in the affairs of the man to whom they were strangers and for whom they had been forced to work? Besides, the others were the stronger force, and resistance would be useless.

After Murza-Khan, foaming with rage, had been securely bound, Djambek gave orders to turn toward the shore. It was high time, for the war-ship was fast approaching.

Elated with their victory, the men bent to their oars with renewed vigor, and the little fleet swept toward the shore, and soon was sheltered behind the jutting reefs.

Djambek, however, was not free from anxiety. If

the commander of the war-ship should suspect that a body of the enemy was quartered here, a fight must follow, and it could not be hoped that the walls of Kardjeti-Tziche would long hold out before the heavy guns.

His first care, after placing the women in safety, was to confine the prisoners in the underground rooms, and then he ordered his men to conceal themselves behind the walls. If it appeared that everything was quiet it was to be hoped that the vessel would not go out of its way to make an attack.

Having completed these arrangements, Djambek was about hurrying to Thamar, when he was met by some of his men driving a prisoner before them.

"He was hiding in the stable," said the leader of the patrol. "We found him buried under the straw."

Djambek uttered an exclamation of surprise, for he recognized in the strange-looking figure—his hair, beard, and clothes covered with straw—his old acquaintance the worthy Totia.

"It is Cherif-Pasha's spy," he cried, looking at the prisoner with contempt.

Totia seemed to take the insulting words as a jest.

"Not at all," he said, simpering. "I was not here as a spy, but as the friend of your bride's poor uncle, and as—her protector."

"A curious way of protecting her, burying yourself in the straw," said Djambek sarcastically. "Put him with the other prisoners."

"But consider, my good Djambek, you find me here as a private person. I am not in official service."

"That will be determined later," said Djambek

coolly. "For the present, at least, you are a prisoner of war."

"Do not forget that your bride's friend is interested in me, and—"

"Silence!" interrupted Djambek angrily. "Daria despises you as Thamar and I do. Your *rôle* is played out, and the Russian commander shall decide what is to be done with you."

At these words Totia stepped closer to Djambek and said in a low tone:

"I have special reasons for not wishing to come into closer relations with your allies. Let me go. You shall not lose by it. Fortune has favored me in late years, and I have accumulated a very fair property, and I would not mind parting with say one hundred thousand piasters as a ransom if you—" Djambek gave him a push which sent him reeling backward.

"Place him in a secure place by himself" he said to his men. "He is a dangerous man, and he must not be allowed to have any communication with the others. Let him be well guarded. I shall hold you responsible for him."

Totia had scarcely been led away, when Mamukia came running up.

"The steamer is at anchor," he said excitedly, "and a boat is just coming ashore."

This was serious. A struggle seemed inevitable, and one in which all the advantage would be with the attacking party. The walls could not long endure a bombardment, and then if they escaped from the ruins the garrison must be exposed to the full fire of the enemy on the open shore. It would be almost the same as total destruction for the corps.

16

Suddenly an idea flashed into Djambek's mind, and he hurried to the court, where there was an entrance toward the shore. "Let no one stir or even show himself," he cried to his men. "I will receive the visitors alone."

He hurried to the landing place just as the boat reached the shore.

An officer landed and approached Djambek.

"*Hosh gelden!* Welcome!" said the latter, saluting the officer in the Turkish manner. "How can I serve you?"

"Are you the master of this place?" asked the officer.

"Since to-day—yes, as we have just buried my poor uncle."

"Indeed!"

"Yes. Did you not see our boats just now out in the bay?"

"You buried him there?"

Djambek sighed. "We were obliged to do so, as he died of a malignant disease," he said mournfully.

"What do you say? You do not mean small-pox?"

"Worse still; we fear it was the—plague." The officer sprang hastily into his boat and commanded his men to push off instantly.

"Have you heard anything of the enemy," he asked as the boat receded from shore.

"Nothing. Everything is quiet here. A few days ago two sick people came from the north where they said things were looking badly. I think my relative must have taken the disease from them. They died the day before yesterday, and my uncle the next day."

The officer seemed to have found out more than he liked. He waved his hand in a parting salutation, and his boat rapidly receded from shore.

Djambek rubbed his hands in satisfaction and hurried back to the castle. From the veranda he could see the boat reach the war-vessel, and a few minutes later anchor was weighed and the formidabable enemy proceeded on her course.

Saved! At last he might press his beloved to his heart! He had but a little time, for, according to his orders, he must take up the march again and proceed to the north.

With a beating heart he opened the door of the room where the two girls had been left. They stood at the window, and were anxiously watching the war-vessel which was just getting under way.

"The danger is happily past," he cried joyously, and at the sound of his voice Thamar turned from the window to throw herself upon his breast. "Have I you again!" he exclaimed with rapture. "We will never part now—but," he added sorrowfully, "I forget; we must again be separated."

"No. You must not leave me," said Thamar imploringly. "You must not go away. Or if you do, take me with you."

"Into battle?" he said with a sad smile.

"You are going into battle?" she exclaimed.

"That was the condition under which I could rescue you from that villian. Unfortunately, my treasure, we can be together but a few moments."

She clung to him, sobbing. "And if something should happen to you, if you should be—" her voice failed in a flood of tears.

"Do not make the parting harder for him," said Daria, laying her hand upon her friend's shoulder. "Hope for the best. Until now fortune has always been favorable; why should it now forsake you?"

Gradually the young girl became quieter.

"I see that I must submit. I will try to be brave. I will hope—hope with my whole heart that you will be preserved to me, dearest. And if Fate wills it that the heaviest of misfortunes strikes me, then I will follow you, my beloved. I swear it!"

"Hush, Thamar. Do not talk so. All will yet end well. I believe with confidence in our star."

She was about to reply when Mamukia's head appeared in the door.

"Murza-Khan wishes very much to speak with you," he said.

Djambek's first impulse was to refuse the prisoner's request, but on second thought he concluded to listen to him.

"I will come," he said curtly. "Farewell, my beloved. We shall soon meet again. I must give this rascal a few minutes, and then we must start."

Thamar turned pale as she saw that the moment for parting had come. She flung her arms about his neck and held him close, passionately, to her soft bosom, as if she could not let him go.

"Oh, Djambek," she whispered with a trembling voice, "you can not know how hard this parting is!"

"Courage, my own! Think of our next meeting, of our coming happiness. You shall hear from me as often as I can send a message. That will strengthen you to bear this last separation."

He drew her close and covered her face with kisses. Then he pressed Daria's hand and hastily left the room.

Murza-Khan had been placed in one of the lowest underground rooms which he had himself made secure with iron bars and heavy doors as a safe place for his treasures.

Djambek entered and curtly asked him what he wished.

"I want to know how long I am to be kept a prisoner in my own house?" said the other, whose hands were still bound behind him.

"Until my superiors decide what is to be done with you."

"And what right have your superiors to dispose of me? Am I their subject? or am I in the position of an enemy in arms?"

"Is that what you wished to talk with me about? If so, it was needless to disturb me."

"Good! Let us come to business, then. What ransom do you demand?"

Djambek smiled scornfully.

"Do you take me for one of your Batoum friends? Were your hands not bound I would strike you in the face for the insult."

Murza-Khan bit his lips, and at first made no reply. Then he said:

"You can not deny, Djambek, but that you are taking a personal vengeance upon me, and that—"

"And have I not a hundredfold right to do so?" interrupted the other angrily. "Have you not acted toward me as a villain? Would not another man have plunged a dagger to your faithless, traitorous heart?"

" Had not the other interposed you would have done so."

" The loss would not have been a great one."

" That may be. But as he prevented it, we need not discuss the matter. Hear me, Djambek. I admit that I have deeply wronged you. I admit your right to take vengeance upon me. I only ask that you will take your vengeance now. What do you wish? Do you condemn me to a heavy ransom? I am ready to pay it. Do you wish satisfaction at the point of the sword? Then, let us finish on the spot. But what do you gain by holding me here like a thief?"

Again Djambek laughed scornfully.

" A ransom! You judge others by yourself. Gold! and always gold! And you will condescend to fight a duel with me! That would, indeed, come cheaper for you, if fortune favored you. Know this. I do not want your gold; and as for a duel, after your shameful betrayal of one you called your friend, I despise you too deeply to think you worthy of crossing sabers with me. Should the fortune of war bring this land under the rule of my allies you will become their subject, and will perhaps be able to give them information on certain points. It is said that your father made himself rich at the cost of those whose sons are now under Russia's protection. If that be true you are the son of a thief, and you can well understand that I intend holding you until the courts can decide about you. You shall make recompense to those whom your father robbed. Now, you know what is likely to happen to you."

Djambek slowly walked to the door.

" You think you are a great war hero, boy!" snarled

Murza-Khan, grinding his teeth. "You play the part of a victorious conqueror. A fine victory, forsooth! capturing a fortress that was not defended! But my day will come, too, when I shall laugh as I strike the traitor to his country in the face, the traitor who has sold himself!"

"What do you understand of such things?" said Djambek scornfully. "You never took arms for your country as long as you could fill your purse in peace. You were always to be bought, and think others are like yourself. But why lose words? I have more important things to do than argue with you on things that are beyond your comprehension."

He left the room while Murza-Khan yelled curses after him.

Djambek proceeded at once to give orders for the detachment which was to be left as a garrison for the place. It was a great comfort to him to know that Ahmed would be there as a protector of the two girls, though there was really but little danger for them, as in case the Turks captured the place, Ahmed would represent himself and his charges as prisoners.

CHAPTER XX.

THE storming of the fortress of Tzichis-tzeri was one of the hardest fought battles of the war. The Turks defended the ramparts with the courage of lions, and again and again were the Russians driven back, leaving thousands of their dead upon the field.

Djambek's corps and the battalion with it finally succeeded in gaining a foot-hold within the redoubt. But not much was gained with that. Upon the fortress itself still waved the red flag with its star and crescent, and it looked as if there must yet be many a hard struggle before the standard would be lowered in token of defeat. But that the fortress must be taken was the fixed determination of the besiegers; it was as if each soldier had sworn it. And it fell finally, but only after a terrible sacrifice.

Djambek had been in a very hail of bullets, but not one had touched him. He had plunged into the hottest of the fight with the beloved name upon his lips, and that name seemed a talisman before which bullets fell harmlessly.

"Bravo, Djambek!" cried the general, as he saw him doing a brave deed, "that shall bring you the cross!"

The cross ! Was it for a medal—a piece of metal to hang upon his breast—that he fought? No. He was forced into the struggle contrary to his real desires. He had given his word. He had become convinced that only by a violent overturning could better things come to his country. And so he fought not for honors, but for his country's and his word's sake. The fierce frenzy of battle, the thirst for destroying which others felt, he had no part in. He did not rush forward with his troops blindly to kill, but he sought and often found opportunities for preventing acts of cruelty.

This was the first, and it should be the last time that he drew sword from sheath to take part in such a slaughter of his fellow-men. That he swore solemnly to himself. No cross, no medal, no promotion should ever tempt him to again leave the path of peace. To him these groans and cries, these fierce passions, this bath of blood, were an utter horror; and after it was over he felt a shuddering grief at sight of the death-strewed battle-field which so many poets have sung in exultant strains. These piles of quivering limbs, these red-black pools of blood, these dead faces distorted with their last agony, filled him with loathing, and he felt a sort of bitterness against those who had made the scene of destruction a possibility. He felt no glow of pride when the commander-in-chief summoned him before him and complimented him on his bravery. He felt rather as if he were a butcher's apprentice praised by his master for having slaughtered an animal with special skill.

He hurried away as soon as he could, and threw a few hasty lines on paper, which he gave his servant to deliver.

"The cruel slaughter is over, my love, and I am
unharmed. But I scarce dare think of thee in a place
so filled with death agonies and cries of pain. I must
away from here as soon as possible. Some one has
already written a song about the 'glorious battle,' but
I can only wonder that rhymes lend themselves to such
cruelties! I must flee far into the forest, far as may
be from this discord of triumphal songs and dying
groans. There I will rest and dream of thee, my
love."

He strode rapidly through the darkness of the
night to carry out his intention of getting as far away
as his duty would permit from the scenes of horror
that surrounded him. He finally reached a spot where
only now and then could be heard an echo from the
camp, and there he threw himself on the ground and
closed his eyes. But the longed-for dream pictures
would not come to him. In vain he sought to shut out
the horrid visions of the battle-field. He spoke aloud
to his loved one as if the sound of her voice might
come to him in reply. In vain. Cries of pain and
groans of agony were the only answer.

Djambek awoke at the first glimmer of dawn
from his feverish slumber. He sprang up and hurried
again to the place from which he had fled at the approach of night. Duty called him as a leader to be
with his followers.

The sun had scarcely risen when General Tasafioff
came riding by.

"Good morning, comrade!" he cried in good
spirits. "Up so early? I thought I should surprise
you asleep." He dismounted and took Djambek by the

arm. "I know what troubles you," he said. "It can be helped. The army begins the march to-day. If I might offer your bride a seat in a rickety wagon which will take her to Kutayis in a couple of days, I should esteem it a favor."

"I accept your kindness with heartiest thanks," replied Djambek.

"Good, then. The matter is finished. My wife, too, has gone to Kutayis. In Aschalzich it was too lonesome and not entirely safe for her, there are so many of these cursed Laz robbers about now. Go and saddle your horse and bring the young ladies here. My wife will be delighted to offer them her hospitality until you are ready to set up your own household gods."

Djambek thanked his good friend heartily and hurried away.

.   .   .   .

It was after sun-down when the wagon train started. It was not a joyous journey, for a part of the wounded were taken along, too.

The larger body of troops remained in the captured fortress and in its near neighborhood, as it was expected that the Turks would make an attack from the sea. Up to this time the hostile fleet had held itself in reserve, but it was more than probable that Hobart-Pasha would yet have a word to say before allowing the Russians the full victory. Consequently, the troops were kept busy day and night, throwing up earthworks and barricades to strengthen their position. Djambek's men worked vigorously and gave a good example to their allies.

"Fine people, these Adjarians," said the commander - in - chief, well-pleased, as he inspected the works. "By the way," he added, turning to Djambek, "you have some prisoners, I believe, at Kardjeti-Tziche."

"Yes, Excellency," he replied. "I was just going to ask you to decide what should be done with them."

"Kapanidze has been speaking to me about them to-day," interposed General Tasafioff. "I understand that the owner of the castle is among them, one Murza-Khan. Kapanidze thinks that the father of the man was from Daghestan, where he acquired great riches through robbery."

"So they say," said Djambek. "Kapanidze must know, however, better than I do, as he is of Daghestan descent."

"It is well; we will examine into the matter," said the commander.

"There is another prisoner, who lately stood very high in Cherif-Pasha's confidence. His name is Totia Nitscheladze."

"What name did you say?" asked General Tasafioff.

"Totia Nitscheladze."

"I know the name, but can't remember at the moment where I have heard it."

"It is said that he was formerly an officer in the Russian service."

"Indeed! We will see about it."

"The simplest way is for us to go there now. There may be some among the prisoners who ought not longer to be deprived of their liberty," said the chief.

Accordingly they set out for Kardjeti-Tziche accompanied by a large escort.

On arriving there, Murza-Khan was first brought before them, and Kapanidze related all the particulars which he knew concerning him.

The commander-in-chief shook his head doubtfully.

" In many cases it seems just that the sins of the fathers should be atoned for by the children," he said. "From what you have told us, Kapanidze, it appears that the father of this man was a common robber, but the man himself is a Turkish subject, and—"

"If I may be allowed a remark," said Djambek, interrupting him, "it is beyond doubt that this district will be ceded to Russia, which would change the circumstances."

" Very true; I had not thought of that," cried the chief, while Murza-Khan gave his enemy a look of hatred. "That being the case, we are bound to keep the man a prisoner until the question is decided."

" As I have no intention of ever becoming a Russian subject," exclaimed Murza-Khan, his voice trembling with rage, "the question can as well be decided now. It is a gross abuse of power to deprive me of my freedom, and I will hold you responsible for it."

" I can manage to bear the responsibility, I think," was the cool answer. "In case this piece of country falls to us, those whom your father robbed will unquestionably have the right to institute process against you for the recovery of their property."

" As I am certain I should have no chance for justice in a trial with your *protégés* I am ready to make a proposition on the spot," said Murza-Khan, trying to speak calmly.

" And what is your proposition ? "

"To transfer my possessions here to the Russian Government for a proper recompense. There are many witnesses who can show that I have enlarged and improved the property. I deny emphatically that my father did any worse than any of the large land-holders of the time in Daghestan. The stronger simply took possession, and that was the end of it. Without doubt the ancestors of this victim," he continued with a mocking glance at Kapanidze, "would have done the same, if they had had the strength and the courage. But we need not dispute about that. I repeat, the Russian Government may have my property for a fixed sum, and can then do with it as it pleases. But for my person and my movable property I demand the fullest freedom, and in that no one can dispute my right."

General Tasafioff whispered a few words to the commander, and the latter nodded in assent and then said, turning to Murza-Khan:

"Your 'right' might be easily disputed, but as you are not a prisoner of war, and are not personally accused of any crime, I will waive that. I will make you a proposition. Give me security that you will appear when wanted, and I will grant you your freedom —of course on condition that you leave the country."

Murza-Khan shook his head.

"It is rather for me to demand security that my property be not injured. But I will not insist on that if I am at once set at liberty."

The commander consulted for a few moments with the others, and then said:

"Very well. We grant your request. You are free."

" But you will give me a statement in writing about buying my property? "

" The real tradesman's spirit," whispered Djambek to the general.

" No," said the latter in reply to Murza-Khan, " for I am unable to make any promises on behalf of those who have charge of such matters. The tribunals must first decide whether anything is to be paid, and if so, how much? "

" You do not seem to understand that my estates are of great value."

" That I do not need to know. The judges will ascertain it at the proper time, and you may be sure no injustice will be done you."

" You are all witnesses of this promise," said Murza-Khan looking at the others. " We will see how much a Russian's word is worth."

" It is worth a good deal, you may be sure," said the commander quietly.

" One thing more," said Murza-Khan. " My boatmen are held here as prisoners. They are all Greeks."

" In that case they are of course free, and you can leave with them."

Murza-Khan bowed and turned to go, but stopped suddenly and said to Djambek, with deep hatred in his tone : " I have a word for you ! Never cross my path again, or it will be at the peril of your life."

" You miserable coward," exclaimed Djambek, his eyes flashing. " Do you think I fear you? "

He took a step forward and laid his hand upon his sword. Then remembering his resolution he stopped.

Murza-Khan satisfied himself with a mocking laugh. "Ruffian!" he said, "do you think I am fool enough to fight? But Allah grant that my revenge come some time!"

He turned on his heel and left the room accompanied by one of the guard.

"Now for the other one," said the commander.

"What did you call him?"

"Totia Nitscheladze."

"Very good. We will see what is to be done with this gentleman."

In a few minutes Totia was led in.

"What is to be done with him?" exclaimed General Tasafioff as soon as he saw him. "I claim this prisoner as mine. I know now where I have heard the name. That is the rascal who had the honor to serve in the same regiment with me once, and whose long fingers emptied the safe one fine night. He escaped justice by flight, but his sentence is still in force —ten years in Siberia, if I remember rightly."

"Put him in chains," commanded the chief curtly.

"Mercy!" cried Totia, falling on his knees. "I will restore all. I am rich now!"

"Did you hear me," said the chief to the guard. "I said, put him in chains." And he turned his back on the groveling wretch.

"Are we through?" he asked. "It appears not. They are bringing another one."

"That is not a prisoner," Djambek hastened to assure them as Ahmed approached. "I owe this man more than my life." And he went to the muezzin, and took his hand. "This brave friend saved my bride and prevented Murza-Khan's escape. He is a man of peace, but at the critical moment he can act the real hero."

" Do not speak of that," protested Ahmed. " It was not right and I—"

" Not right to prevent a murder? "

" You did well," interposed the commander-in-chief. " We are all under obligations to you for not letting him escape.—Remind me, Djambek, that this man deserves recognition for his services."

" If you think me worthy of reward, I pray that it may consist in restoring me to my office."

" And what is your office, my friend? "

Djambek smiled. " He is muezzin at a mosque in Batoum. I believe it must bring him in as much as one hundred piasters * a month."

" Just enough to keep him from absolutely starving," remarked the general, smiling. " Well, put me in mind of it at a favorable opportunity. If we get Batoum, this muezzin shall have the best mosque in the city."

They mounted their horses and rode back to the camp.

A few days later Djambek received orders to occupy Murza-Khan's castle and hold it until the military operations in Asia Minor should be ended.

The fall and a large part of the winter passed before the longed-for news arrived that the war was at an end. On this side the Black Sea both Turks and Russians, worn out with the strife, had for some time ceased from active operations except in occasional unimportant skirmishes, but on the European side the

---

* One hundred piasters equals four dollars and forty cents.

17

contest had been fiercely prolonged, and it had required a crushing defeat to induce the Ottoman leaders to sue for peace.

But finally peace came, and Djambek and his associates could once more sheathe their swords and enjoy the long looked for rest and tranquillity.

CHAPTER XXI

FOR many months now tranquillity had again reigned in the land. The conquered nation had purchased peace at a heavy cost. Thousands upon thousands rested beneath the cool earth—sons, husbands, fathers—mourned by parents, wives, and children. But the genius of war has no thought for these; where a land's policy speaks the heart must be silent. National hatred permits no rival in natural affection, and as for the lives that are destroyed, they are but the small coin of the war indemnity; the larger sums are the gold and the square miles which must satisfy stricken hearts.

Nature was clothed in the laughing tints of spring; everywhere were greenness, bloom, and perfume. Hills and valleys seemed to rejoice aloud in the warm rays and lavish verdure. New life sprang up everywhere —even there where but a little while before Death had with pitiless, brutal hand sowed desolation like wheat.

Djambek sat with Thamar on the veranda of the house at Kutayis where General Tasafioff lived with his family. In the joyousness of nature that surrounded them they had no thoughts for the troubled past, and only looked forward to a happy future. In a few days they would be each other's forever.

The general came out of the house and sat down with them. "There is one thing more to be arranged, which must serve as my excuse for intruding," he said kindly.

Thamar smiled. "The presence of so good a friend can never be an intrusion," she said.

The general warmly pressed the hand she gave him, and continued: "We are agreed then, Djambek, are we, to go to Batoum day after to-morrow?"

"Yes."

"I will accompany you to your estate to see that the official papers are given you to take on your journey to St. Petersburg—your wedding journey, I might say, as you will combine business with pleasure. It is true, it might all be arranged by correspondence, but I think it better that you should present yourself in person to your new sovereign and receive your estates back again from his hands. I learned recently that His Majesty intended, as a reward for your brave services, to confer on you the title your ancestors bore when they were still Georgians. But tell me now, how long a time will the journey to your place require?"

"We can go and return to Batoum in three days."

"Then my wife with Thamar will meet you there on Sunday."

"I trust so."

"Now I have something else to speak about," continued the general, turning to Thamar. "Your courageous young friend who so faithfully nursed the wounded with you, and came so near falling herself a victim to fever, needs rest and recreation. The physi-

cian assures me that with this favorable weather she
will soon recover her strength, but do you not think
a voyage would do her good, and—"

At this moment Daria appeared at the door leading
from the house. Thamar sprang up and went to her,
and putting her arm affectionately about her led her
to the divan. The once rosy cheeks were pale, but the
eyes sparkled again and a smile hovered about the
tender lips as Thamar embraced her.

"We were just speaking of you, Daria," she said.
"You know we are soon going to take a trip to the
north. Won't you go with us?"

Daria shook her head. "What are you thinking
of?" she said, laughing. "Do you think a bridal
couple needs a third person with them to complete
their happiness? Hardly, my dear."

"How can you speak so?"

"Let me stay here, sister. I know I should talk
you to death; and besides that, I don't like to leave
this warm climate for the icy north. I would like to
do one thing, though," she continued, after a moment's
pause. "Let me arrange your house for you while you
are away. It will give me something to busy myself
with, and I should dearly like to make your nest all
ready for you when you return. May I?"

"Certainly, you may. You could give me no greater
pleasure."

"Good! That is all arranged, then," said the general. "And now I will tell you a secret. But you must
not breathe it to any one. It is said that I am to receive an appointment as Governor of Batoum, so that
we shall be neighbors."

"That will indeed be a pleasure to us!" cried

Thamar heartily, while Djambek and Daria added their expressions of pleasure and congratulation.

"Then you will doubtless have the citadel for your residence, and will become acquainted with the historic chamber where Thamar languished in captivity," said Djambek, smiling.

"Oh, Batoum is full of historical reminiscences," added Thamar. "The prison, for example, where a dangerous rebel was confined until he escaped with the help of a muezzin!"

"I presume the city is so full of interesting reminiscences that it would require a whole quarry to furnish tablets enough to record the noteworthy events!" said the general, laughing.

Kapanidze now joined the company, and they adjourned to the garden, where tea was served.

"She still bears the traces of her fight with Death," whispered the young man to Tasafioff. "She is a brave girl!"

"Yes, indeed. She showed courage equal to the bravest soldier."

"Did she not! When one saw how bravely she met danger, how tenderly and pityingly she nursed the sick—one felt like falling on his knees before her!"

The general threw a sharp, quizzical glance at his enthusiastic young friend.

"Ah—ah!" he said, "that is the direction of the wind, is it! Well, curb your impatience until the bridal couple return, and then if you wish to try your fortune you will have my best wishes."

. . . .

The steamer glided swiftly out the harbor. The young couple stood on the deck and waved their hand-

kerchiefs in farewell to their friends left behind until
they were no longer in sight.

"Let us go," said General Tasafioff, giving his arm
to his wife. "Our ship will soon weigh anchor.—Farewell, until we meet again, Ahmed," turning to the
muezzin, who began murmuring words of thanks.
"Not a word. What we have done for you was but
an act of justice. So, good-by for the present. We
shall soon be neighbors."

The muezzin walked slowly to his mosque. He
drew the key from his pocket, and, unlocking the door,
ascended the steps leading to the top of the minaret.
There, his first look was for the steamer, now far away
in the distance. The red disk of the sun had half disappeared behind the horizon. A mass of white clouds
had formed there like mountain crags and cliffs, and
through the mass the half-sun glowed like the open
door of a gigantic furnace, through which there seemed
to flow a mighty stream of molten fire extending across
the sea, a long line of fiery red, glowing, gleaming on
the wide expanse of water. As the sun dipped lower
the glittering path stretched farther until it reached
the shore. And now the steamer reached the gleaming
way, and, becoming every instant smaller and smaller
to the view, a spot of darkness on a field of light, seemed
to glide down that glowing pathway toward the fiery
temple of the sun, and suddenly vanished, as if within it.

The muezzin had followed it with his earnest look
until the dazzling rays blinded his eyes. Then he
stretched out his hands thither, as if in invocation and
benediction, and murmuring "*Selam aleikum!*"* be-

---

* "Peace be unto you!"

gan in clear, vibrating tones, though with something of sadness in his voice, the evening call to prayer:

" Allah ekber, la allahé ullala
Heijha allel fehl-lah.
Eshed de-enni Mohammed-di rasoul ülla."

THE END.

APPLETONS'
Town and Country Library.

PUBLISHED SEMI-MONTHLY.

Bound in tasteful paper covers, at 50 cents each; also in cloth, at 75 cents each
(excepting when price is otherwise given).

1. THE STEEL HAMMER. By Louis Ulbach, author of "Madame Gosselin."

"'The Steel Hammer,' by Louis Ulbach, is not only a splendid bit of fiction, finely conceived and vividly wrought out, but it has the rare merit of appealing to the two classes that go so far toward making up the general reading public. . . . It is this happy combination of objective and subjective treatment which makes of 'The Steel Hammer' a story worthy of Gaboriau, while at the same time it is a study of the human conscience which might have evolved itself from the mind of Balzac."—*The Critic.*

2. EVE. A Novel. By S. Baring-Gould, author of "Red Spider," "Little Tu'penny," etc.

"The machinery of the plot is made the vehicle for vigorous study of character and description of quaint and interesting life in a secluded part of England. Jasper and his brother, Barbara, Eve, and the two seniors, are wrought out with artistic and painstaking skill, and several of the minor personages are studied with hardly less effect. The novel is strong, bright, and eminently readable."—*Eclectic Magazine.*

3. FOR FIFTEEN YEARS. A Sequel to "The Steel Hammer." By Louis Ulbach.

"Though 'The Steel Hammer,' the story to which 'For Fifteen Years' is the sequel, was a fascinating one, it was a comparatively tame prelude to one of the most powerful *dénoûments* possible to conceive. The plots and counter-plots are worked out with a power and devotion which are startling in their intensity."—*Baltimore American.*

4. A COUNSEL OF PERFECTION. A Novel. By Lucas Malet, author of "Colonel Enderby's Wife," "Mrs. Lorimer," etc.

"It would require us to go back to Miss Austen to find anything that better deserved the praise of fine form, fine grouping, fine coloring, humorous delineation, and precision of design."—*London Spectator.*

5. THE DEEMSTER. A Romance. By Hall Caine.

"The spiritual grandeur of its conception and the tremendous nature of the forces engaged raise it to the region of tragic drama. . . . Grandly conceived and grandly executed."—*London Academy.*

6. A VIRGINIA INHERITANCE. By Edmund Pendleton, author of "A Conventional Bohemian." (In cloth. Price, $1.00.)

". . . It has an interest and freshness of its own; in parts it is amusing; in parts witty; here and there wise. The courtesy of the Chesters, their oddities, their reckless acceptance of every claim of exorbitent hospitality, their indolent carelessness, their embodiment of the 'hospitable, out-at-elbow, irrelevant, sympathetic South,' are set forth in a manner which has a sort of fascination."—*The Saturday Review,* London.

7. NINETTE: An Idyll of Provence. By the author of "Véra."

"A very charming Provençal idyll. The author of 'Véra' must be reckoned among the very few English writers who are capable of reproducing the atmosphere of Continental life."—*The Athenæum.*

8. "THE RIGHT HONOURABLE." A Romance of Society and Politics. By JUSTIN McCARTHY and Mrs. CAMPBELL-PRAED.

"The moral is sound. It is one of duty victoriously achieved though at great cost; and perhaps verisimilitude is not strained by the idealization which imputes to the woman's superior strength of renunciation and moral stamina the successful passage through the last and most fiery trial. Incidentally there is much bright description of fashionable life and people."—*New York Tribune.*

9. THE SILENCE OF DEAN MAITLAND. By MAXWELL GREY.

"The story culminates in a scene which is almost unequaled and unexampled in fiction. . . . As a tale of spiritual struggle, as a marvelously graphic and vital picture of the action and reaction of human life, 'The Silence of Dean Maitland' is a book that is destined to an extraordinary recognition and permanent fame in literature."—*Boston Traveller.*

10. MRS. LORIMER: A Study in Black and White. By LUCAS MALET, author of "Colonel Enderby's Wife," "A Counsel of Perfection."

"'Mrs. Lorimer' is not only brimful of cleverness, profuse and careless cleverness, as of one rich in intelligence, and of genuine, softly reflective humor, such as critics love; but of power of a kind so separate that it is hard to characterize without quoting in justification the whole book. It is as a story of rare prominence, alike of humor and of pathos, that we recommend 'Mrs. Lorimer.'"—*London Spectator.*

11. THE ELECT LADY. By GEORGE MACDONALD, author of "Home Again," etc.

"Rich in imaginative beauty and fine insight into the mysteries of spiritual life."—*London Spectator.*

"There are some good bits of dialogue and strong situations in the book."—*The Athenæum.*

12. THE MYSTERY OF THE "OCEAN STAR." A Collection of Maritime Sketches. By W. CLARK RUSSELL, author of "The Wreck of the 'Grosvenor,'" etc.

"Mr. Clark Russell occupies a peculiarly happy position in literature. He is absolutely without competitors. Opinions may differ as to the best writer in almost any other line of work, but there is only one fabulist of the sea, and, in one respect, Clark Russell is a better story-teller than any of his colleagues in other branches of fiction."—*San Francisco Examiner.*

13. ARISTOCRACY. A Novel. (In cloth. Price, $1.00.)

"A very clever and amusing piece of novel-writing is 'Aristocracy,' by an unknown author, who seems to have a sufficient knowledge of the manners and tone of good society in England to satirize them unmercifully, while adhering in a considerable degree to the truth. . . . He also knows how to write an interesting story, and his book has not a dull page in it."—*The Sun, New York.*

14. A RECOILING VENGEANCE. By FRANK BARRETT, author of
"His Helpmate," "The Great Hesper." With Illustrations.

"A very pretty, natural, and refreshing story is 'A Recoiling Vengeance.' . . .
It is a story told in the first person of a struggle for the inheritance of a wealthy
lawyer in a country town, and in its clearness and brightness reminds us not a
little of the manner of Anthony Trollope."—*London Saturday Review.*

15. THE SECRET OF FONTAINE-LA-CROIX. A Novel. By MAR-
GARET FIELD.

The heroine of this story is an Englishwoman, but the events occur principally
in France. In the main the story is domestic in character, affording some charming pictures of life in a French château, but scenes in the Franco-German War
are also depicted, and the action leads up to a striking and most dramatic
situation.

"An interesting story well told."—*Christian Union.*
"Altogether a delightful story."—*Philadelphia Bulletin.*

16. THE MASTER OF RATHKELLY. A Novel. By HAWLEY SMART,
author of "A False Start," "Breezie Langton," etc.

"The Master of Rathkelly" is an Irish landlord, and the incidents of the
story illustrate the nature of the present conflict in Ireland in a striking manner.

17. DONOVAN: A Modern Englishman. A Novel. By EDNA LYALL.
New cheap edition. (In cloth. Price, $1.50.)

A cheap edition of "Donovan" has long been called for by those who have
recognized its merits, and wished to see its influence extended. It falls within
the range of thought stimulated by "Robert Elsmere," and books of its class.

18. THIS MORTAL COIL. A Novel. By GRANT ALLEN.

"Mr. Grant Allen's is a good story, a little burdened with the constant effort
for a sparkling narrative, but fairly true to life, and speaks through its characters."—*The Athenæum.*

19. A FAIR EMIGRANT. By ROSA MULHOLLAND, author of "Marcella
Grace," etc.

"The 'fair emigrant' is a young lady who returns to her father's country for
the purpose of trying to clear his name from the disgrace of a crime with which
he was falsely charged. . . . A very interesting narrative."—*The Spectator.*
"A capital novel."—*Scotsman.*

20. THE APOSTATE. A Novel. By ERNEST DAUDET.

"The Apostate" is a novel of much more than ordinary power, and in a field
somewhat new. In morals it is unobjectionable, and in style noble and impress-
ive. The translation has been carefully done.

D. APPLETON & CO., PUBLISHERS, 1, 3, & 5 BOND STREET, NEW YORK.

21. RALEIGH WESTGATE; or, Epimenides in Maine. By HELEN
KENDRICK JOHNSON.

The time of this story is just before and during the rebellion, but the reader
is carried back to some curious episodes in the early history of Maine, the traditions of which supply part of the material for the plot.

"Out of the common run of fiction."—*Boston Beacon.*

"An atmosphere of quaint humor pervades the book."—*Christian Inquirer.*

22. ARIUS THE LIBYAN: A Romance of the Primitive Church. A
new cheap edition. (Also in cloth. Price, $1.25.)

"Portrays the life and character of the primitive Christians with great force
and vividness of imagination."—*Harper's Magazine.*

"Beside this work most of the so-called religious novels fade into insignifi-
cance."—*Springfield Republican.*

23. CONSTANCE, AND CALBOT'S RIVAL. By JULIAN HAWTHORNE.

"The reader will find a fascinating interest in these strange and cleverly told
stories which are as ingenious in conception as they are brilliant in develop-
ment."—*Boston Gazette.*

24. WE TWO. By EDNA LYALL, author of "Donovan." New cheap
edition. (Also in cloth. Price, $1.50.)

"We recommend all novel readers to treat this novel with the care which
such a strong, uncommon, and thoughtful book demands and deserves."—*London
Spectator.*

25. A DREAMER OF DREAMS. A Modern Romance. By the author
of "Thoth."

"Of an original and artistic type . . . near to being a tremendous feat of
fancy."—*Athenæum.*

"Resembles its predecessor ("Thoth") in the weirdness of the plot and the
incisive brilliance of style."—*London Literary World.*

26. THE LADIES' GALLERY. A Novel. By JUSTIN McCARTHY and
Mrs. CAMPBELL-PRAED.

"It is interesting and racy, and abounds in clever sketches of character and
in good situations. Both authors are, so to speak, on their native heath. . . .
Altogether, the book abounds in amusement."—*London Guardian.*

"An absorbing, powerful, and artistic work."—*London Post.*

27. THE REPROACH OF ANNESLEY. By MAXWELL GREY, author
of "The Silence of Dean Maitland."

"The Reproach of Annesley" will be welcomed by every reader of "The
Silence of Dean Maitland," a novel that has been pronounced by both English
and American critics a work possessing striking power and originality.

28. NEAR TO HAPPINESS. A Novel. Translated from the French
by FRANK H. POTTER.

"The plot is strong and clearly constructed, and the characters are sketched
with marked force and artistic skill. The era of the incidents is that of the
Franco-German War, and the point about which they revolve is a tender love-
story to which a deep dramatic interest is imparted."—*Boston Gazette.*

29. IN THE WIRE-GRASS. By Louis Pendleton.

"An unusually clever novel is 'In the Wire Grass,' by Louis Pendleton (Appletons). It presents a vivid picture of Southern life by a native of the South, and abounds in incidents and characters racy of the soil. . . . The humor is everywhere bright and genuine, and the action uniformly brisk."—*The Sun.*

30. LACE. A Berlin Romance. By Paul Lindau.

"'Lace,' Lindau's novel, of which the Appletons have just published a thoroughly good translation, gets its name from the fateful *rôle* held in it by a marvelous mantle of Brabant lace. This mantle wanders through the mazes of this story like a specter that will not down, and, rarely beautiful as it is, grows in the end into a veritable robe of Nessus. . . . Altogether, 'Lace' is one of the most effective pieces of work that we have seen for a long time."—*Commercial Advertiser.*

31. AMERICAN COIN. By the author of "Aristocracy."

A satirical picture of impecunious English peers in search of fortunes, and of the daughters of American millionaires in search of titles.

"'American Coin' is a remarkably clever and readable story."—*N. Y. Herald.*

32. WON BY WAITING. By Edna Lyall.

"The sentiment of the story is delicate and uplifting, and the style is uncommonly spirited and active."—*Boston Gazette.*

33. THE STORY OF HELEN DAVENANT. By Violet Fane.

"Neither Miss Braddon nor the author of 'The House on the Marsh' could have contrived a more ingenious story than that of 'Helen Davenant.'"—*The Academy.*

34. THE LIGHT OF HER COUNTENANCE. By H. H. Boyesen, author of "Gunnar," "Idyls of Norway," "A Daughter of the Philistines," etc.

The scenes of this story open in New York, but the action soon shifts to Italy. The characters are mainly American and English. The incidents are picturesque, and the movement animated.

35. MISTRESS BEATRICE COPE; or, Passages in the Life of a Jacobite's Daughter. By M. E. Le Clerc.

"A simple, natural, credible romance, charged with the color of the time and satisfying to the mind of a thoughtful reader."—*The Athenæum.*

36. KNIGHT-ERRANT. By Edna Lyall.

"'Knight-Errant' is marked by the author's best qualities as a writer of fiction, and displays on every page the grace and quiet power of her former works."—*The Athenæum.*

37. IN THE GOLDEN DAYS. By Edna Lyall.

"The central figure of her story is Algernon Sidney, and this figure she invests with singular dignity and power. Some of the scenes are remarkably vivid. The escape is an admirable narrative, which almost makes one hold one's breath to read."—*The Spectator.*

38. GIRALDI; or, The Curse of Love. By Ross George Dering.

"'Giraldi' is undeniably a clever book; satirical, humorous, and amusing; full of consistent sketching of character; . . . an original and readable novel." — *The Saturday Review.*

39. A HARDY NORSEMAN. By Edna Lyall.

"All the quiet power we praised in 'Donovan' is to be found in this new story."—*The Athenæum.*

40. THE ROMANCE OF JENNY HARLOWE, and Sketches of Maritime Life. By W. Clark Russell.

"'The Romance of Jenny Harlowe,' supplemented by other sketches of sea life, offer capital reading. The story is exciting enough to satisfy the most exacting on this score."—*The Academy.*

41. PASSION'S SLAVE. By Richard Ashe-King.

"Mr. King is a refined and pleasant writer. . . . His tact is generally beyond reproach."—*The Athenæum.*

42. THE AWAKENING OF MARY FENWICK. By Beatrice Whitby.

"We have no hesitation in declaring that 'The Awakening of Mary Fenwick' is the best novel of the kind that we have seen for some years. It is apparently a first effort, and as such is remarkable."—*The Athenæum.*

43. COUNTESS LORELEY. From the German of Rudolf Menger.

"An exciting novel, the scene of which is laid principally in Germany just before and after the Franco-Prussian War. The characters, which embrace besides the two principal ones a Breton duelist, a lion-hearted Englishman, a Russian diplomat, and others, are presented in a spirited manner."—*Boston Gazette.*

44. BLIND LOVE. By Wilkie Collins. With a Preface by Walter Besant.

This posthumous novel was unfinished at the time of Mr. Collins's death, although in course of serial publication. By means of the ample notes left by the author, Mr. Besant was enabled to complete it along the lines laid down by the author. "The plot of the novel," says Mr. Besant, "every scene, every situation, from beginning to end, is the work of Wilkie Collins."

45. THE DEAN'S DAUGHTER. By Sophie F. F. Veitch.

"The passages in it which deal with the morally distorted and tragic passion of Vera Dormer recall to some extent the vanished hand of the author of 'Jane Eyre.'"—*The Academy.*

46. COUNTESS IRENE. A Romance of Austrian Life. By J. Fogerty.

"This is a charming story, interesting and *mouvementé*, with some highly dramatic incidents. . . . The pictures of Viennese life and manners are admirable, and the descriptions of Austrian country-house life amid the magnificent scenery of the Salzkammergut are most attractive."—*Westminster Review.*

12mo, paper cover. Price, 50 cents each.

New York: D. APPLETON & CO., Publishers, 1, 3, & 5 Bond Street.

*R*ECOLLECTIONS OF THE COURT OF THE TUILERIES. By MADAME CARETTE, Lady-of-Honor to the Empress Eugénie. Translated from the French by ELIZABETH PHIPPS TRAIN. 12mo. Cloth, $1.00; paper cover, 50 cents.

The inside view which these Recollections give of the Court of Louis Napoleon is fresh and of great interest.

"We advise every one who admires good work to buy and read it."—*London Morning Post.*

*M*EMOIRS OF MADAME DE RÉMUSAT. 1802-1808. Edited by her Grandson, PAUL DE RÉMUSAT, Senator. 3 volumes, crown 8vo. Half bound, $2.25.

"Notwithstanding the enormous library of works relating to Napoleon, we know of none which cover precisely the ground of these Memoirs. Madame de Rémusat was not only lady-in-waiting to Josephine during the eventful years 1802-1808, but was her intimate friend and trusted confidante. Thus we get a view of the daily life of Bonaparte and his wife, and the terms on which they lived, not elsewhere to be found."—*N. Y. Mail.*

"These Memoirs are not only a repository of anecdotes and of portraits sketched from life by a keen-eyed, quick-witted woman ; some of the author's reflections on social and political questions are remarkable for weight and penetration."—*New York Sun.*

A SELECTION FROM THE LETTERS OF MADAME DE RÉMUSAT. 1804-1814. Edited by her Grandson, PAUL DE RÉMUSAT, Senator. 12mo. Cloth, $1.25.

*M*EMOIRS OF NAPOLEON, his Court and Family. By the Duchess D'ABRANTES. In 2 volumes, 12mo. Cloth, $3.00.

The interest excited in the first Napoleon and his Court by the "Memoirs of Madame de Rémusat" has induced the publishers to issue the famous "Memoirs of the Duchess d'Abrantes," which have hitherto appeared in a costly octavo edition, in a much cheaper form, and in a style to correspond with De Rémusat. This work will be likely now to be read with awakened interest, especially as it presents a much more favorable portrait of the great Corsican than that limned by Madame de Rémusat, and supplies many valuable and interesting details respecting the Court and Family of Napoleon, which are found in no other work.

New York: D. APPLETON & CO., 1, 3, & 5 Bond Street.

The Dominant Seventh.

A MUSICAL STORY.

By KATE ELIZABETH CLARK.

12mo, half cloth. Price, 50 cents.

A novelette by a young author whose first effort is marked by a charm and grace that commend it to all readers of taste.

New York: D. APPLETON & CO., Publishers, 1, 3, & 5 Bond Street.

THE GAINSBOROUGH SERIES.